LUCK CAN TURN YOUR LIFE AROUND—
BUT ONLY LOVE WILL MAKE YOUR
DREAMS COME TRUE!

Lucky in Love

IS A FAMILY FORTUNE
MORE VALUABLE THAN LOVE?

ZEBRA/0-8217-4054-7 (CANADA:$5.99) U.S. $3.99

CHERYL BIGGS
Family Tradition

"LET ME LOVE YOU, TORI. TONIGHT."

Rand's words were a whisper as his hot breath drifted through her hair.

A moan escaped Tori's lips, only to be swallowed when his mouth descended on hers again. She made no effort to escape his embrace, to deny the swirling passion that had enveloped her, or the desire to be possessed by him.

He had kissed her before, and held her, but not like this. His mouth was working dark magic on her, pulling her into an uncharted world of sensuality that she had never known existed. The hunger of his passion pushed hard against her stomach, as his hands caressed her, one moving over the bare flesh of her arm, the other pressing against the small of her back, and the other cupping her derriere.

Tori's eyes shot open. The other? That was three hands!

She pushed herself out of Rand's arms and whirled around, her eyes wide and searching. Then she saw him. "Uncle Chance!"

He chuckled softly, but guilt was not etched on the handsomely carved face, and he began to fade from her sight.

CHERYL BIGGS

Family Tradition

ZEBRA BOOKS
KENSINGTON PUBLISHING CORP.

ZEBRA BOOKS

are published by

Kensington Publishing Corp.
475 Park Avenue South
New York, NY 10016

First Printing: January, 1993

Printed in the United States of America

For my mother, who has always given me all the encouragement and support a daughter could ask for, and who shares with me a love of the Old South and an unquenchable fascination with the supernatural. Thanks, Mom.

Chapter One

"You know, Tori," the general whispered in her ear, "you are the family's pride and joy."

Tori laughed happily at her partner's comment as they danced gracefully across the ballroom to the strains of the Emperor Waltz. Her voluminous silk skirts rustled softly as the bell-shaped hoop-cage swayed, and the lace petticoats beneath it brushed lightly against her legs. The lilting music filled the cavernous gold-and-white ballroom, drifting out through the open French doors into the sultry night air. Twin crystal chandeliers dripped with several hundred teardrop prisms and sparkled brilliantly, their double tiers aglow with the flames of more than a hundred candles. The golden glimmer of each flickering candle was reflected in the tall gilt-framed mirrors that hung above the room's dual fireplaces and from the dark panes of glass of the half dozen French doors that graced one long wall.

They were the only couple dancing, she a whirl

of lavender silk and antique ivory lace, he a dashing and proud figure in a blue army uniform trimmed with gold braid. The others in the room were either busy in conversation or content to stand aside and watch the passing couple. But that was the usual occurrence when Tori Rouchard took to the dance floor, for she was the family's pride and joy.

"Oh, General, you nearly took my breath away on that last swing." Tori laughed, as she paused between steps to kiss her partner's cheek. She felt the soft whiskers of his bushy sideburns and thick mustache tickle her face and wrinkled her nose. The general was an aristocratic figure of medium height and burly build, with a shock of thick silver hair, matching mustache and short-cropped beard, all of which served to accentuate the brilliance of his blue eyes. But the smile that seemed always on his face whenever Tori was about deftly hid the ache that lay constantly within his heart.

As they resumed dancing, Tori spoke in a mock-serious tone, a thoughtful frown on her face. "It's such a pity you weren't able to run for President, General, as you'd planned. I know you would have won the election against Lincoln's second-term campaign. And if you had, the reconstruction era after the war would have been so much different. You would have been wonderful." This last comment was made just as the music ended. Tori curtsied. "Thank you, General. It is always a pleasure to dance with you."

A loud voice from the far end of the ballroom

suddenly drew her attention. "Tori, someone's pounding on the entry door," Stanton Clemente called. The old man turned his wheelchair around and deftly maneuvered himself toward the dark foyer.

"Gramps, wait for me," Tori ordered, though she knew her words would fall on deaf ears. She grabbed a candelabrum from the fireplace mantel, scooped up a handful of gown in the other hand, and hurried after her grandfather.

Holding the candelabrum high, Tori whispered a sharp curse at the lack of modern conveniences in her home. RiverOaks Plantation was more than 175 years old, and everything about it was authentic, including the oil lamps. There was no electricity, except in the kitchen, and no air conditioning had ever been installed. A private telephone that almost no one had the number to was the only surrender to modern convenience, and it was used only for emergencies.

Another knock sounded just as Tori entered the foyer. The soft glow of the candles lit her way to the door but left the outer reaches of the massive entry in dark shadow.

"Who in blazes could that be at this hour?" she mumbled. "We're not expecting anyone."

"Well, open the door and find out," Stanton said. He pulled his chair to a stop to one side of the door and slipped a hand under the shawl that covered his lap and legs. His fingers curled around the antique Colt .45 that he always kept snuggled there.

Tori swung the door open and, holding the candelabrum high, stared out at the man on her doorstep.

"Well, who is it, Tori?" Stanton tried to peer around the doorframe, found his access inhibited by her hoopskirt, and grumbled again. "Girl, who's there?"

Tori, suddenly mesmerized into speechlessness, continued to gawk at the stranger. He was cast in a conflict of light and shadows from the candles at his face and the pale rays of the moon at his back, encompassing him in an ethereal haze. Tori's grip instantly tightened on the door handle as she gasped and felt shivers ripple through her body. She lifted the candelabrum higher. His blond hair, lying in thick waves, turned to spun gold beneath the candles' glow, his tan to a deep bronze. High cheekbones framed a classically straight nose and hollowed to a strong, square jaw, which looked as if carved from marble, and his eyes were almost the same blue as the midnight sky. His Western-style suit, also a dark blue, was slightly rumpled. It stretched taut across wide shoulders and was cut snugly accentuating his muscled thighs and long legs.

At the sight of Tori at the door, he whipped an ivory-colored cowboy hat from his head and held its brim between his fingers.

Tori's pulse raced, her breath lodged in the back of her throat, and the world began to spin. Time stood still, or rather, in her startled mind, flew backward about a hundred-plus years. He looked like . . . but no, that was impossible! It was a trick of some kind—her eyes, the light, something!

She continued to stare at him, emotions washing over her. The cut and color of the blue suit in the soft haze of light resembled the Union Army uniform the general wore in a portrait that hung in the upstairs hallway, the uniform he'd worn at Antietam, the uniform he still wore.

But that wasn't possible. Was it? The thought had no sooner entered her mind than the words seemed to echo within her ears.

"Yankee! Yankee! Yankee!"

Tori found herself filled with confusion. She closed her eyes, squeezed the lids together, shook her head and then reopened her eyes.

He was still there.

"Yankee! Yankee! Yankee!" she heard again.

She glanced over her shoulder. "Oh, hush, Lila. There are no more 'Yankees' and you know it," she said, not realizing she'd spoken aloud.

"Pardon me?" the stranger said.

Tori turned back and smiled. "I'm sorry, sir. My grandfather asked me a question. But what is it we can do for you?"

"Grandfather?" Named Lila? Rand shrugged the confusing thought away. He was tired, hungry, and slightly frustrated from several hours of flight delays, but he was also awestruck by the sight that stood before him in the doorway. The day's trials had been instantly forgotten the moment Tori had opened the door and her eyes, gold-flecked pools of cinnamon, met his.

11

When he'd stepped from the cab that had brought him out from the airport, he'd had the fleeting impression that the house resembled *Gone with the Wind's* Tara, but he'd never expected to be greeted by Scarlett O'Hara!

Rand found himself repeating the gestures the woman before him had just made. He closed his eyes, shook his head, and looked again.

She was still there.

Diamonds of reflected candlelight played within the curls of her ebony hair as the satiny strands caressed olive-tinted shoulders left bare by the lavender gown's lace-trimmed décolleté. He looked from the plunging neckline to the swell of creamy bosom tucked snugly into the silk bodice, then at her waist, its small breadth emphasized by a wide sash of purple velvet. From the massive folds of the ruffled skirt, Rand's eyes traveled back up toward her face, noting the slender column of neck and the giant magnolia blossom pinned behind one shell-like ear. The flower's sweet, heady fragrance filled the night air around him. Then his gaze returned to meet hers.

She seemed a beauty from the past, a vision of a time long forgotten, and when she smiled again, Rand felt his heart lurch within his chest, its thunderous beat echoing in his ears.

"Well, now, young fella!" Stanton bellowed. He crushed Tori's skirt aside and moved his chair closer to the door. "What can we do for you?" Though he was still wary, one hand wrapped securely around the gun in his lap, there was a faint thread of amusement in Stanton's voice as he watched Tori and the stranger stare at each other.

"Uh-oh, excuse me, sir," Rand stammered, actually noticing the old man in the wheelchair for the first time. He found it difficult to tear his gaze away from the sable-haired beauty, but he finally managed. He offered his hand to Stanton. "I'm Rand Mitchell."

"That's a nice name, young man, but it don't mean a thing to me," Stanton replied, and released's Rand's hand after noticing, and silently approving, the firm handshake.

Rand stood openmouthed at Stanton's response, puzzlement and surprise clearly evident on his face.

"As my grandfather asked earlier . . ." Tori began coolly, and then suddenly a look of recognition came over her face. "Mr. Mitchell? With the room reservation?"

"That's the one," Rand said.

"But we expected you yesterday. When you didn't arrive then, I assumed you weren't coming."

Rand frowned. "I was tied up in a meeting and then my flight was delayed. You didn't rent the room to someone else, did you?"

"Oh, well, no." Her heart had slowed its frantic beat but still refused to return to a normal rate. The candelabrum wavered slightly in her grasp.

"Well, thunder and blazes, Tori, don't keep the young man standing out there. He's a guest—get him in here!" Stanton roared, his voice like a small roll of thunder through the high-ceilinged rooms.

He whipped his chair around and sped toward the dark parlor. "We can visit a spell in here."

Visit—just what she did not want to do. Didn't Gramps realize what would happen if she was delayed in getting back to the ballroom? She threw her grandfather an icy glare, but it was too late. His back was to her and he was halfway to the parlor. She turned to Rand, forced a smile to her lips, and stepped aside to open the door for his entry.

Stanton had several oil lamps lit by the time Tori and Rand joined him in the parlor. He turned toward them as they entered. "I'm Stanton Clemente, son, and this here little beauty is my granddaughter, Victoria Rouchard, but everyone calls her Tori."

Ignoring Tori's angry expression, Stanton kept his attention turned on their guest. "So, young fella, sit down and tell me about yourself. What d' ya do for a living?" Piercing gray-blue eyes fixed on Rand, and bushy gray brows snapped together in amused concentration.

Watching the stranger carefully, Stanton chewed on his cigar, his lips lost beneath a thick fringe of gray mustache. One hand lifted to brush a stray lock of silver-white hair from his forehead.

Tori placed the candelabrum on a marble-topped end table and went to stand behind her grandfather. Her gaze moved around the room nervously, then returned to lock steadfastly on the candelabrum. The flames danced on the candlewicks, wavering, leaning, almost blowing to one side and then righting themselves again. They

14

stretched upward unnaturally, small spurts of orange-and-blue fire, rising toward the ceiling, and then just as suddenly shrank to near invisibility. Luckily, because of the glow from the oil lamps, this wasn't noticed by their guest.

Tori was uneasy as she watched the flames. Something was going to happen. She just knew it. *They* were going to do something. She was unaware she was holding her breath, or that anyone had spoken to her, until her grandfather raised his voice and reached out to gently touch her arm.

"Tori, did you hear me?" Stanton twisted around in his chair to look up at her. A frown drew his generous brows together.

Tori started. "Huh? Oh, I'm sorry, Gramps. I wasn't listening. What did you say?"

"I said, why don't you sit dow . . ."

The sentence was left hanging in the air as Tori suddenly emitted a small mew and dashed across the room. Arms outstretched, she grasped a large vase of flowers as it wobbled dangerously on the edge of the mantel.

Stanton whirled around. "What in tarnation?"

Startled, Rand jumped to his feet at Tori's abrupt movement and Stanton's curse. With a troubled gleam in his eye, he watched Tori lean her head against the mantel, her fingers still tightly clutched around the vase.

Only moments before, as they'd entered the room, he had glanced into the mirror that hung over that mantel and noticed the vase. He could have sworn it had been in the center of the man-

15

tel—not at the end of it, and nowhere near the edge.

"That was a close one, Gramps," Tori said. She threw a smile over her shoulder at the two men. "I guess there must have been a little settling movement in the house or something." The excuse sounded lame even to her own ears, but it was the best she could come up with at the moment. She slid the vase back to the center of the mantel and wiped a nervous hand across her brow.

"Mother warned me they'd make life unusual," she said under her breath, waiting for her nerves to calm so she could turn around again.

"They who?" Rand asked.

Not realizing her words had been loud enough to be heard, Tori jerked up her head at his questioning comment.

She stared into the mirror and saw Rand's handsome face reflected beside and just a little above her own. He was standing directly behind her, close enough that she would have sworn she could feel his breath on her neck and the warmth of his body searing her skin.

Stop it! she ordered herself. Searing her skin, indeed! He was a stranger. And a guest. Tori forced herself to smile as she turned to face him. "Oh, don't mind me, Mr. Mitchell, I always talk to myself. A kind of nervous habit, you know?" A warm flush spread across her cheeks as she realized that the more she talked, the daffier she sounded.

"Come on, Tori, come sit down so this young fella can tell me about himself," Stanton ordered.

He puffed lazily on a thin cigar he held between his lips and pointed to a chair directly opposite where he'd positioned his wheelchair.

Tori, her voluminous skirts swaying gracefully as she walked, moved past Stanton to settle herself on a rosewood-and-green-damask meridienne. The oddly shaped half couch was one of the few seats in the parlor that could comfortably accommodate the antique gown's hoopcage. It had been designed for just that purpose when hoopskirts were the fashion.

"So, young man," Stanton began, "you say you're here on vacation."

"Yes, sir. I've always wanted to . . ."

"Krissy, stop that," Tori whispered, and slapped at the air at her side. Suddenly aware she'd spoken aloud yet again, she glanced up to find Rand and her grandfather staring at her.

Chapter Two

"Is something wrong?" Rand asked, trying to figure out just what it was Tori had been doing.

"Oh, no, no," she stammered, and smiled nervously. "I was just . . . that is, I was . . ." Her mind raced frantically in search of a plausible explanation. "I saw a . . . a spider."

Rand nodded, and Tori gave an inward groan. She could see the skepticism and disbelief in the brilliance of his blue eyes as he stared at her. *Right, Tori,* a spider. *A spider named Krissy.*

"Well, if you're settled now," Stanton said, and looked pointedly at Tori, "can we get back to our conversation?"

"Yes, Gramps. I think we're *all* settled for a while." Tori hoped her grandfather would take the hint and cut his conversation short so that Rand Mitchell would go to his room. She didn't need any more incidents, and certainly not with a stranger to witness them.

"Mr. Mitchell was just telling me he's never been to New Orleans before."

Tori smiled. She was *not* going to encourage this conversation to last any longer than necessary. Maybe if she wasn't too talkative, their guest would get the hint and go up to his room. Of course, she had to admit that if it wasn't for "the family," whom she could feel glaring over her shoulder, she wouldn't be in such a hurry to get rid of him, either. There was something about Rand Mitchell. She wasn't sure exactly what it was, but there was something there she liked, something she'd felt when his gaze had met hers and his lips curved into a smile.

His smile caused Tori's heart to somersault and skip a beat. She tingled with warmth and then caught herself. What was the matter with her? She hadn't acted like this since . . . well, for a long time. And the feelings, although quite pleasurable, were not exactly welcome. She'd fallen in that trap once, and it had proved a disaster in more ways than one. She had absolutely no desire to end up there again.

"What prompted you to visit New Orleans, Mr. Mitchell?" Tori asked, despite her resolve not to talk.

A log in the fireplace suddenly fell from the metal grate and crashed down on the brick hearth. A shower of sparks and ash spurted upward, filled the air and flew straight toward Rand. He moved quickly, jumping up from the seat just before the tiny sparks touched him.

"Dagnab it!" Stanton cursed. "Tori, how in tarnation did that fire screen get open?"

19

"I don't know, Gramps. I guess I forgot to close it." But she knew full well it had been secured only seconds before.

Tori closed the screen and then, seeing Stanton and Rand had returned to their conversation, moved to stand at the doorway that led to the foyer. "Will you please stop all of this?" she whispered into the dark entryway.

The answering words were so faint that she could barely hear them, but they were definitely there. "He's a Yankee! A damn Yankee. Get rid of him."

"Oh!" Tori threw up her hands in resignation. "There are no more Yankees! The war's over, Lila. It's 1993, for heaven's sake." She turned and walked back into the parlor.

Stanton threw her a look that spoke volumes. *Stop speaking aloud into thin air,* his eyes seemed to shout.

Well, so what? Tori smiled back sweetly. *The man probably already thinks I'm a few brain cells short.*

The puzzled look in Rand's eyes was unmistakable, but he didn't ask any questions. Instead, he shifted his position on the green-and-white-brocade-covered settee, his entire body weary with fatigue, and silently cursed the chair's stiff cushion and rosewood carved arms. It was about as comfortable as sitting on a pile of rocks.

"So, young fella, you never did answer my question. What d' ya do for a living?" Stanton asked again.

"I have a ranch in the foothills of California, near a place called Grass Valley. I raise a few horses and some cattle, but to support myself I own a few small stores here and there." It was the truth . . . almost. He looked back at Tori and once again found himself fascinated. She was beautiful, the perfect image of a Southern belle straight out of the past, except that she seemed to continually talk to someone who wasn't really there.

Tori felt his gaze on her and looked up. Blazing blue eyes met the smoldering richness of gold-flecked brown, and for a moment each was aware of nothing but the other.

Stanton chuckled as he watched the flush that spread across Tori's cheeks. The soft sound yanked Tori and Rand from their reverie.

"I hope I haven't inconvenienced you folks by showing up late." He smiled as Stanton made an inane and long response. Rand's mind wasn't on the old man's conversation, but rather on the beautiful creature sitting next to him, who with merely a smile had sent his blood boiling and caused his heart to thud madly in his chest. But it was the old man who was doing most of the talking.

"Tori," Stanton said then, "why don't you get us some coffee? Mr. Mitchell's had a long trip getting to our part of the country. Must be pretty tired." He watched in amusement as his granddaughter tried not to openly glare at him.

"In that case, Gramps, I'm sure Mr. Mitchell would rather go up to his room and retire for the night," Tori said sweetly. Too sweetly. She'd had time to regain her composure and now more than ever wanted Rand Mitchell gone, at least for the moment, before something else happened.

"Actually, I'd love a cup of coffee," Rand replied, surprising even himself. It was the last thing he wanted. The thought of bed seemed so good that his tired body was ready to mutiny against him, to declare war on his traitorous emotions, but he'd been unable to help himself. At the moment the thought of tearing himself away from the gorgeous but mysterious mistress of RiverOaks was just not appealing.

"Very well," Tori said. Her tone dripped saccharine sweetness. "I'll only be a minute."

"I'm afraid she isn't quite pleased with me right now," Stanton said. "Inviting you into the parlor to talk kinda put a damper on her activities for the evening. No, no, don't get up," he added as Rand began to rise. "Wasn't anything we won't be doing again another time."

"I guess, from the way she's dressed, that you open the house to tours on the weekends?"

Stanton nodded and smiled slyly. "Yeah, we do that."

A few minutes later Tori returned carrying a silver serving tray, and the tantalizing aroma of milk-sweetened chicory coffee filled the room. "I hope you don't mind *café au lait,* Mr. Mitchell?"

"Always willing to try anything once," Rand said, and extended a hand toward the proffered cup.

Their hands brushed, delicate olive against bur-

22

nished tan. Their eyes met, locked, and quickly looked away, but both had felt the surge of warmth, the tremor that passed through them, and each was left to silently puzzle and try to deny the feelings. But the others who were peering into the room, unseen, became all too aware of the result of that innocent touch and disliked what they feared was happening.

"So, young fella," Stanton said, "what are you going to do while you're here? See some sights?"

"Please call me Rand."

"Okay, Rand. What have you got planned for yourself?" Stanton repeated.

"I'm not sure. I'd like to take a riverboat cruise. Other than that, I don't know yet. Any suggestions?"

"Sure do. Tori here runs a travel agency. She's got some of the best tours of the Vieux Carré—the French Quarter, in case you didn't know—the original part of the city. If you need someone to show you the sights, she's the best there is."

Stanton avoided looking at Tori as he blithely continued. "Why don't you drop by her office tomorrow? It's down by Jackson Square in one of the Pontalba buildings. Anyone can tell you where that's at. She's a hell of a guide. Taught her myself." He smiled proudly and finally allowed his eyes to meet Tori's, then wished he hadn't.

Tori shot her grandfather a look that dripped icicles.

"That sounds great." Rand turned to Tori. "If you don't mind?"

23

"Actually, Mr. Mitchell, *I* don't conduct the tours. My guides do that. I run the agencies."

"You run them yourself? You're the president?"

"Yes, since my parents died a few months ago."

"I'm sorry," he said, as if the knowledge were new to him, when actually he'd been fully aware just when and how her parents had died.

"Thank you."

"How many locations do you have?" He hoped he wasn't being too obvious.

Tori smiled, pride squaring her shoulders. "We have ten in Louisiana, two in Texas, and two in Mississippi. I'm negotiating a Florida location now, and we have plans to open five more in the next two years."

Rand smiled. This was better than he'd hoped for.

Chapter Three

"Abram will show you to your room, Mr. Mitchell," Tori said a few minutes later, and rose from her seat to put an effective end to the conversation. For the past ten minutes she had been holding her breath and waiting for the roof to cave in over their new guest. It hadn't yet, but that didn't mean it wouldn't if she didn't get him to his room, which was no guarantee of safety either, since *they* could go anywhere they pleased and she could do nothing about it. But she wanted to talk to them, and that meant getting Rand Mitchell out of earshot.

Rand rose, taking the hint. "I'm sorry. I didn't mean to keep you up, but you're right, it is getting late." He smiled and Tori felt the cool resolve she'd tried so desperately to maintain in his presence begin to melt. "I'll see you tomorrow then? About eleven? At your office?"

She nodded and threw her grandfather a "wait until I get you alone" look.

Abram entered the room as if on cue and waited

by the door for Rand. Tori glanced at him in relief. How he always seemed to know when she wanted or needed him had forever been a mystery, but one she was grateful for. She felt a tug at her heart as she gazed at the old man. He had aged considerably in the past twenty years, but then he was eighty-five years old, a year older than her grandfather, but not as robust looking. He'd always given the appearance of being frail. His six-foot body was as thin as a rail, and his ebony skin had acquired so many wrinkles over the years that he resembled a prune. She almost laughed. A prune with a thick bush of white hair.

She waited in the foyer until Abram shuffled onto the second-floor landing and began his slow descent of the wide, curving staircase. Satisfied that his reappearance on the stairs meant that their guest was safely in his room and out of hearing range, Tori reentered the parlor. What little amusement she'd felt at the earlier events was gone.

Stanton raised his hands to hold her off. "Now, Tori, don't go —"

"I'll deal with you later." She threw him a baleful look meant to instill fear in his old heart, which she knew from experience would do nothing of the sort.

Tori stopped at the doorway to the ballroom, propped clenched fists onto her hips, and stared into the dimly lit room. "Well, dear family, I certainly hope you are all satisfied with that little performance you gave tonight." She looked around, but no one appeared. "Oh, now you've decided to be quiet. Well, it's too late." She walked into the ballroom. "And what about Southern hospitality? Have you forgotten how to extend it?"

She paused, but there was no answer. "Why didn't you all just lift him from his seat and toss him out the front door? I know that's what you wanted to do."

A deafening silence filled the room. "I swear, one of these days I'm going to open that door and there's going to be two men standing there in white coats ready to take me to the looney bin, and it will be your fault."

Again she paused, and again there was no answer. Tori stamped her foot on the highly polished hardwood floor. "Damn it, answer me. Can't any of you get it through your heads that the war between the North and South is over?"

"Maybe for the Yankees, but we're not done with them yet," came a deep, drawling voice at her ear.

Tori whirled around, but there was no one there. She threw up her hands. "This is ridiculous. This whole argument is ridiculous."

"Ain't no use talking to them, Tori," Stanton said. "You know they're the stubbornnest bunch of—"

Near the door, a large fern in a heavy porcelain pot set atop a small marble-topped table suddenly crashed to the floor. The pot shattered and shards of gilt-edged porcelain flew across the floor amid a spray of dirt and bits of twisted, broken fern.

"That's enough," Tori said. She looked at Stanton. "And you be quiet before they break something else." She turned back to the ballroom. She couldn't see them at the moment, but they were obviously there. "Now listen to me, all of you. You can't keep judging everyone who comes to this house by whether or not he's a Southerner. It's 1993 for cripe's sake, not 1865."

"You wouldn't have yourself in such a turmoil if you stopped letting them damn Yankees into our home."

Tori spun around abruptly and caught sight of her long-deceased great-great-great-aunt, Lila Rouchard. The woman stepped back and her image began to fade.

"Don't you dare disappear on me," Tori snapped.

Lila's eyes flared with indignation, and her almost emaciated body trembled with rage as she glared back at Tori. She had never been a pretty woman, with dark eyes set too far apart in an extremely thin face, her long nose and thin lips; the years and circumstances had taken a heavy toll on Lila, until her personality had grown almost as harsh as her aged features.

"Tori, your aunt Lila nearly swooned when she saw that young man enter the parlor. She thought . . ." The general shrugged. Everyone already knew what Lila thought—the Civil War was not over and anyone not born and bred in the South was not only a Yankee, but their sworn enemy.

Tori sighed and turned to Lila. "All right, Aunt Lila, what's going on this time? You've never swooned a day in your life, or since, for that matter, so what's this all about?"

"It's just like last time," Lila spat out. She whipped a fan from the pocket of her black hoopskirt. She had donned black at the time of Dominic's death at Gettysburg. She had continued wearing it when Chance had been killed on his riverboat, *The Lilac Queen,* while he was trying to smuggle guns downriver to Confederate troops. Though she had lived many years past the war's end before her own demise, Lila had never returned to colors. She snapped open the fan and began to flutter it in front of her face. "You let another Yankee into our home. Isn't one of those filthy creatures here enough?" Her gaze flickered to the general as if to make her point while she screeched the question. Defiance, pride, and outrage flashed from her eyes.

"Just because your fiancé never came back from the war and you died a spinster is no reason to constantly harangue my husband, Lila," Miriam Rouchard Buckner said. The petite brunette held her husband's arm and stared up at him with soft, love-filled blue eyes.

"You may be my cousin, Miriam," Lila said, "but that doesn't give you the right to talk to me like that. Especially since you married a traitor."

"That's enough," Tori said again. Both her humor and patience were near to evaporating. The whole situation was ridiculous, but it was one she had grown up with and found delightful most of

29

the time. This was not proving to be one of those times. "Mr. Mitchell is not a Yankee. He is a guest in this house and—"

"I won't have it! You hear? I just won't have it!" Lila fanned herself furiously and began to pace like a tiger on the prowl. She stopped and stuck her face nearly into Tori's. "You have no regard for my feelings, young lady. Or theirs." She jabbed a bony finger toward the others. "My brothers died defending the Confederacy. And we almost lost this plantation."

"Tori, your aunt Lila is upset. Perhaps we should discuss this another ti—"

"Do not dare to speak for me, Ambrose Buckner," Lila snarled. She rushed up to whack her fan soundly across his arm for emphasis.

Tori stifled a laugh. It was like watching David swat at Goliath.

"Lila, Ambrose may have fought on the wrong side, as far as we are concerned, but he is a part of this family. He has a right to be here," Dominic said, his rich voice melodic in the stillness that had followed Lila's tirade.

Startled at the tall Creole's defense of the general, Tori stared at Lila's older brother, who stood directly across the room from them. He was poised before one of the tall gilt-framed mirrors that hung over the mantelpiece. She had always thought of him as the handsomest man she'd ever seen. His black hair curled in ragged waves over the faded butternut-colored collar of his gray Confederate uniform and framed a face whose features were aristocratic and finely chiseled to perfection. His stance was still defiant, and his rich brown eyes remained full of pride for the cause he'd died for at the battle of Gettysburg.

Dominic caught Tori's gaze, the tall gilt-framed mirror at his back reflecting nothing more than the candlelit parlor, Stanton in his wheelchair in the doorway, and Tori standing alone in the center of the ballroom.

"Right?" Lila said, and sniffed. "How can you, of all people, defend him? Why, for all you know it might very well have been Ambrose who fired the shot that killed you."

"He was never that good a shot," Dominic said. His eyes twinkled with mischief.

Tori threw him a thankful glance.

"Humph! The war almost destroyed this family, and having Ambrose Buckner in our midst all these years is just a constant reminder of what *they* did to us." She turned her wrath back on Tori. "And you, disrespectful child, keep allowing those . . . those people into our home."

"Dominic's right," Laura Rouchard said softly, and moved to place a hand on her husband's arm. Dominic's wife was as petite, blonde, and beautiful as her husband was tall, dark, and handsome.

"Tori, what the hell's going on?" Stanton boomed suddenly, his patience beginning to wear thin. He knew *they* were giving her a hard time— that was obvious—but witnessing a one-sided argument struck him as pointless.

"I think the Rouchards are about to declare the

31

Civil War reopened," Tori quipped, glancing at her grandfather.

"There was nothing 'civil' about it," Lila snipped angrily.

"Excuse me," Tori said, "The War between the States." She turned back to Stanton. "Aunt Lila has it in her mind that Mr. Mitchell is a Yankee threatening our precious home." Even through the anger and frustration she felt, Tori couldn't help but chuckle at her own words. But if anyone other than Stanton or Abram overheard her, she knew they'd think her crazy as a loon.

"Well, a woman scorned never does forget, that's what I always say," Stanton grumbled. "You ask me, that soldier who run off and left her most likely figured she was just too damn ornery to live with the rest of his life."

"You shut that old man up, Victoria, or I'll make him sorry he was ever born," Lila screeched. With more speed than Tori would have given her credit for possessing, Lila snatched up a candelabrum from the mantel and waved it toward Stanton's head.

"Put that down," Tori ordered. The humor of the situation was quickly waning.

Stanton eyed the candelabrum warily as it seemed to float through the air of its own accord, the candles flames doing a frantic dance on their wicks in an effort to stay lit.

"Tori, keep her away from me!" Stanton shouted. A bit of panic in his eyes belied the growl of his words.

Tori quickly stepped in front of her aunt.

The candelabrum came to an abrupt halt, and Lila glowered at Tori.

She sighed and placed a hand on the old woman's shoulder. "Please, Auntie, no more trouble. The war's over. Can't we just forget it?"

Lila snatched her hand away. "Never," she snapped. "I will never forget. I may have to spend eternity sharing RiverOaks with this thing—" she jabbed a finger toward the general, "—but I do not have to like it, or welcome another of his kind into my home. And I won't."

"Nor will I," came a deep, resonant voice from the shadows of the foyer.

Chapter Four

"Oh, Lord," Tori moaned as Chance Rouchard stepped into the room, and the fray.

"Now what?" Stanton demanded. He looked around the room for what had made Tori groan and saw nothing, which wasn't unusual since only she could see them.

"Hello, Uncle Chance," Tori said.

"Humph, more like Uncle Trouble," Stanton grumbled.

Chance Rouchard, Dominic and Lila's older brother, threw Stanton a cursory glance and then proceeded to ignore him. He approached Tori and Lila, his black hair glistening beneath the glow of the chandeliers, one errant lock falling forward to dangle carelessly on his wide forehead. Piercing gray eyes looked down from his six-foot-three-inch height to meet Tori's cinnamon gaze. He wrapped an arm around her shoulders. "Tori, honey, I know you want to continue with your grandma's tradition of opening the house to visitors, but Lila is right. It is just too difficult for us to live with the presence of yet another Yankee under our roof, even temporarily."

"Live?" Tori said, almost choking on the word. She wanted to laugh. At the same time she was so angry with them that she wanted to scream. "But that's just the point. You're not alive, any of you."

"Touché, Tori!" Stanton yelled. "You tell 'em, girl."

"I'm going to roll that old man right out of this house," Lila said, and made a threatening move toward the handles of Stanton's wheelchair.

"Lila, please, leave Gramps alone."

Lila whirled around, her hoopskirt swaying about her legs, the soft silk of her black gown causing the barest whisper. "You'd best start worrying about what Ashford's going to think of this, young lady," she said haughtily.

"Ashford?" Tori echoed. "What in heaven's name has Ashford to do with any of this?"

"Ashford is a gentleman, a good Southern gentleman," Lila answered. "I'm sure he has every intention of asking for your hand in marriage, but he may not do so if you continue to flirt with that Yankee." Her fan whipped up a small tornado between them, and Tori felt the wispy curls at her temples move.

"Ashford is a friend, Auntie—nothing more. And I am not flirting with anybody."

"I doubt Ashford would agree. After all, he has been your escort for over a year now."

She decided to ignore that one. Lila would never be convinced that Tori shouldn't marry Ashford, even if she didn't want to. "Mr. Mitchell is a house-guest, for cripe's sake. It's not like I went out troll-ing the streets for him." Though she couldn't think of a better catch if she had.

"But you did consent to escort him around the city tomorrow," Chance said. His tone was almost surly.

Tori stared at him in disbelief and bewilderment as he raised a hand to straighten the pale blue silk cravat at his neck. A diamond stickpin was nestled in its center.

"I give tours for a living," Tori retorted.

"You run a multimillion dollar company. You have guides who give the tours," Chance re-counted.

Tori threw up her hands. "This is ridiculous."

"Tori's right," Dominic said, drawing everyone's attention. The worn gold braid on his faded and frayed gray uniform glowed softly in the candle-light. "For the life of me—" he paused and smiled wistfully at his own choice of phrasing "—I don't know why she puts up with us." He looked at his sister and brother. "I think it's time we all said good-night. We can talk about this later."

Tori found herself suddenly standing in an empty room, except for the presence of her grand-father.

"They gone?" Stanton asked. He wheeled up be-side her.

"Yes, Gramps, they're gone. For now," she added.

"Good. Think I'll go to bed." He wheeled

around and called for Abram, who instantly appeared in the doorway.

In the foyer, Rand stepped away from his position just to the side of the parlor doorway and mounted the stairs. He hurried back down the hallway toward his room. He slipped past the door and closed it quietly behind him. What the hell had that been all about? He sat on the massive poster bed that dominated his room and stared, unseeing, out at the moonlit night. Who in blazes had she been talking to? He lay down on the bed. Whoever it had been, they hadn't answered, or if they had, he'd never heard them. Could she have been on the telephone? He hadn't dared look around the doorway for fear of being seen, but the moment he thought of a telephone he shrugged the possibility away. There were no phones at RiverOaks. At least, according to the brochures on the place. But then maybe that was just for the public, to keep up the image of authenticity.

That had to be it. She'd been arguing with someone on the phone. But with that decision made, another popped up to nag at him. But why did she keep talking about the war being over? And referring to a Yankee being here?

Rand closed his eyes. What was going on here? He tried to tell himself it didn't matter, yet knew that for some reason he didn't even understand, it did. And it shouldn't. In a few days he'd have gotten what he wanted and be on his way home. The thought didn't make him feel as good as it once had. His mind drifted back to the one-sided conversation he'd overheard. He felt a tightening deep within him at the thought of Tori, and a vision of her wrapped securely in his arms filled his thoughts, and that did make him feel good.

Tori stood at a window in the dimly lit parlor and looked out at the grounds of RiverOaks. What had it been like in their time, she wondered, before the War between the States had destroyed their world? She turned and moved to the fireplace, picked up a poker, and stoked the fire. A soft chortle escaped her lips. She was so used to living with them, hearing their tales of what life had been like back then, living with the past, that when she'd first opened the door to Rand Mitchell, seen his blue suit and ivory hat, she'd thought he was a ghost. The ghost of a yankee soldier.

She shook her head. He probably already thought she was crazy. She grew suddenly serious as she remembered the shiver that had raced through her when their hands had touched. He'd felt it, too, she knew. She'd seen it in his eyes. The surprise. She moved to extinguish the oil lamps that sat on twin cherrywood tables at either end of the settee. Well, she'd just have to be pleasant, give him his tour, thanks to her grandfather, and then ignore him for the remainder of his stay. A fling with some California rhinestone cowboy was just not on her agenda, now or ever.

* * *

The next morning the alarm clock's jarring ring shattered her dreams and brought her bolt upright. Tori looked at the clock in disbelief. It couldn't be six o'clock already. She grabbed the shrilling timepiece and jabbed its button down. The room was abruptly plunged into silence.

"Thank heavens," she said, and sighed. She lay back, rolled over, and groaned. Her eyelids didn't want to stay open, and she'd swear her limbs were filled with lead. She felt as if she hadn't slept one wink all night. Instead, her mind had been plagued by images of Rand Mitchell. She sat up. "All right, get hold of yourself, Tori," she admonished herself. "You're acting as if you were sixteen." She lay back against the pillows. Sunlight streamed between the heavy rose damask drapes that had been closed against the night and bathed the room in a golden glow. Tori glanced around the room that had been hers since the day she'd been born, twenty-eight years ago. Every piece of furniture had been in the room for more than a hundred years. A tall armoire, its arched top piece a mass of carved flowers, stood against one wall beside a white, Italian-marble-faced fireplace. Above the fireplace hung an oil painting of Tori and her sister. She felt a lump in her throat as thoughts of Krissy filled her mind. She'd been in the car the night of the accident. Their parents had died instantly. Seventeen-year-old Krissy had lived a few hours, long enough for the ambulance to get her to the hospital, long enough for Tori to get there, and then she'd joined their parents. Tori wiped away the mist of tears that filled her eyes and forced her gaze from the portrait. It was caught by a cheval mirror that stood in one corner of the room.

She laughed at her own reflection. "Why is it that in the movies a woman wakes up in the morning and looks gorgeous? I wake up and look like I've just fought a hundred-year war."

With a sigh, she dragged herself from the warm, cocoonlike mound of covers, enjoyed a quick shower, indoor plumbing being one of the few conveniences ever installed at RiverOaks, and began to dress.

She looked down at the lone shoe on the floor. "Oh, no, not again." Only one lay on the floor where she'd set them last night. Before going to bed the night before she had carefully laid out the clothes she'd wear that day: an orange silk blouse and matching flared skirt. It was an extremely flattering and feminine outfit, and after selecting it she had almost changed her mind, worrying that somewhere in her subconscious she had chosen it with Rand Mitchell in mind. She had placed her orange Caressa shoes on the floor in front of the armoire, side by side. Now there was only one.

Suspicion flared, followed by a spurt of annoyance, but she forced herself to remain calm and searched the room thoroughly.

It proved fruitless. "I knew it," she grumbled. "I just knew it." Getting up from her knees, Tori grabbed her purse and hobbled from the room and down the stairs. She paused in the middle of the foyer, clenched hands on her hips. "All right, Lila," she said, "this isn't going to work, so give it back." Silence surrounded her. "Lila?"

"Good morning, Miss Rouchard," Rand said, stepping around the corner of the parlor entryway.

Oh, Lord, she'd forgotten he was in the house. She tried to hide her bare foot behind the shoed one, nearly lost her balance, felt her cheeks warm and knew they were probably clashing horribly with her blouse. Her gaze met his. Another mistake. She found herself nearly drowning in their depths. Damn, the man oozed more sex appeal than anyone she'd ever met. She felt her pulse race and silently cursed herself for being silly. "Uh, good morning."

"I thought I heard you talking." The questioning look in his eyes made her even more nervous than his words. "Oh, I, uh, was talking to myself. Thinking out loud, you know?" She tried to smile. "I was looking for my shoe, and, uh, berating myself for misplacing it." She sounded like an idiot. What's more, she was acting like one, and she couldn't seem to help herself.

"I saw a shoe out on the porch behind the kitchen earlier when I stepped out for a breath of morning air." He looked down at her feet. "I think it looked just like that one you have on."

It can't be this easy, Tori thought. "Uh, thank you," she mumbled, and hurried past him toward the kitchen. She found the shoe, exactly where Rand had said it was, and slipped it on.

41

When she reentered the kitchen Stanton was sitting at the table, but Rand was nowhere in sight.

Good, she could make her escape. She smiled and moved to kiss Stanton's cheek. "Well, Gramps, I've got to get to the office. I'm going to have dinner with Ash tonight, so don't wait up, okay?" With that, she made for the door, hoping to escape before he could respond. The scowl on his face at her mention of Ashford was already more response than she needed.

"Maybe after you and our new guest do the town today you won't be so interested in going to dinner with that fop," Stanton said.

She gave her grandfather what she hoped looked like a reproving glare. "Gramps, we are not going to *do the town*. I am going to give him a tour, that's all, just like any other customer. And Ash isn't a fop. He's a very nice man." And that was exactly how she'd always thought of him: a very nice man, and she wasn't going to marry someone because he was nice. She and Ash had been dating for a little over a year, but neither was serious about the relationship. They were friends. They'd practically grown up together. Ash liked his freedom, but he also liked a pretty woman on his arm, a steady companion, and someone he could have fun with. Tori fitted that bill. She needed the relaxation her times out with him gave her, and didn't have to worry that he would get serious and want more. That wasn't Ash.

"Hah!" Stanton said. "Rand Mitchell ain't just like any other customer, Tori, and you know it. I seen the way you two looked at each other last night. Sparks was flying, and don't bother to deny it."

"Gramps, please," Tori said. It would be just her luck for Rand Mitchell to walk in on their conversation. Or worse, be in the next room and listening to every word. She dropped her voice to a whisper. "He could be an ax murderer, for all we know. Or escaped from prison or something."

Stanton waved a dismissing hand at her. "Ahhh, and he could be just the man to kick these ninnies around here off their high horse, and be a match for you, too, kiddo."

She smiled and opened the screen door. "I'll get home as soon as I can."

"I'll be up," he said. "You can tell me all about your exciting dinner with Ashford Thibeaux III."

"Be careful," she said, and laughed, "or I might just do that."

She pulled her red Porsche Carrera into a shadowed porte cochere. The narrow carriage entrance ran alongside an old building in the French Quarter that had once been the town house of a very prosperous plantation family. It was now a perfume shop and the owner rented Tori a space to park her car. The old Pontalba buidings, where her office was located, a block away, faced the square and had no space for cars.

It was early, not quite eight, and the air was already heavy with the sultry heat of another summer day. The streets were still quiet, the throngs of tourists that migrated to New Orleans every summer not yet out and about. This was Tori's favorite time, when she loved the quarter best, when she could actually feel its past, the people who had built it, lived in it, and fought for it.

She locked her car and began to walk toward her office, her gaze drifting over the surrounding buildings that she knew so well. Just about every structure in the quarter dated back to the seventeen or eighteen hundreds, and were a combination of Spanish and French architecture, since for years rule of the city had flip-flopped back and forth between the two countries. Their walls were all stuccoed, their paint faded to a soft pastel pink, brown, cream, or green. Tall cypress shutters adorned windows and doorways, iron balustrades supported intricately designed wrought-iron galleries, and wide, arched carriage entrances led to bricked patios lush with ferns, azaleas, and jasmine vines.

"Hey, *chérie,* you not going to say good morning to me?"

Tori paused and looked into the doorway she was just about to pass. She smiled. "Sorry, Gus," she said to the manager of Maspero's Exchange, a small coffeehouse set on the corner of St. Chartres. "Guess I was daydreaming."

He nodded. "I seen me Jean Lafitte this morning. Plain as the nose on your face. Sitting at that table there." He pointed to a table in the corner that reportedly had been the scene of Andrew

44

Jackson's meeting with the famous pirate to secure his aid against a British invasion of the city. "Appeared outta nowhere, then, poof, gone." He laughed heartily at the prattle he usually saved for his paying customers.

"Next time tell him to hang around so I can meet him, too." She waved to the old man and resumed her pace. "Then again, I think I can do without another one of *them* in my life," she mumbled to herself. But her mind wasn't really on Lafitte, or Jackson, or even on work. It was on a tall man with blond hair that looked like strands of pure gold, and eyes that reminded her of a moonless, stormy night.

She rounded the corner and moved along the wide walkway that separated Jackson Square from the building where her office was located. She glanced across the square at a building identical to her own. They were of brick and dated back to 1851 when the Baroness Pontalba had built them as the city's first apartments. She had also been the one responsible for the landscaping of the square, and for changing its name from Place d'Armes, which Tori secretly liked better, to Jackson Square, in honor of the city's hero of the time, Andrew Jackson.

Stepping into the air-conditioned coolness of her office, Tori was not surprised to find it already a hum of activity. Her secretary, Sherrille, was sketching out an itinerary for the proposal of a jazz tour while listening to someone chatter in her ear on the phone that was propped on her shoulder.

Leslie, one of the guides, was handing out maps and brochures of Bayou John's Swamp Jaunt to a group of Midwest retirees.

"Tori," Sherrille said, as she placed the phone back on its cradle. "Your client is already here. I gave him coffee and let him wait in your office."

A frown knitted her brow, and Tori felt a sense of confusion. Client? What client? Taking the cup of coffee Sherrille held out to her, Tori opened the door to her office and tried not to show her surprise.

Rand Mitchell lounged casually in the antique Victorian chair that sat facing her wide desk, the chair's rosewood trim and brocade padding nearly obscured beneath his solid frame. His long legs were stretched out in front of him, one booted foot propped across the other, muscular arms crossed over his wide chest.

How in blazes had he beaten her here?

Rand looked up lazily and smiled. "Good morning—again," he drawled.

The deep, sultry tone of his voice seemed to reach out to her, caress her, and sent a shiver up her spine. Her fingers tightened around the coffee cup. Oh, why had her grandfather done this to her?

Rand's gaze slid over her easily. Rarely did he mix pleasure and business, but then rarely did he ever find himself wanting to. Last night he had become entranced by a vision of loveliness from days long past. Today, in the light of the morning sun, he found himself confronted by one of the most beautiful women he'd ever seen. But it wasn't just

46

her beauty. There was something else about her that drew him. He just didn't know what it was. He watched her walk around the desk, her thick hair, the blue-black color of a raven's wing, sparkled as if sprinkled with diamonds. She glanced at him and the soft brown of her eyes suddenly reminded him of a desert at dusk.

Tori's gaze shot toward a corner of the room as if she'd heard something. Rand looked over his shoulder, saw nothing, and turned back to her.

"I—I'm surprised to see you here," she said. "I mean, I thought you were still at the house."

"I left right after we spoke in the foyer. I had some phone calls to make." He rose and moved slowly around the room, looking at the books on her shelves, the pictures of her parents and Krissy, the small stuffed dog her father had given her for her eighth birthday.

The room suddenly seemed too small to hold two people.

"So, where are we going today?" He turned back to her and pinned her with his gaze.

Her mind groped frantically for a way to get out of spending the day with him and found none. At least none that sounded logical or sincere. "I, um, haven't decided yet." She moved to sit in the tall wing chair behind her desk and plunked her coffee cup down, then watched in horror as hot brown liquid splashed up one side of the mug and sloshed all over her desktop. She dabbed at it with a piece of paper. "Well, I remember you said you wanted to take a ride on a riverboat."

"Yes, but at night. I'd imagine it's more romantic that way." The gleam in his eyes was anything but innocent.

"Oh." Tori felt her face warm. Suddenly an image of them standing on the deck of *The Natchez*, bathed by the pale light of the moon, their arms around each other, flitted into her head, and with it the urge to know what it would be like to be kissed by him, to feel his lips press to hers. She stiffened in alarm. What in heaven's name was the matter with her?

Chapter Five

A knock sounded. Both Tori and Rand looked at the door as it swung open even before she could utter a response.

Ashford Carlisle Thibeaux III stood framed in the doorway, then, without waiting for an invitation, he entered. With three strides of his long legs he was across the room and standing beside Tori. He regarded Rand, who had settled back into the chair before Tori's desk, but it was a cursory glance, one obviously meant to dismiss him as nothing more than one of Tori's paying customers.

"Victoria, sweetheart, I just wanted to drop by and remind you of our dinner date for tonight." He slid a thigh onto the corner of Tori's mahogany desk, leaned toward her and pecked her cheek with a quick kiss. "We're joining the Devereauxes, so don't get lost in your work and forget."

Tori stole a quick glance at Rand and wished instantly she'd refrained. His opinion of Ashford was written all over his face. In fact, it couldn't be any more blatant if it was flashing in passionate pink

49

neon. She turned back to Ash and smiled. He was a gentleman and considered in most circles as one of the most eligible bachelors in New Orleans. "I haven't forgotten, Ash. I'm looking forward to it," she said sweetly. Her voice oozed sugar, so much so that she almost cringed. What was she doing? She never played games like this. Ash took her hand in his, a proprietary gesture that was unusual for him. She felt a twinge of surprise.

Rand felt a flash of disgust. Obviously Tori viewed Ash as handsome, charming, and debonair. He saw a ninety-pound weakling who seemed pompous, rude, and conceited. His gaze raked over Ash. Lord, was this the type of man she went for? The man's double-breasted blue silk blazer, complete with gleaming gold eagle-imprinted buttons, and gray slacks were obviously tailor-made and cost top dollar, and his silk hose and Italian loafers were most assuredly very expensive. And he absolutely glistened gold: a silk handkerchief that fluttered from his breast pocket, a bracelet that encircled one bony wrist, a Cassini watch the other, and a thick chain nestled in the dark hair that grew at the base of his throat. Rand wondered if the dark hairs that curled out from the open V of his shirt collar ever attached themselves to the chain. Could be painful, he mused, and smiled wickedly to himself at the thought. What the hell did Tori see in this overdressed, gold-laden peacock?

"Well, dahling," Ashford drawled, sounding like a very bad imitation of Rhett Butler, "I know how sometimes you just bury yourself here in the office with all this silliness about work, but we can't let that interfere with our plans, now can we?" He nudged the bottom of Tori's chin with his forefinger, completely unaware of the glint of indignation that flashed into her eyes at his condescending gesture and remarks. "I'll pick you up here at seven-ish."

Tori felt her temper flare at his cockishly possessive attitude but she squelched it, puzzled. This was not like Ashford. She rose from her seat and forced a smile to her lips. "Ash, I'd like you to meet Mr. Rand Mitchell. He's a guest at River-Oaks."

Surprise registered in Ashford's eyes. He swung around, hip still on Tori's desk, and looked at Rand. "Guest?"

Rand smiled. The man was upset that he was staying at RiverOaks. The smile widened and Rand stood so that Ash, in his present position, had to look up at him. Rand forced himself to offer his hand and almost cringed when Ashford's handshake turned out to be nothing more than a weak movement of his wrist.

"I'm giving Mr. Mitchell a tour of the city today," Tori said, all too aware of the sudden tension in the room.

"You? But you never give tours anymore."

"Well, I'm making an exception for Mr. Mitchell." She smiled and gave a reassuring pat to Ashford's arm.

"How nice," Ash replied nastily. He turned his gaze on Rand, but the smile that curved his lips did

51

not warm his eyes. "I'm curious, Mr. Mitchell, just how did you manage to get the president of Rouchard Travel to give you a personal tour?"

"I asked," Rand said simply, and felt like laughing when Ash's face nearly turned purple. Why he was needling the man he had no idea, but it felt good. "Actually, Mr. . . ."

"Thibeaux," Ashford said, clearly miffed. "Ashford Carlisle Thibeaux III."

"Yes, well, how about if I just call you Ash?" Rand said, and continued without waiting for a reply. "As I was about to say, Ash, last night during my visit with Tori—" Rand glanced at Tori and smiled suggestively "—a very pleasant visit, she graciously consented to be my personal guide today."

"Last night?" Ashford echoed. He turned a shocked gaze on Tori. "Your so-called family night?"

If she'd been able to put her hands on a two-by-four at that moment, Tori knew she would have given serious consideration to splitting the thick wave of blond hair on Rand Mitchell's head. As it was all she could do for the moment was give him a look that could have turned the summer air of Death Valley to frost.

She slipped her arm around Ashford's and walked him to the door. "We'll talk later, Ash. I'll be ready at seven."

Still obviously piqued, Ashford leaned down and brushed his lips across Tori's. "Yes, seven." He looked over her shoulder at Rand and, with a sly grin, patted Tori's rear as he turned to leave.

Her little mew of shock was not lost on Rand.

"Well, he's quite a —"

"Never mind," Tori snapped. She grabbed her purse from the desk and called back over her shoulder. "If you really want to see New Orleans, Mr. Mitchell, then I suggest we get going. Sherrille, I'll be out for a few hours." She walked from the office without a backward glance. If Rand Mitchell wanted a tour, then he could just follow her.

She walked briskly through the crowd of tourists who had gathered about the square during the short time she'd been in her office. Many of the sidewalk artists were still setting up their displays and hanging their paintings from the wrought-iron fence that surrounded the square. She didn't pause until she was beside the bronze statue of a mounted Andrew Jackson that was the centerpiece of the square.

She stopped at the granite base of the statue nd turned abruptly back to Rand. "This statue," she said in a monotone, "was placed here by the Baroness Pontalba in 1856 in honor of Jackson's defense of New Orleans against the British in 1814. The square itself, before that time, was called the Place d'Armes."

Rand crossed his arms over his chest, stood with his feet at a wide stance, and watched her in amusement. She was angry with him for making Ashford the wimp jealous. Good. He smiled to himself, but made sure the amusement did not show on his face.

53

"The inscription on the base—" Tori pointed to the granite and kept her gaze averted from his—"The Union Must and Shall Be Preserved' was carved into it on orders from Major General Benjamin Butler during the Civil War when his troops occupied New Orleans. On either side of the square—" she indicated the two-story brick structures "—are the Pontalba buildings, erected in 1851 by the baroness as apartments. The church—" she turned toward St. Louis Cathedral at the eastern edge of the square "—was—"

"Time out," Rand interrupted. He held his hands up as if in surrender. "If we're going to go through the entire day with you doing your impersonation of a very impersonal tour guide and me playing history-minded tourist, I'm going to fall asleep on my feet."

"I *am* a tour guide, kind of, and you *are* a tourist," Tori said coolly. She tried not to look at him, not to be caught by those fathomless blue eyes. She had already determined that every time she did, her heart seemed to melt a little and her pulses began imitating the Indy 500.

"Can't we accomplish a tour *and* enjoy it at the same time?" Rand said. "I'd like to get to know you better, Tori." He tried to keep his tone light and found it not an easy task. She had surprised him. Hell, he'd surprised himself. A romantic interlude was not the reason he had come to New Orleans, but ever since he'd set eyes on Tori Rouchard, it seemed to be the only thing on his mind. And he didn't even know why. She was beautiful, that went

without saying, but he'd dated a lot of beautiful women, and none of them drew him, intrigued him, as Tori did. She reminded him of a butterfly. Beautiful and delicate in appearance, with an air of fragility about her, yet he sensed that beneath that facade was a strong will and a lot of mettle. There had to be, he reasoned, for her to run Rouchard Travel. A butterfly made of steel. No wonder Jason had failed.

"We don't need to be friends to have a good tour, Mr. Mitchell," Tori said. She desperately tried to avoid looking into his eyes.

He took a step closer to her, and she felt his nearness as intensely as if he'd touched her. She tried to take a deep breath and found it ragged, her mouth dry.

"No, we don't have to be, but it would make the day a whole lot more enjoyable," Rand answered, taking her hand in his. "And we could start by you calling me Rand."

His thumb rubbed slowly and teasingly over the knuckles of her hand as he stared down at her, waiting for her answer.

"All . . . all right, Rand," Tori choked out.

"Good." His tone changed from low and seductive to jovial. "What say we start with breakfast? I'm famished."

"How about Brennan's?"

He shrugged. "You're the guide." He cupped her elbow lightly with his hand and they turned toward the cathedral.

They were halfway through the square when a

burst of wind swirled up in front of them. It swooped back down to the ground and then shot up directly into Rand's face, smacking him with dirt, pebbles, and bits of dry leaves and nearly blinding him.

"What the hell?" he sputtered and threw up both of his hands to cover his face. He rubbed his stinging eyes frantically, tears of pain welling up and flowing over his now red and irritated lids. "Damn, where did that come from?" He blinked several times in an effort to refocus his vision.

Tori caught a flash of black out of the corner of her eye and turned to see a frail-looking woman in an old-fashioned hoopskirt, its hem skimming the surface of the walkway as she moved hurriedly away from them. Her bony shoulders were shaking up and down, as if she was laughing.

Lila! Tori looked quickly from her aunt to Rand and back at the retreating old woman again. That freak of wind had been no accident. Anger and frustration warmed her breast. It was becoming painfully obvious that the next couple of weeks, while Rand was their houseguest, were not going to be peaceful.

Within minutes they had walked the few short blocks from the square to Brennan's restaurant on Royal. "This is one of my favorites," Tori said as they were seated at a table on the patio, "and one of the city's oldest."

"Very romantic." He looked at their surroundings with an appraising eye. On two sides of the courtyard was brick wall that was nearly covered with a profusion of ferns and vines, while the other two sides were the restaurant itself, an old house whose gallery had been screened and set with tables. An ornate fountain stood in the center of the courtyard.

Tori blushed. She hadn't thought of the setting when she'd suggested Brennan's. If she had, she would have taken him to The Waffle House, which had about as much romantic ambiance as a fish shack. She flipped open the menu and just as quickly closed it and set it down. A waiter, dressed in a tuxedo, appeared at her side.

"Eggs Hussarde," she said. "And *café noir*."

Rand looked at her and then at the waiter. "Whatever she said is what I'll have, too." Hopefully it wasn't fish eggs and some kind of fancy espresso coffee. He hated that stuff.

"So, what do you have planned to show me today?" he asked, leaning on the table and pinning her with his gaze.

"I thought we'd start with a drive out to Chalmette Battlefield." She almost sighed in relief as the waiter appeared with their coffee and allowed her a reason to look away from him. His eyes were absolutely mesmerizing. She practically put a stranglehold on the cup.

Rand took a swallow of his coffee and slammed the cup back down on the table as he jerked forward and choked, sputtered, then coughed.

Tori tried not to laugh.

"What the hell is this stuff?" he asked, staring at her.

"Coffee," she said, and tried to keep an innocent expression on her face. "Black."

"Yeah, but how long did it brew—twenty-four hours?"

She smiled. "No. It's chicory coffee. Most restaurants serve it unless you ask for something else. But if it's too strong for you . . . " She let the challenge hang unfinished.

Rand settled back in his chair and met her gaze and the challenge of her words. "It's fine. But as long as we're translating the food, why don't you tell me what I ordered for breakfast? Eggs on fire?"

Tori laughed, a melodic sound that reminded him of the tinkling of wind chimes on a rippling breeze. Before she had a chance to answer, the waiter reappeared with the meal in question and placed their plates on the table before them.

Rand looked at the food suspiciously. He could see the rounded edges of two pieces of thick, toasted bread. On top of them were slices of ham. That was all he could identify. The mountain of color that topped the toast and ham consisted of a light brown layer of something, then white, which he guessed might be eggs, and some kind of yellow sauce had been poured over the entire thing. A slice of tomato sat to one side of his plate. Well, at least he knew what that was.

"It's toast and ham with *marchand de vin* sauce, which is in turn topped by eggs and then hollandaise sauce. It's really delicious."

"Uh-huh," Rand muttered, reserving his opinion

until he tasted it. He was usually a steak-and-pota-toes man. Fancy sauces and weird concoctions of food he left to other people's palates.

Tori furtively watched him eat. He wasn't like Ash, who normally picked at this and that and left most of his meal uneaten. Once Rand decided that he liked it, the Eggs Hussarde vanished rapidly from his plate.

"Well, I'm glad to see that my choice didn't dis-appoint you," she said as he finished the food and lifted the coffee cup to his lips.

He looked at her steadily for several long sec-onds before answering. His eyes held hers captive, sending her the ageless, unspoken message that al-ways passed between a man and woman attracted to each other, and for just the briefest of moments Tori felt as if the world had disappeared and they were the only two people left in the universe. "I doubt if anything you could do would disappoint me, Tori," he said finally. Of course, that wasn't quite true; there *was* one thing, but he didn't want to think about that now.

Chapter Six

Tori pulled her car into a parking space, turned the ignition key off, and shook her head. Her wind-whipped hair cascaded over her shoulders. She laughed. "I must look like I stuck my finger in a light socket."

Rand looked at her dark hair, touseled into a mane of waves and curls about her face, and smiled. "You look beautiful," he said. The honey-smooth tone of his voice wrapped around her and sent a glorious shiver of warmth through her.

Tori tried to ignore it. She didn't want to feel anything for Rand Mitchell. It would only complicate her life further, and she certainly didn't need that. She had enough problems just trying to stay on top of the company's dealings, a job she had never wanted in the first place. She'd majored in marketing in college, and had been very happy as the marketing director for Rouchard Travel. Being its president had never been one of her aspirations, but that had no longer been a choice when her parents had been killed. It wasn't as if it was hurting her love life, anyway. She didn't have one. A fleeting sense of guilt swept over her at thought of Ashford, but she shrugged it away. That relationship was strictly platonic, and that was the safest kind, at least for her. The family, or rather their past actions, had convinced her of that. *They* would never accept someone like Rand Mitchell even if she was interested in him. Her interests didn't matter. They had refused to accept Tom, her former fiancé, and that time of her life had proven one big disaster. She still felt a little of the hurt whenever she thought about it. And as far as the family was concerned, they considered Rand, as they had Tom, a Yankee, and as such, their sworn enemy. She slipped her dark glasses back on and climbed from the sports car.

Rand straightened to his full height and Tori found herself admiring his length. A white polo shirt stretched taut across his broad shoulders to accentuate their breadth, then tapered to a narrow waist. He wore beige slacks and dark cowboy boots, both a compliment to his long legs.

Tori suddenly wondered how her body would fit to his.

"I thought this was a battlefield," Rand said, unconsciously jolting her from the sensuous thoughts. He took her hand in his as they walked down a path that was bordered with a wide field of lush green grass on one side, and a row of polished black-and-brass cannons on the other.

"Uh, it is. Or it was." She ordered her heart to stop its ridiculously frantic pace and followed his

61

gaze to the mansion at the opposite end of the field. It was hard to think with his fingers entwined with hers.

"Then what's that?" He pointed to a large mansion at the opposite end of the open field.

"That's the Beauregard House. It was moved here long after the battle. It was basically in ruin and relocated here for restoration. That confuses a lot of people at first."

"Beautiful old place," Rand said, and considered it with a practiced eye. It would be a good tour headline. The house was two stories in height, its outer walls painted a soft pastel pink. Six tall white Corinthian columns graced the front with railings and balustrades between each on both the main and second-story galleries, and supported a roof whose graceful slope was interspersed with dormer windows.

"Most of the old plantation homes were. Unfortunately quite a few of them were destroyed in the name of progress."

The rooms in the old house seemed surprisingly small to Rand, especially in comparison to those at RiverOaks. They moved through them, paused at an exhibit or two, and stepped out onto the back gallery, which overlooked the river. Tori moved toward the steps that led down to the sloping garden at the same moment Rand did. Her shoulder collided with his. At the same time, unnerved by the accidental contact, she missed a step. Rand grabbed her shoulders and pulled her back to him. He had meant only to prevent her fall, but once his hands had touched her and he'd felt her body pressed against his, rational thought left him.

Tori found herself unable to move as she felt one of Rand's arms slip around her waist. Her breath was caught in her throat, and her heart was pounding like a snare drummer's stick gone out of control. With his free hand he reached to entangle his fingers within the curls of hair that brushed her shoulder, then let the silken blue-black strands slip through his fingers, slowly.

A tiny shiver rippled over her skin, leaving her nerve endings tingling in anticipation.

He felt her tremble and tightened his embrace. "Thank you," he said, his voice a hushed rumble.

Tori frowned, confused. "For . . . for what?" she croaked, the effort to speak almost too much for her constricted throat.

"Giving me an excuse to hold you. I've wanted to since the first moment I saw you."

His gaze moved slowly over her face, then drifted downward, to the open V of her silk blouse and to the swell of bosom beneath the thin fabric. Her breasts were crushed against his chest and he could feel her heartbeat.

"We . . . we should continue on your tour." The words were little more than a tumble of raspy breaths, barely audible, nearly incoherent.

"I am," Rand said. His eyes, as much as his arm, held her in place against him. He lifted a finger to her face and moved it lightly over her bottom lip, a feather-light touch that sent a new rush of shivers through her.

She looked down at the hand that had moved to run slowly along the curve of her cheek and down to her jaw. It was a strong hand, powerful, and its touch caused sensations to erupt within her that she didn't want to feel, and yet longed to continue.

He cocked his head, lifted the hair from her shoulder, and pressed his lips against the curve of her neck.

Tori started, but did not pull away. The flesh beneath his lips burned, as if touched by flame, while heat raced through her veins. Rand's arms enveloped her and held her to him, his hands warm and strong on her back. Her own hands slid over his arms. She felt the sinewy muscle and the power within those ropy contours. She tried to inhale deeply, felt the breath snarl within her breast, and the fragrance of him invade her already swirling emotions. A tangy scent, a redolent of pine-covered mountains and snow-capped peaks, emanated from him.

When his lips left the side of her neck, Tori felt suddenly deserted. Her eyes opened just in time to see his mouth descending on hers. She let her eyelids drift closed again, suddenly as helpless to deny him, to push away from his embrace, as if they were fused together, body to body.

He had said he'd wanted to hold her, to kiss her, since the moment they'd met, and now she, too, was forced to admit to herself that was exactly what she'd wanted, in spite of the consequences, which she knew would be dire.

The sparkling reflection of the sun on the river,

the movement of tourists in the house behind them, and on the lawns before them, the droning of the movie being show in the parlor, documenting the house's and battlefield's history all disappeared from her consciousness and faded into nothingness. Only Rand existed, this mysterious man who had walked into her life only a few short hours ago, and changed her world.

His lips brushed lightly over hers, a caress that left her yearning for more. Her hands slid upward, moving over his shoulders until her fingers threaded their way into the ragged strands of hair that curled over the back of his shirt collar. She leaned into him, letting her length meld with his.

His mouth returned to capture hers in a kiss that was neither a gentle brushing nor a savage claim but a branding of her senses. She felt the hot, moist tip of his tongue at the corner of her lips, and then it slid into her mouth, demanding her acquiescence and conquering any last shreds of resistance that might still lurk within her.

Her own tongue moved to entwine with his, sparring, taking and giving caress for caress, a duel of the senses, a challenge to pent-up and long-denied emotions.

For long seconds after Rand's mouth lifted from hers, Tori stood with her eyes closed, savoring the feel of his arms around her, a band of strength that she could lean on, as she had on her father. For six months she had tried to do it all on her own, determined to need no one, to step into her father's shoes and run the company, take care of her grandfather and Abram, and oversee the plantation. But with one kiss, one mind-shattering kiss, she had to admit to herself that she didn't want to do it on her own anymore, didn't want to be the strong, independent businesswoman she had been forced to become.

"Now look what's happened because of your fiddling around and making us late," Lila snapped. Her glare jumped from Chance to Tori and Rand, still embracing, and back to Chance. "What are we going to do now?"

"This," Chance said, with a twinkle of mischief in his dark eyes. He stood beside Tori. "He's not the one for you, you know," he said softly.

Tori's head whipped around and she stared at her uncle. A groan slipped from her throat. "Go away."

"What?" A frown tugged at Rand's brow as his eyes filled with confusion at her words.

She should never have let things go this far. It was wrong. She was asking for trouble, and seeing Chance and Lila here meant she was going to get it if she didn't put a stop to this . . . now. She tried to twist away from him.

Though puzzled, Rand did not release her. His arms held her waist, his eyes hers.

She moved her hands to the front of his shoulders and pushed against them. "Let me go, Rand." Her tone was curt, yet pleading.

His arms fell away from her.

He was looking at her as if she'd lost her mind.

She knew that look well, had seen it a dozen times on other men's faces, dates that *the family* had also not approved of.

He reached out for her. She flinched and pushed his arms away. "No, I can't."

"Tori, what's the matter?"

"I . . . we . . . this is no good. Not between us." She shook her head and glanced toward the door to the house.

Chance smiled and bowed deeply, an exaggerated gesture of the usually gallant act, and stepped back. "I'm sorry, honey. We just don't want to see you hurt, and he *will* hurt you, if you let him."

"He's a Yankee," Lila said. Her fan fluttered in front of a wrinkled face that was smug with satisfaction. "You know the rules, Tori. He'll never get the acceptance you need, you know that, and without it, no good can come of this relationship."

The remainder of the day had gone completely and swiftly downhill, from a late lunch at an outdoor café where Tori had smiled and chatted with everyone except Rand to a brisk walking tour of the French Quarter with Tori the Professional Guide rattling off facts and figures of historical data about the city and its past inhabitants.

By the time they returned to her office he didn't know which emotion was strongest—the desire to take her into his arms again and feel the seductive press of her body against his, or the urge to wrap his fingers around her pretty neck and strangle her.

Squelching his flash of temper and trying to ignore the heat of desire that simmered within him,

Rand forced a lightness to his voice that he was far from feeling. "How about accompanying me to the best restaurant in town for dinner?"

It was well past closing time, and the agency offices were dark and deserted. She fumbled to unlock the entry door, then turned to look at him and found him directly behind her, their bodies only inches apart. Her gaze met his and the smoldering darkness of his eyes drew her to him, their fathomless blue depths beckoning her to a world she had never seen before. She steeled herself against the invisible threads of that hypnotic lure. "No, thank you, Rand," she said curtly. "I have a date with Ash." With that she opened the door, entered, and snapped it closed in his face.

Chapter Seven

The restaurant was crowded, but then Antoine's, which enjoyed a reputation as the city's oldest restaurant, was always crowded. People they knew kept stopping by their table to chat, and Ashford was being so overly solicitious to her that Tori was ready to scream. She didn't like people being nice to her when she felt like ripping someone's head off. It was annoying to have to smile, to exchange pleasantries and be gracious when she'd rather snarl.

"Tori, whatever is the matter with you?" Ashford asked for the umpteenth time. He reached across the table to pat her hand with his long, slim, expertly manicured fingers. "Did you have a bad day, *chérie?*"

"Yes!" At the smug look on his face she was immediately sorry she'd admitted her day had been anything less than perfect.

"Well, it's no wonder, having to spend it with

that Rand Mitchell person. But I don't understand why you insist on working, anyway, *chérie*. I mean, the Rouchards are one of the oldest families in New Orleans. And you are one of the wealthiest women in the South, if not the whole country. It's not like you *have* to work, Tori. I've never been one to accept women working."

"And just who should run the company, Ash—my grandfather?" Tori snapped. Her nerves were frayed, but that wasn't really Ashford's fault and she knew it. Most of the time she found him charming. Tonight, for no apparent reason, she was finding him annoying. Extremely so, and his condescending attitude was enough to make her see red. She couldn't seem to keep her mind on the moment. Instead she kept thinking about Rand, and that was doing nothing for her mood.

"He needs help," Lila whispered, looking at Ashford in disgust. "I've never seen anything so pitiful." She fluttered a fan in front of her face and the white lace pelisse collar that encircled her scrawny neck rippled slightly over her nearly flat breasts.

"Sure isn't like in our time," Chance said, and shook his head.

"Whatever happened to sweeping a woman off her feet?" Lila griped. "The dolt's been courting her for over a year now, and still nothing! What in blazes is he waiting for?"

70

No sooner had she spoken than Chance was across the crowded restaurant and standing beside Ashford.

"Oh, Lord," Lila muttered. "Does he always have to take me so literally?" Her eyes rolled heavenward.

Suddenly Ash's arm was jerked upward and pushed toward Tori's face. His fingers stiffly but gently brushed over the skin of her cheeks, lightly flickered down the long column of her neck, and then skipped back up to trace the curving line of her jaw, which had nearly dropped open in shock at Ash's gesture. He sensed her surprise, but knew it didn't come anywhere close to his own. He was not one for public display of sincere affection, but at the moment it seemed he had no choice in the matter. There was a hard, gripping pressure on his wrist, as if something were holding him, moving his arm and hand for him. He tried to jerk away and the pressure tightened.

Ash nearly bit his tongue at the short shock of pain that seared through his arm.

Abruptly his chair slid sideways, half-thumping, half-gliding with such force and haste that Ash barely managed to retain his seat.

Lost in her own thoughts, Tori didn't hear Ashford's muted squeal or see the shadow of panic that flashed across his face and turned his normally golden skin momentarily stark white.

71

He gripped the table and looked around quickly, but there was no one nearby.

Tori, moved by Ashford's gentle touch and sudden display of affection, smiled, still too immersed in her own thoughts to sense the fear he was trying desperately to squelch. She felt his hand tremble slightly as it held hers and experienced a flash of guilt. Ash was usually demonstrative and showy, everything done with a sense of flash and daring, but never sensitive. Maybe he was trying to soothe her bad mood.

"I'm sorry for being such a grump tonight, Ash." She laid her other hand on his arm. "I guess it was just too long a day. Would you mind if we called it an early evening?"

Ashford forced a smile that was more of a grimace. Suddenly something held the back of his head, like a steel vise, and he found his face pushed toward hers. His lips rammed against her cheekbone.

"Ash, are you all right?" Tori pulled away from him. She gingerly touched the cheekbone he had just plowed into and frowned. She looked around suspiciously, but saw no one.

He nodded and stood abruptly, so fast that he nearly knocked his chair over. He didn't know what the hell was happening, but at the moment, he didn't care. All he knew was that he wanted out of this restaurant, and the quicker the better. The pressure on his wrist and head suddenly disappeared, and he found himself in complete control of his physical self again, but the lump of fear in his throat had momentarily paralyzed his vocal cords and the coiled knot of panic in the pit of his stomach still threatened to reverse the course of his recently consumed dinner.

Tori walked beside him out of the restaurant, and though she tried to look casual, her gaze kept darting furtively toward Ashford. What had gotten into him? If this were Rand beside her, she thought, she'd suspect Lila and Chance of having done something to him, but they never bothered Ash—they liked him.

In contrast to the busy restaurant, the streets of the French Quarter were relatively quiet, with only a few tourists still wandering about the narrow sidewalks. Several times a carriage filled with tourists passed them, and as the steady clip-clop of the trotting horse echoed against the still, sultry night, Tori's mind conjured up images of another New Orleans, a grander, more elegant, slower-paced New Orleans, and a time she sometimes wished she had lived in. In the distance, a shrill whistle announced the approach of one of the riverboats that catered to the city's never-ending throng of tourists.

With each step they took, Ashford felt his rubbery legs turning back into flesh and blood, and the tremble, which had nearly crashed his knees together on the way out of the restaurant, had subsided. By the time they reached Tori's car, he had managed to regain his composure, or at least most of it, as long as he didn't think about what had happened.

She unlocked the driver's door of her sports car, then turned to say good-night to Ashford. His arms slipped around her waist and he drew her to him, the curves of her breasts crushed against the white silk of his shirtfront. His mouth claimed hers in a soft, moist kiss.

Tori rested her hands on his shoulders, tasted the apricot brandy that lingered on Ashford's tongue, and felt the warmth of his hands as they caressed her back and held her to him.

"Well, it's about time that boy did something!" Lila said, and rubbed her spindly hands together in glee. A wide grin split the ancient-looking face as she watched the two embracing figures within the shadows of the porte cochere. A single flambeau on the wall high above the couple illuminated the area, the dancing flames within the glass sconce bathing them in an aura of warm golden light.

Chance nodded in agreement. "Yeah, he sure is slow. Never took me any year to get my way with a pretty young thing." He chortled as vivid memories of *The Lilac Queen* and the numerous female passengers of the riverboat who had visited his cabin drifted through his mind.

"That's enough of that," Lila said irritably, and rapped his arm with her closed fan. "Tori's not like those trollops you used to carouse with. She's family, and a lady."

"Yeah," Chance sighed, resignation evident in his tone. He touched the diamond stickpin that nestled within the folds of his silk cravat and then straightened his shoulders. "Well, it doesn't look like he needs any more help from us. Let's go."

Tori tried to respond to Ashford's kiss, she really did, but her heart just wasn't cooperating, to say nothing of her mind. Images of Rand Mitchell kept flitting through her mind's eye to play havoc with her concentration, which was about nil. As her hands slid over Ashford's thin, rolling shoulders, she couldn't help but remember the feel of Rand's muscular curves and aura of strength. Ashford's kiss, which could almost be described as kitten gentle, instantly evoked a memory and a comparison to Rand's mouth on hers, hungry, demanding, and tantalizing.

Ash pulled her closer, the circle of his arms tightened around her, pressed her gently to his tall, lean body, and recollection of Rand's hard, sinewy length surged through her mind. She pulled away from him and fumbled with her car keys, buying a moment to compose herself. What was the matter with her? Ashford always kissed her good-night, and it was usually a pleasant experience. True, stars never soared through the sky and burst into brilliant showering sparks, wedding bells didn't go off inside of her head, or any bells at all for that matter, and rockets didn't zoom past, but it had been comfortable. She liked their relationship. So why, tonight, did she feel so frustrated and empty? And why couldn't she stop thinking of Rand Mitchell, a man she hardly knew?

Only a few short blocks away, in the midst of a crowded bar, jazz music blared loudly, and Rand struggled with the very same thoughts and emotions that were plaguing Tori.

He had come to New Orleans to size up the new owner of Rouchard Travel. Her father had been a shrewd businessman, and not interested in selling his company. Elliott Rouchard had also managed to avoid Rand's attempts at a forced takeover, though that had been a pretty farfetched idea to begin with, but not one he'd given up. He had hoped the daughter, now that, with the death of her parents, she was the new president, would be an easier mark. But ever since he'd met her, business had been the last thing on his mind.

Rand set his beer mug down on the table and looked around the crowded bar, though his thoughts were far from what his eyes were seeing. What the hell was the matter with him? He dated lots of women, beautiful women, and none had ever had the effect on him that Tori

Rouchard seemed to have. He could barely think of anything else — and that was dangerous. He wanted that company, damn it, and getting emotionally involved with her could ruin everything. He had come to New Orleans to uncover her vulnerabilities, to find out what caused the woman who'd inherited a megacorporation to turn down every offer to sell it. He had hoped to find something that would tell him how to get her to at least negotiate, to consider his company's offers instead of flatly rejecting them.

But now he wasn't even sure he could go through with his own plan, and he sure as hell didn't like to think of resorting to what Jason called Plan B.

Several diners at a nearby table suddenly burst out in a gale of laughter. The sound drew Rand's gaze and pulled him from his thoughts, causing him to realize just how tangled his emotions had become since arriving at River-Oaks. He was supposed to be here on business, uncovering anything and everything that would help him in securing Rouchard Travel. Instead he was sitting alone in a damn bar and brooding over a woman he barely knew.

He thought of where she was at that moment, with Ashford Thibeaux III. An expression of utter distaste screwed up his face. The mere thought of Tori in that wimp's arms sent a shudder of revulsion through him.

Suddenly the glass of beer he'd set on the table tipped and fell to its side, the foamy golden liquid splashing across the small wooden table, over the edge, and directly into his lap.

"What the . . . ?" Rand gawked at the toppled glass in disbelief. His hand had been nowhere near it, and no one had bumped into the table.

Across the crowded room, Lila Rouchard laughed and turned away. It was time to go home.

Chapter Eight

Rand pulled his rental car to a stop before the house. It appeared dark, as if everyone had already retired for the night. On the wall beside the entry door, a flame danced within a gold-plated glass wall sconce. It cast a macabre glow over the entrance of the old mansion. Shadows hovered around the front door and wide, pillared gallery and fluttered eerily with each flicker of the tiny flame.

"If this doesn't look like a haunted house, I don't know what the hell does," Rand mumbled. He climbed the shallow, fan-shaped stairs that led to the gallery and reached for the shiny brass handle, but as his fingertips touched it, the door opened.

"Good evening, Mr. Mitchell."

"Uh, good evening, Abram." Rand entered the foyer, which was illuminated by a lone candle on an antique skirt table set against one wall, its back mirrored to give ladies of the past a glimpse of their hemlines, shoes, or whatever else they needed to see past or beneath the voluminous bell shape of their hoopskirts. He had learned that today in his tour with Tori. The single candle gave the foyer an unearthly look. "Great place to make a horror movie," Rand mumbled to himself.

"We have been approached," Abram said. "About films."

Rand turned sharply, unaware he had spoken loud enough for the old man to hear. He smiled, hoping his words hadn't offended him. "Is Miss Rouchard still up?"

Abram closed the front door and moved to pick up the candle. "She has not yet returned this evening," he said, and shuffled to the staircase. "If you will follow me, sir, I will show you to your rooms."

"I think I'll stay up awhile longer, if it's all right. I'm not really sleepy. May I browse a bit in the library?"

"Certainly, sir." He handed Rand the candle.

"Won't you need one?" Rand asked, as Abram began a slow ascent of the stairs.

The servant didn't bother to turn around or pause. "No, sir, thank you." He disappeared into the darkness that engulfed the top of the staircase.

Rand entered the library and removed the glass top on one of the hurricane lamps that decorated the room. He touched the candle's flame to the lamp's wick and then replaced the sconce, as well as the lamp's pink rose-etched glass top. A rosy glow settled over the room and turned it warm and welcoming. He began to study the books set onto the shelves of a floor-to-ceiling bookcase that covered two walls of the room. The volumes, all bound in leather that had cracked and darkened with age, were mostly classics. There were also numerous volumes of poetry and several dozen on politics and war strategies, but it was the ten that seemed to be journals or old family diaries that piqued his curiosity. He reached to retrieve one.

Without warning or obvious cause, two small books on the shelf above where he had reached toppled forward. One struck his outstretched arm, which deflected it from bashing his upturned face, the other hit his shoulder, the pointed ends of its cover gouging his flesh before it tumbled to the floor.

"Damn it." He looked up in search of the obvious reason for the books' fall, but no cat peered down at him. He bent to pick up the books. So why had they fallen? He felt the short hairs on the back of his neck prickle and looked around the room. He was alone. The house was quiet. And there had been no earthquake or settling that he'd felt. Yet he didn't feel alone. In fact, he had the distinct sensation he was being watched.

He looked at the volume he'd picked up from the floor. It was a biography of Robert E. Lee.

Rand moved toward a chair set beside the glowing lamp.

"He's defiling that book with his Yankee touch," Lila said. She snapped her fan closed and threw Rand a scathing glare. "Robert signed that book for me, and that . . . that creature is contaminating it."

"Why don't I—" Chance's sentence was abruptly cut short when he noticed Tori step across the threshold of the library. He immediately faded into the dark shadows at the edges of the room, grabbing his sister's arm and dragging her with him.

"Oh, I thought my grandfather was in here," Tori said, noticing Rand.

He turned to see her standing in the shadow of the tall doorway. Pink lamplight touched the apricot silk of her skirt and blouse, and turned the delicate threads to a diaphanous veil about her body, and her hair, which cascaded in waves across her shoulders, to a blanket of glistening ebony. His chest tightened and he felt a hot, simmering ache deep within him. He wanted her. If he accomplished nothing else on his visit to New Orleans, he knew he had to have Tori Rouchard, had to know the fiery passion he sensed lay beneath the quiet surface of her beauty.

"I wanted to talk to you before you retired," he said finally, unable to take his eyes from her. What was it about this woman that so mesmerized him? That made her different from all of the other women who had been in, or were still in, his life?

Tori took a step back from the doorway. She'd only come to the library because she'd seen the light and thought Stanton had waited up for her. She didn't want to talk to Rand. There was something about him, something that drew her. She liked him, and *they* didn't, and that meant all she would accomplish by allowing something, anything, even friendship, to develop between them was emotionally dangerous. She'd been through that mill with *them* once, and had absolutely no intention of repeating the mistake. She was not ready to commit emotional suicide. "I don't think we have anything to say to each other, Mr. Mitchell." She tried to smile to soften her words. After all, it wasn't his fault that the mildest of flirtations on her part could bring a battle down around his ears that would make Pickett's charge look like a high school parade. But it *was* something she could prevent. "What happened today shouldn't have, that's all. I'm sorry." She turned to go. "I really need to retire. I have a full schedule for tomorrow."

He had not missed the fact that she had reverted to calling him *Mr.* Mitchell. He swore beneath his breath. He moved to the doorway as Tori hurried toward the stairs and called after her, "I'll be at your office by eight."

But instead of going to her room, as soon as she felt certain he'd gone back into the library, Tori moved to the door at the rear of the foyer. It was identical to that of the entry, a delicate fanlight overhead and narrow lace-covered side lights next to the door. She stepped quietly onto the dark gallery and moved down the steps into the moonlight. She took a deep breath, and a satisfied sigh escaped her lips. Night was one of her favorite times on the plantation, one of the few times, she thought, that it was truly peaceful. In spite of what a lot of people thought of so-called haunted houses, the spirits who inhabit them do not always stir at night. She moved around the garden slowly, enjoying the fragrance of the night-blooming jasmine whose vines twisted around and clung to several of the back pillars of the house. The pale light of the moon touched the garden and transformed it into an expanse of iridescent shapes and curves. The dark green leaves of the giant live oaks that dotted the landscape turned silver beneath the moon's glow, the rosebushes to ragged fronds of gold, and the thick, waxy leaves of the magnolia trees glistened emerald.

Tori smiled. Her home was a magical place, a place like no other, and she loved it, and *them,* though when they acted up she always found herself wondering why she didn't just have them exorcised. But of course she'd never do that, any more than any of her ancestors had. Most of them left her alone a goodly part of the time, but then, there were thirty-five of them. She remembered her parents and sister and amended her thought. There were thirty-eight of them now, though she knew it would take them a while before her parents or Krissy would actually be able to appear to her. She thought back to the others. Many weren't happy with the times and events they'd witnessed pass and were just as happy to stay grumpily to themselves. Others, like Lila and Chance, weren't content unless making themselves, and their opinions, explicitly known. And none of them could ever agree on anything—except who was wrong for Tori. *That* they always seemed to agree on, whether she did or not. Thank heavens it was only her father's side of the family, and those who married into it, who refused to leave River-Oaks. If she'd had to contend with relatives of every member who'd also married into the family she might just refurbish the old *garconnière* and leave the house to *them*.

She wandered slowly through the quiet gardens, and let the serenity of her surroundings envelop her and calm the ragged edges of the nerves that had begun to fray the moment Rand Mitchell had appeared on the doorstep of River-Oaks. The night was still, only the barest hint of a breeze wafting across the land from the river several miles away. An owl hooted from

85

deep among the boughs of a nearby oak, and Tori smiled. She put thoughts of her family aside and let her mind dwell on the man whose kiss had brought feelings alive within her that she hadn't felt for a very, very long time. And she wasn't sure she wanted to feel them again. What was it about him that sent her into a tizzy every time he came near? No good could come of it, that was evident. Anyway, she had to keep her mind on business. The company was growing, and this was not the time for her to have her concentration elsewhere. Her father had left the entire company to her, had entrusted her with what it had taken him a lifetime to build. She couldn't risk anything happening to it, and she couldn't sell it no matter how good an offer she got. She just couldn't do it. She'd feel as if she was betraying her father's trust, or selling off her heritage. But she had to admit, the offers she'd been getting lately were very good ones — and all from a man named Jason Newhall, whom she knew nothing about.

She paused beside a pond set in the middle of the garden. It was surrounded by a brick walkway and at the opposite end from where she stood an old gazebo sat in the shadow of the overhanging limbs of an oak tree. Spanish moss dripped from the tree's gnarled centuries-old branches to faintly touch the gazebo's spired white roof. Tori leaned forward and looked down at her own reflection in the pond. The moon at her back created a halo of glistening gold around her head and turned the water's surface to a glimmering mirror.

A deep sigh blew from her lips. Life had been so much simpler a few years ago. Her father had headed the company, and even though she'd been head of marketing, hers had almost been a part-time job, if that. She had been able to take time off whenever she'd wanted, even to taking off with only a moment's notice. Traveling had been a pleasure, a thrill. Now it was part of the job, but it wasn't fun anymore. She looked long and hard at her own image in the water. She'd laughed more then, too. Except when *they* had caused Tom to leave her. Tori had honestly believed him strong enough to deal with them, but she'd been wrong. She wouldn't make that mistake again.

Suddenly another face appeared, and Tori drew back, startled.

Rand's hands caught her shoulders before she backed into him. "I guess we both had the same idea about how to end the evening," he said, though the encounter had been no accident.

Tori whirled around. The heel of one shoe caught in the brick that surrounded the edge of the pond and she was thrown off balance. For the second time that day, Rand Mitchell's strong fingers clasped her arms, steely bands of strength that held her in place and prevented her fall. Shaken, her heart dancing to a rhythm that threatened to send it bursting from her chest, she pulled herself from his hold and moved a few steps away. "Sorry," she mumbled, feeling foolish for her reaction. "I thought I was alone." She almost laughed at her own words. At RiverOaks, she was never alone, but he didn't know that. She sat down on a marble bench set in an alcove of boxwood hedge.

Rand stood beside the pond. "I didn't mean to startle you. Would you rather I left?"

Tori avoided meeting his eyes. She shook her head, though she knew she should scream, yes, please, go away before it's too late. Instead she said, "I—I like to come out here sometimes at night. It's so peaceful here."

A leaf from one of the tree branches overhead fluttered down and into the midst of several tiny fireflies that flitted over the pond. Their tiny glowing bodies caused them to look like a shower of diamonds dancing atop the water's surface, blinking and sparkling as they looped and soared through the air.

"I can see why you like it." The deep drawl of his voice reached out, slid over her skin like warm honey, and left pinpricks of sensation behind that caused her to tremble involuntarily. "This place, your home, has a sense of timelessness about it. A kind of foreverness."

She smiled. He didn't know how true his words were.

He turned toward her and their gazes met and fused. Moonlight touched his hair, vanquished any shadows that might dare to lurk within the flaxen waves, and turned the bronze hue of his tanned flesh to golden velvet.

If he pulled her into his arms again, claimed her lips with his, held her in his powerful embrace, would she feel the same aching stirrings she'd felt that afternoon? Would passion overcome her better judgment again, and leave her helpless to his will? To his desires?

Suddenly a shadow moved between them, and a flash of alarm swept over Tori. *They* were here! She made to rise from her seat, ready to intercept whatever *they* had in mind.

"Tonight in town I was—" His words were cut off with a strangled gasp.

Tori watched in horror as Rand fell backward toward the pond. His arms flailed the air and a look of sheer confusion, and just a bit of fear, widened his eyes.

"Rand!" she screamed, and jumped to her feet. She grabbed for him. Her fingers brushed his shirt sleeve but could find no hold.

His backside hit the surface of the pond with a loud *kerplop* and water flew up around him like a small tidal wave. The orange and white koi that lived in the shallow pool swam frantically in all directions. Water splashed over the edge of the pond and onto the bricks, rippled out atop the walkway and lapped at Tori's feet.

She looked around. At least one of them was here, she knew it, but no one was appearing to her, which, under the circumstances, was no surprise. Her gaze dropped back to Rand.

He had hoisted himself to a sitting position and was staring up at her. His wavy hair was now plastered flat to his head. Rivulets of water glistened silver in the moon's glow and trickled down his face. A drop fell from the tip of his nose to cause a ripple on the pond's now quiet surface, just as one of the koi swam across his lap.

Tori didn't know whether to laugh, cry, or get mad. She looked at Rand. "Are you all right?" she mumbled, and almost strangled on a laugh she struggled to suppress.

Rand looked at her as if her question were the most insane thing he'd ever heard. He had felt hands on his chest. Someone had pushed him, yet he could swear Tori had been several feet away. He moved to rise. "How'd you do that?"

In the sudden rush of water that poured from his rising form back into the pond, Tori didn't hear the accusation.

The koi scattered and darted to the other side of the pond again, and water dripped from Rand's soaked clothes as he stood. A small puddle of water formed around his feet. She would deal with *them* later; right now she could no longer contain herself. A laugh burst from her lips and echoed in the still night.

"Very funny," Rand said, and tried to shake some of the water from himself. "Are all your guests treated to such a gracious bath?"

"I'm sorry, but . . ." She shrugged, and laughed again, totally chagrined but unable to help herself.

His flash of temper disappeared immediately. He held out a hand to her. "Actually the cool water felt good. Maybe you'd like to join me in another dip?" A devilish smile curved his lips.

The next morning, true to his word, Rand arrived at Tori's office promptly at eight o'clock. But he was not the first to arrive. When her secretary showed him into Tori's office, the smile on his face that had been directed at Tori, who sat behind her desk, was immediately replaced by an unconscious scowl.

"Mitchell," Ashford said, as if announcing the fact that he knew Rand's name. "What are you doing here?"

"Meeting my tour guide," Rand replied. He threw Ash a satisfied smile.

"Victoria isn't a tour guide, Mitchell," Ash sneered. "She's the president of the company, in case you didn't know."

"I do know. That's why I insisted she be the one to show me the city, Ash," Rand said, purposely using the abbreviated version of the man's name, which he had already sensed aggravated the hell out of him. He smiled widely. "I never settle for second best." Though his words were directed at Ashford, he looked intently at Tori. He felt burning heat deep within him and begin to simmer. Damn, but she was gorgeous. And he wanted her. Maybe more than he'd ever desired a woman in his life. He settled into one of the chairs set before Tori's desk. "So, what are you doing here, Ash?"

"Just stopped in to see Tori on my way to an early morning meeting, if it's any of your business, Mitchell."

Tori's gaze flitted from Ashford to Rand. What was it with these two? Were they under some misguided illusion that she couldn't hear them? Couldn't speak for herself? Make her own decisions? She rammed her pen back into its brass holder and shoved aside the papers she had been about to sign.

"Well," Ash said, before Tori had a chance to open her mouth. He slid his hip from the corner of Tori's desk and stood up. His tan slacks slipped elegantly into place around his long legs, and he shifted his thickly padded shoulders beneath the obviously expensive brown sports coat. "You should feel honored, Mitchell. After we're married, Victoria won't be working anymore, let alone conducting tours for strangers."

Tori gaped at Ashford, her eyes wide. "Ash,"

she gasped, and nearly choked on the single word. What in blazes was he babbling about? Marriage? When had he planned that? And why?

Ashford smiled at Tori, then paled slightly. Her face was flushed tomato red, but whether from embarrassment or anger he wasn't sure — and he didn't intend to stick around long enough to find out. He moved hastily toward the door, well aware that he'd best escape before her shock wore off and she found her voice. "See you tonight, *chérie*," he said, and waved back at them.

Tori slammed a hand down on her desk. "Of all the —"

"Something wrong?" Rand asked, and smiled slyly. He knew damn well what was wrong. Over a cup of coffee that morning with Stanton, Rand had discovered quite a bit about Tori. Like the fact that she and Ashford had grown up together, that she'd been dating him for over a year, but that marriage, as far as Stanton knew, hadn't been considered, let alone discussed. And the old man had made no secret of the fact that he did not like Ashford Thibeaux III, and had no intention of seeing his granddaughter married to him if he could help it. The conversation had been terminated abruptly when Stanton's coffee cup had fallen over and hot liquid poured all over the table. Rand could have sworn that Stanton's hands had been clasped together in his lap, but then things don't just topple over by themselves.

"No, Tori snapped. "Nothing's wrong."

"Would you like to have breakfast somewhere?'

"No."

"How about a riverboat ride?"

"No."

"Tour some of the old plantations?"

"No."

Rand smiled and rested a foot on his knee. The black leather of his cowboy boot shone softly beneath the light that filtered into the office from a window set among her bookcases on the wall behind him. "Well then, what would you like to do today?"

"Move to Canada," she said snippily, and then laughed at her own words. "Sorry, Ash just made me mad."

Rand stood. "So, breakfast?'

She looked at the mound of papers on her desk. "I really should get some work done, since I missed a day yesterday."

Rand placed both hands on her desk and leaned across it toward her. "Will the company fall apart if you're gone?"

"Well, no, but . . ." She grabbed a stack of papers and drew them in front of her.

He moved around the desk. She looked up at him as he moved to her side and took her hand. He put an expression of pleading on his face. "Please, ma'am," he drawled, "just break-fast?"

She knew she should say no. She should call in one of her guides and appoint her to Rand as his personal tour guide for the day. But she didn't. "Okay, breakfast."

When she rose from behind her desk, Rand noticed that she'd dressed more casually than the day before. Her legs were encased in a pair of light wool cream-colored slacks that fitted snugly to her hips and, when she turned to re-trieve her purse, he took note, cupped her der-riere to perfection. A sleeveless silk blouse, the same color as her slacks, draped over her breasts and, nestled between them, hanging from a delicate gold chain that encircled her neck, lay a tiny watch, its face made up of ro-man numerals, its circumference encrusted with minute points of topaz. He felt the inseam of his Levi's turn snug and forced his thoughts to cool. *Down boy,* he told himself. *Remember, this is business.*

She strode toward the door, opened it, and turned to him. "Coming?"

He exited, and just before closing the door behind her, Tori stuck her head back into the room. "Don't come with us," she whispered hur-riedly.

Chapter Nine

"But I have work to do," Tori said, though even to her own ears her words sounded less than convincing.

"Can it wait?"

"Well, yes, but that's not the point. We have acquisitions coming up, new locations readying to open. I have a million things to do."

"Just today, Tori." He reached across the table they were sitting at and took her hand. "Just give me today."

Surprisingly the time passed in a whirl of pleasurable experiences. She neither saw nor heard *them,* yet there was always a part of her on edge, alert, listening, watching for them to appear. Tori knew, deep down inside, that she should keep some distance between herself and Rand, if for no other reason than to prevent the trouble she felt sure was brewing at RiverOaks. All morning, despite her reluctant agreement to spend the day with him, she had offered excuses why she needed to get back to the office, and

he had overcome every one of her excuses. Even
her own guilt at neglecting the company didn't
hasten her back to the office. She felt almost as
she had before the accident, before she'd become head of the company . . . and it felt
good. She felt happier and more carefree than
she had in months. When they walked beneath
the Dueling Oaks in City Park, he reached for
her hand and entwined his fingers around hers.
She felt a little leap of her heart and returned
the pressure of hand holding hand. By late
afternoon, as they browsed in the Vieux Carré,
Tori knew her heart was in serious jeopardy of
being lost to him—permanently, and the thought
both thrilled and terrified her. She took him to
all her favorite places: a drink at Maspero's Exchange, and another at the Napoleon House. In
Betty's Doll Shop, Rand bought a handmade
rag doll of a Southern belle for his sister, and
at Madame Labat's Perfumery a box of soaps
for his sister.

By the time they walked out of the Cabildo,
the old government building that now served as
a museum, dusk hovered over the city, and as
the light of day slowly disappeared, so, too, did
the obvious traces of modern society that had
invaded the quarter over the years. The narrow
streets gradually became devoid of automobile
traffic and the camera-clicking, sunglass-bespec-
tacled tourists. Glass-enclosed wall sconces had
been lit on the walls of the old buildings, lamp-

light glowed from behind lace-draped windows, and the echoing clip-clop of the carriage horses whose drivers catered to tourists filled the air. A peaceful serenity settled over the landscape, broken momentarily by the whistle of *The Natchez* as it announced its impending departure from the docks.

Rand grabbed Tori's hand. "Come on, let's take a riverboat ride."

The Natchez's whistle blasted again as Rand and Tori ran up the gangplank, which began to rise almost the moment they stepped from it.

"Made it," Rand announced needlessly, and laughed. He hadn't felt so good in a long time. Of course he usually spent his days in a boardroom, or scouting out prospects of new acquisitions, not running around the countryside playing tourist.

The riverboat began to pull away from the dock and a Dixieland band in the boat's lounge began to play. The spirit-rousing cadence of "Camptown Races" filled the air and helped to enhance the mood of yesteryear.

Tori moved to the railing and wrapped one arm casually around a gleaming white balustrade. The steady whoosh-whoosh sound of the massive red paddlewheel at the boat's stern seemed almost to keep pace with the music, and sent a fine spray of water on anyone standing too close.

Rand slipped an arm around Tori's waist and

pulled her closer to him. "Ummm, that's better."

She smiled, and a small sigh escaped her lips. She had planned on only going to breakfast with him. She had a ton of work to do at the office: building rentals to approve, leases to sign, managers to consult, and an advertising campaign to put the finishing details on. There was no room in her life for a relationship right now, long or short term, and especially one that wasn't going to work, anyway. It couldn't — everything was stacked against it.

In the corner of her eye, she caught a sudden flash of movement a few feet away and stiffened, almost afraid to look. When she forced her head to turn, her gaze to penetrate the shadows beneath a set of stairs against the cabins wall, she saw nothing. A sense of relief swept over her. She hadn't seen *them* all day, and it had been wonderful — no surprise appearances, no nagging little threats, no disasters. She turned back to look at the horizon and stared out into the distance without really seeing anything. They hadn't appeared to her since this morning. A sense of apprehension filled her. Now she was worried because they *hadn't* appeared. She closed her eyes for a brief second. Lord, they were driving her crazy.

Memory of that morning in her office brought with it recollection of Ashford. What in heaven's name had gotten into him, talking marriage like that? The subject had never even come up between them before, and that was all right with her. She was fond of Ashford, always had been, but she was not in love with him, and though she didn't want to hurt him, she certainly had no intention of marrying him, whether *they* liked it or not.

Rand's arm tightened around her waist. "Do your tours include a ride on *The Natchez?*" he asked, interrupting her thoughts.

She nodded absently. "Some of them." She kept her gaze glued to the horizon. She had to. Her heart felt as if it was beating a million miles a minute. For some insane, inexplicable reason, Rand Mitchell had the ability to turn her senses inside out and upside down with a mere glance. A touch was dynamite. Her conscience nagged at her that she was asking for trouble, and she did her best to ignore it. She would probably regret her decision, but she couldn't deny that she was enjoying herself, and being with Rand. Especially being with Rand.

The sun had begun to slip from the sky and its dying rays cast a brilliant pink glow over the city in the distance. The ancient buildings of the Vieux Carré took on an almost ageless look, while the newer downtown buildings, the tall skyscrapers that edged the northern horizon of the quarter, reflected the descending globe's brilliance in their glass-paneled walls. The river itself had been turned to a blanket of wavering iridescence, the dip of each wave a murky green, its curl turned gold, its tip silver.

A bell rang.

"That's the bell announcing dinner," Tori said, and pushed away from the railing.

The band, dressed in red-and-white-striped vests, ruffled green satin armbands and black bowlers, stood at one end of the room and continued to play as the meal was served, while the tourists who packed the lounge hummed along. Within minutes people were filing out onto the small dance floor, unable to resist any longer the urge to move their feet to the old melodies. Rand, to his own surprise, felt exactly the same. The only dancing he'd done in recent years had been at formal affairs, charity fundraisers and society parties, where couples waltzed, did the fox-trot, or in some cases, merely swayed to the music. It was something a person did to be seen, a calculated move in a business prospect, or the seduction of a beautiful woman, or a gesture to pay a compliment to a hostess. But this was different; for maybe the first time in his life that he could remember, he had no ulterior motive, unless it was that he wanted Tori in his arms again.

He turned to her, placed their plates on a nearby counter, and swung her into his arms. A soft laugh echoed deep within Tori's throat and her eyes, dark and sultry, blazed with the flame of tiny gold sparks. The scent of magnolia enveloped him as she surrendered herself to his embrace, a heady fragrance that at once made him think of times when riverboats plied the Mississippi and belles wore hoopskirts and flirted from behind fluttering fans. Rand nearly laughed at himself. What was he doing, turning into a romantic? The thought was ridiculous. He had business to consider here, and if he mixed a bit of pleasure with it, so much the better . . . as long as in the end he got what he wanted—Rouchard Travel.

His arm around her waist held her tight, his hand on her back pressed her against his tall length, while his other hand curled around hers and held it cradled against his chest. She was soft and warm in his arms, and she was incredibly desirable to him. With her breasts crushed against his chest, her hips melded to his, Rand's imagination began to conjure up images that proved sweet torment to his already hardening body.

He led her around the dance floor in a graceful sweep, and Tori felt as if the world had shifted into slow gear, its pace slackened to match that of the soulful music. Outside, the sun had finally disappeared. The many windows of the lounge, framed with red velvet curtains, glistened black, and reflected the golden glimmer of the overhead chandelier. Tori looked up at Rand. The chandelier's light shone on his hair, turning each strand to a ribbon of flaxen silk, and shadowing the ruggedly cut contours of his face, creating finely honed planes and valleys. Her gaze dropped to the open collar of his shirt, and the small hollow at the base of his neck. Beneath the hand that rested atop his shoulder Tori could feel the hard contours of muscle, the strength and power that was separated from her touch only by the thin fabric of his shirt. With each step he took, his body spoke to hers, hip to hip, thigh to thigh, chest to breast, and each touch aroused a plethora of new sensations within her that she was finding almost impossible to resist or deny.

Rand's hand slid slowly down to rest at the curve of her spine. Through the sheer silk of her blouse Tori could feel the touch of his fingertips against her back, like spots of flame that burned her flesh and sent radiating heat through her body. She leaned into him, an unconscious surrender to the aura of virility that surrounded him and drew her.

"It's true what they say about Southern women," Rand said huskily. "They are the most beautiful and seductive in the world."

Tori's hand slid from his shoulder to the back of his neck, her fingers running through the strands of hair that curled over his collar. She could feel the curve of his jaw at her temple, the beat of his heart as her breast pressed to the wide rock-hard wall of his chest, and the warmth of his breath on her bare shoulder.

The music stopped, but Rand did not release her, and Tori made no effort to slip from his arms. A few seconds later, when the band began to play again, Rand stepped slowly to the lilting beat. Tori followed him easily, every nerve of her body seemingly alert to the slightest sway of his so that they moved together as one.

Her apprehension forgotten for the moment, Tori looked up into his face, intending only a glance, but suddenly found herself unable to look away, her gaze a captive of the blue eyes that stared intently into her own. Her breath was swept away and her heart began to beat in hard, almost paralyzing strokes. Mesmerized by the eyes that held hers, Tori's gaze moved over his dark, lean face, over the harshly formed features that were neither soft nor hard, golden brows that curved sardonically over those riveting eyes, and a lone dimple that appeared in his right cheek when he smiled.

So lost was Tori in the magic of his embrace and the sensations that stirred within her that she did not notice the glares of two very familiar figures standing in a far corner of the lounge.

"I need some air," Rand whispered in her ear as the music ended. He turned Tori toward one of the open doors that led to the deck. Night immediately enveloped them as they left the glaring lights of the lounge behind and strolled toward the paddlewheel at the riverboat's stern. The sky had turned to a sweeping vista of dark infinity, its blackness broken only by a sliver of saffron moon and a sprinkling of stars, all glistening like precious stones scattered over a blanket of ebony velvet. In the distance the shoreline of New Orleans twinkled against the night, the tall office buildings in the background reminders of the twentieth century, while at the river's edge the ancient Vieux Carré glowed softly, the steeple of the St. Louis Cathedral a palely lighted sphere in the center of antiquity.

"This is why people come to New Orleans," Tori said, staring at the landscape. "Because yesterday, the past, is still alive here."

Rand's arms once again encircled Tori's waist and he pulled her toward him.

She went willingly into his embrace, no longer conscious of a reason to resist him, or heedful of the perilous ground she had just stepped upon.

One hand moved to her neck, warm and vibrant against her skin, burning wherever it touched, leaving a brand upon her flesh, invisible, yet as permanent and real as if seared with a hot iron. His fingers moved to entwine within the thick, swirling strands of hair at the base of her neck, and tilted her head to receive his kiss.

With a willingness of their own, Tori's arms slid around Rand's shoulders, embraced the breadth of muscle they moved over, and held to the strength, the power, that emanated from him.

His mouth descended on hers, his kiss a demanding caress, at once an edict for acquiescence and an entreaty for passionate response. His tongue moved over her bottom lip, a feather-light touch that sent a tidal wave of delicious shivers through her and left her trembling in his arms. She opened her mouth to him and felt the dueling, flicking stroke of his tongue on hers. It had been madness to kiss him. She knew it the moment his lips claimed hers, but she had been unable to help herself, unable to resist the temptation to know the touch of his lips. His mouth explored hers in what seemed a timeless caress, his tongue an instrument of sensual seduction, hungrily tasting and teasing. An aching need began to gnaw within the depths of her being, and her body turned to flame, a burning fire that scorched every cell and fiber and left her floating in a languorous haze.

Sanity and reason tried to push their way back into her mind. She moved her hands to his chest and made an almost involuntary attempt to escape him.

Rand felt the slight push of resistance and deepened his kiss. Whatever his intentions had been when he'd come to New Orleans, they were for the moment forgotten, vanquished the moment his mouth pressed to hers, consumed by the fire of need that had swept over him, a need created by her touch, her kiss, a need that made him forget everything but the desire to possess her.

Long seconds passed, the music played on, the paddlewheel continued its steady plowing of the murky water, a light breeze wafted over the boat and skimmed gently across Tori's bare arms, and Rand continued his assault on her mouth. He kissed her with a mastery like none she had ever experienced, an expertise that drained away her urge to resist, banished the shadows of fear that still lurked in the back of her mind, her heart, and filled her instead with an ache to know the depths of this man's passion. His lips cajoled, caressed, and demanded. They moved from her mouth, across her jawline, and beneath the lobe of her ear.

"Let me love you, Tori," he whispered. His hot breath drifted through her hair. "Tonight."

A moan escaped Tori's lips, only to be swallowed when his mouth descended on hers again. She made no effort to escape his embrace, to deny the swirling of passion that had enveloped her, or the desire to be possessed by him.

He had kissed her before, and held her, but not like this. His mouth was working dark magic on her, pulling her into an uncharted world of sensuality that she had never known existed. The hunger of his passion pushed hard against her stomach, as his hands caressed her, one moving over the bare flesh of her arm, the other pressing against the small of her back, and the other cupping her derriere.

Tori's eyes shot open. The other? That was three hands!

She pushed herself out of Rand's arms and whirled around, her eyes wide and searching. Then she saw him. "Uncle Chance!" she gasped, the words ragged as she fought for breath. She stared, shocked, at the dapper gambler who leaned, only a few feet away, against the riverboat's carved white balustrade.

Chance chuckled softly, but guilt was neither in his dark eyes nor etched on the handsomely carved face. He began to fade from her sight. "Just a reminder, Tori, dear," he said. "He's the wrong one."

"Don't you disapp—"

"Tori," Rand said, and touched a finger to her shoulder. "Who are you talking to?"

Her mouth snapped closed and she whirled around. Oh, Lord, her mouth had gotten ahead of her brain again.

A frown shadowed his brow and his eyes, those penetrating moons of dazzling blue, seemed to be looking straight through her and into the dark, secret depths of her soul. If she were the swooning type, she could just have fainted. But she wasn't, and she'd never been any good at faking such things. Or, if he were more like Ash, she could just laugh softly and excuse it as a momentary lapse of sanity, very acceptable in some Southern circles. But then there were already more than enough people in New Orleans who, through the years, had suspected the Rouchards of being a bit "touched," thanks to the family's shenanigans. No sense adding more fuel to that fire. "I, ah, I thought I felt someone's hand on . . ." She blushed. "I mean . . . it wasn't you and—"

"And you thought it was someone named Uncle Chance?"

A groan almost slipped from her throat. "No, I was just thinking of something, about my uncle, and I got confused, and . . ." She was babbling, making no sense whatsoever, and each word that spilled from her lips only seemed to make the situation worse. She closed her mouth, shrugged, and turned away to look out at the night. The city was growing closer as the boat made for port, the tour nearly over.

Chance was right—Rand was the wrong one for her. The look in his eyes a moment ago, that skeptical "am I in the company of a lunatic?" look, told her more than words ever could that he would never understand about *them*.

He reached for her hand. She jerked it away, as if his touch had scalded her skin.

"I—I have to go home." She turned and walked toward the lounge.

"Tori," Rand called after her, "we're on a boat."

Chapter Ten

The ride home from town seemed agonizingly long. Tori sat slumped in the passenger seat of the car while Rand drove. She refused to utter more than a few grunts to his questions, and once they pulled up in front of the house, she jumped from the car and ran inside, leaving him to find his own way. By the time dawn crept through the window and into his room, he'd spent an almost sleepless night tossing and turning, but whether his nagging worries were more because of Tori herself, or the fact that if he'd blown it with her he might also have blown acquiring Rouchard Travel, he wasn't sure. He just knew he felt miserable. Damn miserable, and it wasn't a feeling he was used to. Getting himself together was another hapless adventure. First he nearly broke his big toe when he accidentally rammed it on the edge of the metal tub Abram had brought to his room and then filled with water for Rand's bath. Then he pulled a button from his shirt and had to change to another one, caught his shorts in the zipper of his slacks, though he breathed a sigh of relief that his shorts were the only thing that got caught in those ugly little teeth, and last, nicked his chin while shaving. When he finally made it downstairs for breakfast, his mood was surly and his temper short. He found Stanton at the table and Abram hovering near the stove, but Tori was nowhere to be seen. He took the cup of coffee the old servant handed him and, with a mumbled thanks, sat down.

"She went to work already," Stanton said, a sly twinkle in his old gray eyes.

Rand looked at him and frowned.

"You wanted to know where Tori was, didn't you?" A smug smile lifted the corners of his bushy mustache.

"One of these days I'm going to throttle that old man," Lila said, and snapped open her fan. "Then maybe he'll mind his own business."

Chance smiled. "Don't count on it, sis."

Rand stood and waved off Abram, who had been about to prepare him a plate of food. "I've got some business to take care of today. I think I'll drive into town." He needed to use the telephone, and Abram still insisted there wasn't one at the plantation.

"Jason? Any progress?" Rand asked sharply.

He looked past the public telephone and across the street toward Tori's office building.

"Not much."

"That's not the kind of answers I pay you an extremely generous salary and commission to give me, Jason." Rand's voice was rough, edgy, and reflected the anger roiling within him and the lack of patience it created.

Jason Newhall was his vice president, and the most trusted and valued employee Paradise Tours had. If anyone could manage a purchase or a takeover of Rouchard Travel Jason could. "What's the problem now?"

"Same one. The daughter inherited almost the whole applecart, and she's not in a mood to sell even a seed. Every approach we've made, to her or her attorney, has been met with a staunch no. They won't even negotiate."

"Aren't there some relatives who own percentages of the company?"

"Yes, cousins mostly."

"Go after them. Find what they want and can't afford, and offer it to them." He hung up the phone without saying goodbye and looked at the glass front of Tori's office. She'd walked away from him last night. Maybe not literally, but she had all the same, and he'd paced his room practically all night trying to figure out why it bothered him so much. True, women didn't usually walk away from Rand Mitchell, but something told him that wasn't entirely what was eating at him. He still wanted her. Despite everything, and knowing that when she found out who and what he was, she would hate him, he still wanted her. It was probably the only way to satiate this damning hunger that was gnawing at his gut, a hunger that had erupted in him the moment he'd laid eyes on her, and had been preoccupying him ever since.

"He's not going to give up," Chance said.

"She walked out on him last night," Lila retorted, looking totally satisfied.

"That won't stop him, Lila, believe me." He stared at Rand as he started to walk across the square toward Tori's office. "He reminds me of myself."

Lila whirled on her brother, aghast. "Have you gone out of your mind? Comparing yourself to a Yankee? Why, if it wasn't for them you wouldn't have been blown to smithereens on that boat of yours."

"Come on," Chance said, ignoring her comment. He began to fade.

Rand walked into the reception room of Tori's office. Her secretary, Sherrille, recognized him at once. *A good employee,* Rand thought. *We should keep her.*

"I'm sorry, Mr. Mitchell, but Tori's not here.

She had an appointment and won't be back today."

He nodded, thanked the woman, and left. Great, a whole day and nothing to do. *Try a little business,* he thought. After obtaining directions, he headed for the public library. Paradise Tours needed all the advantage it could get to pull this off, and a little more research into Rouchard Travel's background wouldn't hurt.

Three hours later he'd learned nothing he hadn't already known, except that Tori's family had been one of the few in the South who had managed to hang on to their plantation after the Civil War. They'd maintained some investments in England rather than turn every cent they had into Confederate notes. Though, from what he'd read, they had done quite a bit of that, too.

He wandered around the quarter aimlessly, going into one store after another. When his stomach growled loudly, he realized with a start that he hadn't had a thing to eat all day. He stopped at a small café and sat at one of its outdoor tables. The blonde waitress, obviously a local college student, flirted outrageously with him, and Rand paid no attention.

Damn, he'd never ignored a beautiful woman before. Especially one who was practically throwing herself at him. What the hell was the matter with him?

An hour later he passed a florist's shop, and on impulse, went in.

Tori pulled a pale yellow dress of sheer silk from her armoire and tried to ignore the bouquet of long-stemmed red roses that sat on her dressing table. Abram had arranged them in a crystal vase and carried them into her room shortly after she'd come home, but she'd yet to open the card. She didn't have to open it to know who the flowers were from. Ash didn't send flowers. He'd always said it was silly, because they just died the next day, anyway.

She slipped into the dress and a matching pair of heels, ran a brush through her hair, letting it flow loose over her shoulders, and picked up her bag. Ash was probably already downstairs waiting, and he hated to be late when they had reservations.

But rather than Ash, it was Rand who waited in the spacious foyer at the bottom of the wide staircase. He didn't smile as she descended, but his eyes bored into hers, as if searching for something, something she was neither ready nor willing to give. "I came by your office today," he said simply.

She nodded. Her secretary had told her. "I know."

"Were you avoiding me?"

The uncertainty in her eyes disappeared, replaced by a cool glimmer. "I have a business to conduct, Mr. Mitchell, and I had a meeting today. An important one."

The comment reminded him of the agency, and he suddenly wondered if her reason for refusing his own company's offers was that she was considering another laid on the table by one of his competitors. "Made some money, I hope," he said, attempting a light voice and hoping the comment was subtle enough, yet pointed enough, to draw some kind of response he could calculate.

"Advertising campaigns are always important."

He nearly sighed with relief. Acquiring Rouchard Travel was vital to his expansion plans. "Did you get my roses?"

"Yes." Her voice warmed, but the coolness did not entirely leave her eyes. "Thank you, they're beautiful, but if you'll excuse me . . ." She heard Ashford's voice coming from the parlor, and sudden fear of what her grandfather might be saying to him chilled her. "Ash is waiting."

Rand reached for her arm, the words *Let him wait* already formed in his mind and ready to slip from his lips, when he pulled back and let her go. That wasn't the way to get to Tori Rouchard.

"You've been dating my granddaughter for over a year now, Thibeaux," Stanton said pointedly. He wheeled himself to within inches of a still-standing Ashford. "I guess I should have

116

asked before this, but frankly, I never thought you'd last this long. What are your intentions toward Tori?" He watched with a perverse sense of satisfaction as Ashford's nervous fingers twisted the stems of the daisies he'd brought for Tori and practically decapitated the blooms.

"Actually, sir, I've, ah, I've proposed to Tori, but we haven't set a wedding date yet." He looked down at the flowers in his hand. Where *had* they come from? Somehow, and he was at a loss to explain how, they had suddenly appeared on the front seat of his car. He hadn't noticed them until he pulled up to the entry of RiverOaks and then just figured someone, evidently while his car had been parked in the quarter earlier, had lost their use for them and tossed them through his open window.

"You've what?" Stanton growled. He gripped the armrests of his wheelchair and nearly flew from its seat.

"He's going to ruin everything," Lila said. She swept behind Stanton's wheelchair. "A fast little turn around the gallery should put him back in his place."

Chance stepped between his sister and Stanton. "Not now, sis." He turned to watch Ashford. "Later."

Ash straightened his shoulders and returned Stanton's stare, though his color had rapidly gone from golden bronze to ashen gray. "I proposed. And she accepted."

"Accepted? Humph, that I find hard to believe." His eyes narrowed. "Anyway, we'll just see about that," Stanton groused. "In my day a young man asked the girl's family for permission to court her, let alone marry her. I didn't hear you ask me for permission to do anything, not that you'd get it."

"Gramps!" Tori groaned, as she entered the room and heard enough of the conversation to tell her what was happening. She threw him a look that would have prompted Attila the Hun to flee in terror, but didn't seem to raise a single hair on her grandfather's head. "We have to go, Ash, it's late." She grabbed his arm and practically pushed him through the foyer and out the front door.

He helped her into the car, and just before closing her door, and almost as an afterthought, offered her the now bedraggled bouquet.

"Flowers?" She looked up at him in surprise.

He nodded, closed the door and walked around the glistening black Jaguar to the driver's side. Her surprise was not lost on him, but he was not about to explain that the flowers hadn't been his idea.

He slid into the driver's seat and glanced down at the flowers, set between him and Tori now, where she'd placed them. He started the engine. Someone had to have thrown them into his car earlier. There was no other explanation for their appearance. "I've made dinner reservations for us at Commander's Palace."

"The Palace sounds wonderful, Ash," Tori said, and slipped a cassette into the tape player. In truth, the old mansion in the Garden District that had been turned into a restaurant was elegant, and the food delicious, but it was Ashford's favorite spot, not hers.

"Commander's Palace?" Chance quipped from the backseat. "That's not where the dolt should be taking her. If he's going to make her stop thinking of that Yank, then he needs somewhere quiet and romantic, someplace away from the city, where you can look out at the stars and moon."

Tori turned in her seat and looked into the back of the car. She could have sworn she heard talking.

"Well, *we* know that, Chance," Lila agreed haughtily, "but obviously *he* doesn't." She snapped open her fan. "And a lot of good those flowers did. He practically mutilated them."

"Well, it was a good idea, anyway, but maybe I can fix where we're going." With a twinkle of mischief in his dark eyes, Chance immediately materialized in the front seat, between Ash and Tori.

Tori jumped toward the door panel. "Oh, no," she groaned.

"What's wrong?" Ash asked, turning to look at her.

119

Chance made to grab the steering wheel.

"Everything," she moaned, and threw her uncle a scathing glance.

"Chance Rouchard, what in tarnation are you doing?" Lila cried. "You don't know the first thing about operating a horseless carriage."

Tori gripped the sides of her seat. Maybe she should just move to the North Pole. They wouldn't follow her there—too cold, and too far north.

"How hard can driving this thing be?" Chance said, and laughed merrily. "You just point this wheel to where you want to go and push down on this little pedal on the floor."

"You're going to get Tori killed and ruin everything."

Tori whirled around to look at Lila. "What are you two trying to do?" she demanded frantically.

"Ask him!" Lila snapped, and pointed a bony finger at Chance's back.

Tori turned her gaze on Chance, who merely smiled wickedly back at her.

Ash gaped at Tori as if he thought she'd lost her senses. "I'm driving us to the Palace. What do you think I'm doing?"

The steering wheel spun to the left and took a suddenly wide-eyed Ashford's hands with it. The long, sleek Jaguar swerved into the center of the road and headed directly for an oncoming car. Tori shrieked. Ash grappled with the wheel. The Jaguar lurched back into its own lane only seconds before what surely would have been a fatal collision.

"Chance, I'm going to kill you!" Lila screeched. She struggled with her hoopskirt and tried to climb back onto the seat after having been thrown to the floor.

"Little late for that, sis," Chance said gaily.

Tori took a deep breath and maintained her grip on the armrest.

"That was close," Ash said, and wiped a hand over his brow. "I don't know what happened. The steering wheel just flew out of my hands. We must have hit a pothole in the road and it jerked the tires, or something like that."

"Right, or something," Tori said, and glared at Chance.

He merely smiled widely and shrugged. "Sorry, my dear, I'm not used to these confounded things."

"You're not supposed to be," she retorted.

Ash frowned. "I'm not supposed to be what?" He made to round the corner. "Blast, the wheel won't turn." He cursed and strained to force it.

"You're going to get us killed!" Tori cried, and reached for Chance's arm.

"I'm not doing it," Ash snapped.

Her hand went through Chance's arm and slapped Ashford's thigh. He jumped. "Hey, what was that for?"

She groaned and slumped back in her seat. It

121

was no use. *They* were in control, and there wasn't a thing she could do about it. She watched the quickly passing landscape as the car zoomed up South Claiborne, leaving the Garden District and Commander's Palace far behind. The Jag careered around several other cars and a tour bus.

"Tori, the damn car's out of control!" Ash yelled. "I can't stop it!" He tried to stomp his foot on the brake and felt something kick his leg away.

They sped through a yellow light. "You're supposed to stop for a yellow light!" Tori yelled at Chance.

"Oh." He looked over his shoulder at her. "What about a red one?"

"I know about the lights, Tori," Ash said, almost spitting the words out, "but tell the car."

She whirled around to look out the front window, instantly stiffened in fear, and instinctively jammed her feet against the floorboard. "Stop!"

"I'm trying to!" Ash yelled back.

The car sped through another intersection. "Too late," Chance said, and chuckled. "Hey, this is fun once you get the hang of it."

"Which you haven't," Lila snipped.

Tori glanced from the road to Ash. He was a picture of pure terror. His hands gripped the steering wheel, knuckles white, jaw clenched in a grimace. "It's out of control, it's out of control," he blabbered. His eyes were wide, nearly bulging from their sockets as his gaze jumped from the road to his hands and back to the road. "Its out of control, it's out of control." He yanked on the steering wheel.

"Oh, no you don't, sonny," Chance said.

A sharp jab to Ashford's ribs pitched him forward and momentarily knocked the air from his lungs. He pulled his foot from the gas pedal, but the car kept going. He tried again for the brake, and again his leg was kicked away.

"Uncle Chance, please," Tori pleaded.

"I'm leaving," Lila announced, and abruptly disappeared.

Ashford reached for the ignition key.. It was the only thing left to do that he could think of. Just as his slim fingers touched it, something icy cold and unearthly closed around his hand and held it in place, the pressure threateningly close to crushing. He jerked his hand back and started to pray, the words tumbling off his tongue at a frantic pace. "Now I lay me down to sleep, I pray the Lord my soul to keep. If I should die—" It was the only prayer he could remember, and he groaned at the words and clamped his mouth shut.

"Ash, listen to me," Tori said, and gripped his shoulder. "We'll be okay. Ash?" She shook him. "Ash?"

The car made an abrupt turn, and Tori was thrown against the door. When she pushed her-

self upright again, she saw that they were bar-
reling straight for the Huey Long Bridge. "Oh,
no," she moaned.

Ashford glanced down at the speedometer and
bit his upper lip in an effort not to scream. "A
hundred miles per hour." He looked at Tori.
"We're going a hundred miles per hour!"

They sped across the bridge, the silver trusses
of the long structure that spanned the Mississippi nothing more than a blur.

The car swerved onto the winding River Road
and sped down the two-lane foliage-bordered old
highway.

Horror-struck, Ashford snapped his eyes shut
and screwed his face into an expectation and denial of impending disaster. He no longer even
pretended to steer the car.

The sleek Jaguar began to slow, turned off
the road, and onto a dirt driveway. It came to
an abrupt stop beneath a giant live oak tree, its
gnarled, ancient limbs draped with curtains of
Spanish moss that hung so low as to skim the
hood of the car. The engine switched off.

Silence embraced them, broken only by
Ashford's raucous wheezing as he tried to
breathe past the knot of fear that clogged his
throat.

Chapter Eleven

The Tchoupitloulas Plantation house sat like a small jewel in a grove of ancient oak trees. Its wooden walls were painted a pale gray, and its Colonial blue shutters gleamed in the flickering light of several tall flambeaux that lined a narrow walkway leading to the entrance. If not for the many cars that crowded the small parking lot set to one side of the house, one might readily believe that it was still a home, and that it was the 1800s, rather than 1993.

While they waited for their dinner, Ash gulped down three martinis in rapid succession. After the third, his trembling had finally subsided to a mild shake, but his gaze kept darting around the room, as if he expected the old house to come alive and devour him.

"Now look what you've done," Lila said, gracing Chance with a baleful glare. "He might as well be in a coma for all the romance that's left in him tonight."

"Oh, button up." He felt a swell of disgust as

he watched Ashford down another drink and look fearfully around the room. "What a sot. He's too much of a milquetoast to be in our family, anyway." He waved a finger at Ash. "Look at him."

"And I suppose you have a better idea?"

"No, but I will, just give me a while. I'll think of something."

"That's what I'm afraid of."

Silence was a cold companion in the car on the way back to RiverOaks. Ash wanted to know what had happened earlier, who Tori had been talking to while they'd zoomed down the road out of control, and she couldn't tell him. Well, that wasn't exactly true. She could, but she wasn't about to. In his present state, he might drive her to a sanitarium rather than home.

Ash pulled the car up before the fanning steps of the RiverOaks entry and killed the engine. Without a word he slipped from the car and walked around to her side.

On the dark porch he bent to kiss her cheek. She had wanted to talk to him tonight about his declaration of their intent to marry, but with what had happened, she thought he'd had enough trauma for one night.

Suddenly the front door swung open and light poured onto the gallery from the foyer.

"Well, welcome back, you two," Stanton declared loudly. He beamed up at them.

Tori stared at her grandfather as Ashford began to mumble. "Goo . . . good . . . good evening, Mr. Clemente. I was just . . . saying good-night to Tori."

"Yes, it is a good evening. Watched the sun go down hours ago. Beautiful sight, just beautiful!" Stanton bellowed. "But why say good-night, Ash?" He smiled slyly and waved a hand toward the parlor. "Still plenty of evening left. Come on in, son, join me for a cup of coffee." He spun his wheelchair around. "Tori, have Abram bring us some coffee, why don't you?"

Tori grew immediately suspicious. Why was he being nice to Ash?

They followed Stanton into the parlor.

"Hey, Ash, Tori, how was your evening?" Rand drawled. He extended a hand to Ashford.

Tension, as well as the sudden presence of a half-dozen uninvited family members, immediately filled the room. Tori felt like screaming. Then she felt like laughing. If Ash and Rand knew how many others were in the room, their attention all centered on them, they'd probably run out of the house in a panic and never return. Chaos was just around the corner—she could feel it—but there was absolutely nothing she could do about it, short of kicking both men out of the house, which might make things even worse.

Ashford's demeanor changed abruptly when he saw Rand. Suddenly the events of the evening were forgotten. His shoulders squared and a purposeful gleam lit his eyes. He wrapped a possessive arm around Tori's waist and pasted a smile on his face. "Mitchell," Ash said a bit too loudly for the quiet room, "nice to see you again." He extended a hand, and his eyes narrowed in an ever so slight wince as the two shook hands.

Tori glanced across the room. Lila and Chance stood to one side of the fireplace, looking none too happy, though Chance seemed to be smugly pleased with himself. The general and Dominic stood just behind her grandfather, and Miriam and Laura sat on a settee against the wall and chatted in low tones.

Tori excused herself and went into the kitchen to help Abram with the coffee, but found it unnecessary. He was already loading a tray. She made a hasty return to the parlor. She didn't dare leave the room for too long. World War III might erupt.

She took a seat on the settee next to Ash, leaving Rand standing beside the fireplace, and averted her gaze from him. But she could feel his eyes on her. Damn, what was there about him that both drew and aggravated her to no end? She didn't know the first thing about him—not who he was, what he was, nothing—yet her heart did silly little flip-flops every time he was around. It was ridiculous.

Abram entered the room carrying a large silver tray laden with a coffee urn and cups, and went directly to a sideboard set against the far wall.

"So, Ash, what kind of business are you in?" Rand said.

Tori ignored their conversation as she caught a movement beside her grandfather and suddenly realized Chance had disappeared. She nearly groaned. Now what? She looked around hurriedly.

"Oh, Lord," she whispered. She looked at Rand, then Ashford. Neither had noticed . . . yet. She tried to keep a smile on her face and rose from her seat. Casually, she hoped.

The men continued to talk, and she moved toward Abram as fast as she could without drawing their attention.

The servant's hands flailed the air, swatting here and there at a half dozen sugar cubes that danced around his head. With each swat, the cubes spun away, zipped and looped through the air, and successfully evaded his grasp.

Tori stole a look back at Rand, Ash, and Stanton. They were still engrossed in somewhat sparring conversation and seemingly unaware of the commotion going on only a few feet away from them. At least Rand and Ash were; she was pretty sure Stanton had noticed.

She stepped to Abram's side. "Stop it!" she

demanded in a whisper, and looked not at the old man, but at the sugar cubes.

They kept flying merrily around in the air.

"Put that down," Abram hissed. His old black hand grabbed at a cube as it swooped down before his face. It looped away, and before he could duck, zoomed back down and bounced off of the end of his nose.

"Chance," Tori said, trying for a reprimanding tone. She fought to suppress a giggle. "Stop this."

"Lawdy, you peoples are more trouble than you're worth!" Abram swore. He shook his head and ducked as another cube lifted from the small silver bowl and went floating upward. "Like a bunch of little children, always into something."

Tori giggled, then caught herself. This was no time to be amused. "Uncle Chance, please, stop this," she whispered fiercely. "Stop, or I swear I'll find some way to make you sorry." She held her breath and hoped the bluff would work.

The barest whisper of a laugh sounded close to her ear. "No woman has ever managed to make me sorry," Chance said.

Tori spun around toward his voice. No one was there, at least no one she saw, but to her relief the sugar cubes, like gently falling snowflakes, drifted downward and settled back into the silver sugar bowl.

"Thank you," she said. Suddenly she noticed

the silence in the room and turned. The three men were staring at her. Stanton appeared amused. Ash looked as if he was now totally convinced she was some kind of voodoo woman. Rand's expression indicated that, at the moment at least, he wasn't sure what to believe.

"Magic," she said brightly, and forced a huge smile to her lips. How did *they* always manage to get her into these situations? "My, um, father taught it to me when I was little. I just get the urge to try my hand at it every once in a while." She turned away and busied herself arranging the cups. She could feel her face burning. Blast, she was probably as red as a tomato. She poured the coffee, lifted two saucers, and handed one to Ash, the other to Rand. Ashford mumbled a stilted thank-you and threw a furtive glance past her to the sugar bowl on the sideboard.

"If you don't stop this, you're going to scare him away for good," Lila said, and slapped Chance's arm with her closed fan.

"Maybe we should." He glowered at Ash through narrowed eyes. "The man's a milquetoast if I ever saw one. Tori needs a man, not a worm."

"Tori needs a man of her own breeding, not some Yankee heathen."

Rand set his cup on the mantel and reached for Tori's hand before she could turn away. His thumb moved slowly, lightly, over her knuckles, and his eyes locked with hers, fusing midnight blue with cinnamon brown, holding her gaze. Ever so slowly, his head lowered, though his eyes never left hers, and he pressed his lips to the back of her hand, a feather-light touch that sent shivers up her arm, hot and tingling, to blend with the accelerated beat of her heart. "Thank you," Rand said softly.

"I think he's winning," Chance said, and nodded toward Rand and Tori, who had yet to pull her hand from his.

"Sweet talk, that's all it is," Lila griped. "She'll see through him soon enough."

Ash gawked at Rand in outright indignation. "I suppose Victoria hasn't had an opportunity to inform you that we are formally engaged now."

Tori spun around in surprise, and the smile on Rand's face disappeared.

"Engaged?" he said, his tone flat.

"Not by a long shot!" Stanton bellowed. He wheeled himself up before Ash. "I told you earlier, *Ashford—*" he put a sneering emphasis on Ash's name"—*I* haven't given permission for anything here."

"Gramps," Tori said, in an effort to defuse the situation, "I'll handle this later."

"There's nothing to handle, except to show this self-righteous whippersnapper where the door is."

"Gramps," Tori said again, the word nearly a groan.

Ash scurried around Stanton and took Tori's hand from Rand's, nearly jerking it from his grasp. "It's all right, *chérie,* I must be going, anyway. I have an appointment with the bank in the morning, but perhaps we can meet for lunch?" He urged her toward the foyer.

"Uh, yes, fine," she said. She had to get this marriage thing straightened out with him, but she didn't need an audience. Especially one that included Rand Mitchell.

The next morning Tori had no difficulty convincing Rand that she'd couldn't act as his personal tour guide again. He didn't ask. In fact, when she left the house she noticed that his rental car was already gone from the driveway. She felt a twinge of disappointment and quickly pushed it aside. It was good that he was off on his own. She had work to do, lots of it.

At exactly eleven-thirty, Ashford sauntered into Tori's office, a bouquet of red roses in one hand, a box of candy in the other. She looked up from the mound of papers on her desk that she'd been trying, unsuccessfully, all morning to muddle through, and gasped. She'd forgotten she had half promised to lunch with him. The morning had already proven a disaster. She had a ton of work to do and had accomplished nothing. Absolutely nothing. Instead, her mind had played little daydream games all morning, conjuring up images of Rand, memories of how his arms felt around her, remembering the burning caress of his lips on hers, the seductive, utterly delicious sensation of his tongue as it dueled with her own.

She rose to greet Ash and instantly regretted it when he swept her into his arms and planted a huge kiss on her lips, then swung her about him.

She laughed, despite her apprehension. This was definitely not the Ashford she knew. "Ash, what's gotten into you?" she said as her feet touched the ground. She made to slip from his arms but he held her tight.

"I just came from Magnolia Acres."

At her puzzled expression he continued, his words flowing forth like water through a burst dam. "The retirement home they just built over by Lake Ponchartrain. You know, the luxury one."

She nodded.

"Well, I wanted to see it first, before I did anything, and it's perfect. Stanton and Abram will have the time of their lives there, I just know it, so I went ahead and put a deposit down on one of the units." He ignored her frown of puzzlement and hurried on. "Then I stopped by to see this realtor friend of mine." He waved a hand in the air. "Well, he's an acquaintance, really. Anyway, he assured me that this is a perfect time to put RiverOaks on the market, and he thinks he knows someone who would be interested in buying the company, too."

Tori's mouth fell open in shock.

"He claims he can get top dollar for both. Says there are always people clamoring to latch on to those plantation houses, though for the life of me I can't see why. Musty old things. He calls them romantic sales." Ash shook his head. "Humph, romantic. More like pouring money down the drain, if you ask me."

"Ash—"

"He's going to stop by here later this afternoon so you can sign the papers and discuss price with him."

"Ash—"

"So, doesn't that sound great?"

"Ash—"

"Oh, I almost forgot, I also stopped by the cathedral and reserved us a date for next month. I figured why wait? The father told me we lucked out. They've been booked solid for months, but he just had a cancellation, so we're in!"

"Ash!" Tori practically screamed.

"What?" He looked at her in seeming surprise and total innocence.

"I don't believe you did all that."

"Well, once I got started, it just kind of took off. Of course, you still have to get your gown, and we have to make up a guest list, and decide

135

where we should honeymoon, but . . ."

"That's not what I mean and you know it."
She set the flowers and candy on her desk. "I
meant, I don't believe you did all of that without consulting me."

"Consulting you? We talked about it the other
night. I asked you to marry me, and you said
yes."

"I never said yes."

"You did."

She decided to try a different tack; this one
wasn't working. "I have absolutely no intention
of ever putting my grandfather or Abram in a
home, luxury or not, and I am not selling
RiverOaks. I thought you always said you didn't
really want marriage. Isn't that what you've always said, Ash? Why marry when you don't
want any children? Aren't those your words?"

"Yes, but I've changed my mind. And we can
get a nanny."

"No."

"Why not?"

"I mean, no, I'm not going to marry you."
She tried to lighten her tone. "Ash, we've been
seeing each other for over a year, and it's been
nice, but . . ."

"This is that cowboy's fault," Ash snapped.
"You're in love with *him*, aren't you?"

"No."

"Then why won't you marry me?"

* * *

Tori thought about Ashford's question for the rest of the afternoon. She totally ignored the work on her desk, had her phone calls held, and paced the office, stopping only when her secretary entered with a cup of coffee for her and warned that she was about to wear a path in the carpet.

Ashford's question had stuck in her brain like a thorn. It nagged at her, demanded an answer, and echoed continuously until she thought she'd go crazy. She couldn't marry Ash because she didn't love him — it was that simple. But it wasn't Rand's fault. Or was it? That's the part that kept gnawing at her. If Rand Mitchell hadn't come to RiverOaks, if she'd never met him, would she have eventually married Ashford?

She shook her head. No, she wouldn't. Before the accident, maybe. She'd been more easily led then, had let other people influence her decisions and coerce her into doing what they wanted. But no more. All that had changed, gradually, as she'd taken over her father's position in the company. She'd had to change, or lose everything.

She picked up her purse and headed for the door. This whole thing was insane, and she was wasting time thinking about it. She had work to do, a company to run, and she was piddling away her time fretting over someone she barely knew, and feelings that were better left ignored.

"You should have accepted his proposal, Victoria," Lila said.

Tori stopped at the door and turned back to face her aunt. She was in no mood to mind her elders, as her father used to say. Rather, she had a devilish urge to strangle them, for all the good it would do. "Why, because he's a born-and-bred good little Southern gentleman?" She regretted the tart words almost the moment they rolled off her tongue, but her annoyance at their shenanigans still grated on her nerves.

Lila's eyes narrowed and her pointed nose lifted higher into the air. "No, because he's the right one for you."

Chapter Twelve

Rand stood on the moonwalk overlooking the Mississippi and stared out at the river without really seeing it. Minutes before he'd slammed down the receiver of a public pay phone and cut off the droning words of Jason Newhall. Nothing was going right this time, and for some reason he was at a loss as to what to do about it. Jason wanted to continue his maneuvering for a forced takeover of Rouchard Travel, but, like the last time they'd tried, it wasn't working, and trying to buy Rouchard Travel hadn't met with any success, either. Jason had presented Tori and her attorneys with two offers in the past two weeks, both substantial, even generous, and both had been flatly rejected. The proposals had been given no consideration, and there had been no negotiations. Tori was being just as staunch in her refusal to sell as her father had been, and the few people who existed who held partial interests in the company, all Rouchard relatives, either also refused to consider selling, or were off jaunting around the globe and couldn't be found.

"Damn." Rand slammed a fist down on the wooden railing before him, then cursed again as pain shot through the side of his hand. He'd faced other situations like this before, and he'd always gotten what he wanted. Always. Why was this time so different?

Across the wide river the streetlights of the city of Algiers began to glow against the darkening sky, and with the disappearance of the sun, the river had turned from a murky green to glistening black.

A loud whistle pierced the air. Rand turned to see *The Natchez* pull away from the wharf and head out on its evening cruise. It passed the raised levee where he stood, and the sounds of Dixieland music echoed from its lounge, the steady whoosh-whoosh of the riverboat's huge red paddlewheel a reminder of days long past and of a night not so long ago.

Rand felt a sudden tightening deep within himself, and a simmering heat in the pit of his stomach as he watched the boat pass. He had stood on that deck only hours before and kissed Tori, held her in his arms, and felt the pliant mold of her body pressed to his. He hadn't been thinking of business then, of ulterior motives and driving ambition. The gnawing ache of need that thought of her aroused in him deepened, and with it, anger at himself. He had let

140

a pretty face sidetrack him, divert him from his intentions—and that had been his mistake. That was why, so far, he'd gotten nowhere.

He should do what he had planned on doing when he'd come to New Orleans. Get close enough to Tori so that she'd tell him why she was being so stubborn about selling, and maybe shed some light on what he'd have to do to get Rouchard Travel.

From now on he would steel himself against the feelings that stirred within him every time he was around her, at least the ones that threatened to take his mind off what he needed to accomplish. This was no time to let foolish sentiment or daydreams get in the way of his plans. Too much was riding on this deal. He took a deep breath and turned to leave the moonwalk. The acquisition of Rouchard Travel was critical to Paradise Tours. More so now than ever before. Too much work, too many manhours, and too much planning had gone into it to walk away from it now. And there was no reason to, in spite of the fact that for the past forty-eight hours all he'd been able to think about was bedding the woman whose company he wanted. Rand smiled to himself. But wasn't that exactly what he'd come here to do?

He walked slowly across Jackson Square. He would accomplish what he'd come to New Orleans to do, and damn anyone, including Ashford Thibeaux III, who got in his way.

141

* * *

Tori rolled down the car window and let the wind whip at her face and hair. Lila was right, of course. Not about her marrying Ashford; she wasn't about to do that just to please *them*. But she was right about Rand's being wrong for her. It didn't matter that Tori was attracted to him. She sighed deeply. There was no sense lying to herself. It wasn't just infatuation, or a simple case of being drawn to a handsome face. It had gone beyond that the moment he'd kissed her at the Beauregard House. She was in dire danger of losing her heart to him. She'd been trying to fight it ever since, but every time she was around him, the thought that it was a nearly lost battle assailed her.

"Ashford's right," Lila said. She suddenly appeared in the passenger seat.

Startled, Tori jumped, and her hand jerked on the steering wheel. The car swerved toward the center of the road. She grabbed the wheel and yanked it back. The small sports car took a sharp corner, barely missed colliding head-on with a pickup truck laden with crates of squawking chickens, and swerved back into its own lane.

Tori gripped the wheel tightly in an effort to stop the shaking of her hands. "You could have gotten us both killed with that stunt."

"Really?" Lila's tone dripped with innocent sarcasm.

Tori looked at her aunt again and suddenly realized the content of her words. She laughed. "I guess that didn't come out right."

Lila waved a dismissive hand at Tori. "Well, you wouldn't have such problems if you were in a carriage. These things—" she screwed up her face in disgust "—are atrocious. Zipping people around like flies on an apple. Why, no one takes the time to enjoy things anymore." She looked out the window. "Like what you're passing. Look at old Gabe Valcorye's house, all closed up and run-down. And to think, Gabe used to give some of the best soirées. Why, I remember . . ."

"Things change, Auntie. And so do people," she added, wishing her aunt would get the hint. It wasn't 1860, no matter how hard Lila tried to believe it was.

Lila sniffed. "As I was saying, Tori, Ashford is right. Your grandfather and Abram would be much better off in a home than roaming about the plantation all day. You two could marry and—"

"I'm not marrying Ashford."

"You're just upset with us because we've been trying to help."

Tori snickered. "Help? Is that what you call what you and Chance have been doing?"

"Yes, and as I was saying, you two could marry and live at RiverOaks, and have children, and—"

143

"He doesn't want to live at RiverOaks."

"Oh, that's nonsense. Of course he'd want to live at RiverOaks."

Tori shook her head. "No, he wants to sell it."

"Sell it?" Lila yelped. Her dark eyes blazed with fury and indignation. "Sell RiverOaks?" she gasped again. "Why, the nerve of the boy. I'll kill him."

Tori smiled. "I thought you wanted me to marry him."

Lila promptly disappeared.

"Well, so much for Ashford," Tori said to herself. Her smile widened just a bit.

The soft strains of a familiar song drifted to her from the radio and pulled her thoughts from the present to a time several years before, and to another man whom *they* hadn't approved of. She had ignored them then, too, and accepted Tom's proposal of marriage. But the moment they saw her engagement ring, their little skirmishes against Tom turned to all-out war. She should have known it would happen, but she'd let her heart get the better of her. Even her father, who'd been alive then, couldn't stop them.

The music drew her attention again, and as memories drifted through her mind, her light mood departed as quickly as it had appeared. She didn't want to go through the pain of loving a man and then losing him. She wouldn't.

Not for anyone. She'd rather remain single for the rest of her life, and she just might do that if a man never came around whom *they* approved of and *she* loved. That seemed to be a pretty big order. The tall wrought iron gate of RiverOaks appeared in the glow of her headlights and she turned the car in to the driveway. She would definitely not go through that heartache again.

She pulled her car into the old carriage house. Anyway, what was she worrying about? She liked Rand, but she wasn't in love with him. Though she knew she easily could be. And he certainly had given no indication that he had any "long-term" feelings for her. As the nose of her car crept into the dark carriage house and its interior was lit by her headlights, she glanced to the side and slammed on her brakes. She looked in dismay at Rand's rental car. "Great. Just great." She thought about sneaking in the back door, then shrugged. Stanton would most likely see her, if he hadn't already spotted her car as it passed the house. No way would he let her get upstairs without comment.

She mounted the entry steps on tiptoe, carefully opened and closed the front door with little more than a whisper of sound, and headed across the foyer toward the staircase. She was almost safe. Just a few more feet.

"Tori, come on in here," Stanton called, as she tried to pass the door to the parlor. "Abram made us all a little buffet dinner."

All? Did that include their houseguest? A long sigh escaped her lips. Was there even the slightest possibility she could be lucky enough to find it was just her and her grandfather? She set her briefcase down on a chair in the foyer, along with her purse, and walked into the parlor.

The heavy damask drapes were already drawn against the night, and flames danced in the grate of the parlor's white marble fireplace. Only the glow of the fire, and that of an oil lamp on a table beside her grandfather, lit the large room. Its outer edges remained cloaked in shadow.

"Hi, Gramps, how'd it go today?" Tori almost sagged in relief to find he was alone. Maybe somebody up there liked her, after all. She sat down on the settee.

"Abram and me been trying to figure out where we seen our houseguest before," he said bluntly.

Tori frowned and paused in the process of kicking off her shoes. "Seen him before? You never mentioned that to me. What makes you think you've seen him before?"

Stanton shook his head and continued to gently caress one end of his bushy mustache. "Don't know, really. Abram and me, we just got this same feeling. Been talking about it for a few days. We've both seen him, that's for certain. Problem is, neither of us can come up with where."

"In a movie maybe? On TV? The news?"

Stanton shook his head again. "Can't say for certain, but none of that sounds right."

Tori slumped back on the settee. "You talked to him about his business. What about that?"

Stanton shook his head. "All he says is he owns a couple of stores."

"Stores? Like boutiques? Sports equipment?"

"Good evening," Rand said.

Tori nearly jumped out of her skin. His voice seemed to waft out from the shadows of the foyer and envelop her. A delicious tingle raced across her skin. She spun around and stared at him. How long had he been there? She tried to ignore the sudden acceleration of her pulse, and forced a smile to her lips. "Gramps was just saying he thinks he's seen you someplace before but isn't sure where."

Rand returned her smile. He had heard the tail end of their conversation as he'd descended the stairs in the foyer. He shrugged and shook his head. "Ever get out to California, Stanton?"

"Never had reason to go there," the old man responded. "Used to go into Texas a lot, though, hunting, but haven't gone back in—" he scrunched his brow in thought "—maybe thirteen, fourteen years."

Rand shook his head. "That would have made me about fifteen the last time you were there."

147

He smiled. "I think my first trip to Texas was about two years ago. How about Arizona? Ever been there?"

"Nope."

"New Mexico?"

"Nope."

"Nevada?"

"Nope."

Tori watched the two men and suddenly felt a tickle of uneasiness. For some reason she had the distinct impression that Rand was hiding something. Or being evasive. But for the life of her, she couldn't rationalize why she felt that way.

"Gramps said you own a chain of stores. What kind?"

"Oh, different types," Rand responded off-handedly, and moved to stand before the fireplace. He rested a booted foot on the brass fender that skirted the hearth, laid a bent elbow on the mantel, and turned all his attention on Tori. "Mostly tourist-type shops." It wasn't *really* a lie. Travel agencies catered to tourists. "But I don't want to talk about me. Or business. I'm on vacation. I want to know about you. About this house, your family, the Rouchards' history here."

"Our history? Why?" Tori asked, and laughed, though his comment had made her more nervous than she wanted to admit. "Are you really a writer planning on doing an exposé on us or something?" She'd been approached by writers before, usually when they were bored, nothing in the world was really happening, and they'd somehow tripped over the old rumor that the Rouchards, all the way back to the beginning of time, were slightly crazy.

"No, my interest is strictly personal."

The comment hung in the air, the underlying currents of its meaning sizzling like a live wire between them. His gaze was riveted on Tori, refusing to allow her to turn away or avert her own eyes.

"Like what?" Stanton demanded. He turned his wheelchair to face Rand, and pinned him with his own piercing gaze.

"Like I would very much like to court your grandaughter," Rand said, his eyes never leaving Tori's. "That is the proper way to ask permission, isn't it?"

Tori felt icy fingers trip up her spine. This was it. She knew it. *They* would go berserk now. She tried to maintain a semblance of reserve and shot a nervous glance around the room.

It remained calm, which was more than Tori could say for herself.

Abram, who had quietly shuffled into the parlor only moments before, handed first Tori, then Stanton and Rand, a plate of salad and cold cuts.

Rand sat on the settee beside Tori. His thigh

brushed against hers, and she jumped as if touched by flame. She tried to subtly move away from him and found the antique sofa unaccommodating.

She glanced around the room again. It remained quiet. Almost too quiet. It was like waiting for an atom bomb to drop through the roof. She picked at her food. "So, did you do some more sightseeing today?" she said finally. Maybe *they* were asleep.

"Good evening, Tori," a deep, resonant voice drawled in her ear.

Chapter Thirteen

Tori nearly choked on the piece of tomato she was just swallowing. She looked over her shoulder. Chance smiled down at her and winked.

"Just wanted to let you know, your aunt Lila's in a real dither tonight, so be careful." He instantly disappeared before she could question what he meant, or why he was warning her.

Tori turned around and slumped against the back of the settee. "Oh, great," she mumbled. "Just absolutely great."

"What's wrong?" Rand asked.

She looked at him in puzzlement, then realized she'd spoken aloud. It was becoming a habit, and he probably was beginning to think of her as a blithering idiot. If he wasn't, then he was certainly one. "Nothing." She stabbed at a piece of lettuce. "What were we talking about?"

"About what Rand did today," Stanton offered.

"I had some business to take care of. Phone

calls and such. He looked at Tori. "I came by your office, but you weren't there."

"I had a meeting."

"I wanted to take you to dinner."

She smiled. He was not going to make keeping a distance between them an easy task. But it was one that had to be, even if he didn't know it.

"Be careful," Chance whispered teasingly in her ear.

She slapped at him and hit Rand's shoulder instead. The blow pushed his arm forward. The plate he held tilted, food slid across its surface, and dressing-covered leaves of lettuce, tomato chunks, beans and shrimp tumbled onto his lap.

"Oh, I'm sorry," Tori mumbled, mortified at what she'd done. She grabbed a linen napkin from her lap and began plucking the remains of his tossed salad from his thighs.

He made no move to either help or stop her, but merely watched and struggled desperately to hold back both a smile and the desire that was coursing through him and hardening him to steel at the light touch of her fingers so near his need. God, but he wanted her, maybe more than any woman he had ever met.

"Are you just going to stand there and watch this, or are you going to do something?" Lila grumbled. She flapped her fan in front of her face, creating a small tornado that ruffled the wisps of gray-black hair at her temples.

"What are you trying to do, take off and fly with that thing?" Chance drawled mockingly, and waved a dismissive hand at her.

She snapped the fan closed. "Stop trying to change the subject. Maybe Dominic refuses to interfere in this, or help us prevent another Yankee from invading this family, but I thought I could count on you." She pointed a bony arthritic finger at Rand and Tori. "Look at them."

"I am looking, and I don't see anything happening."

"Then you're blind, just like your brother. She's falling for him, as if it isn't obvious to anyone with two eyes and a brain." She sniffed. "But then I always did wonder if you actually had the latter."

Chance wrinkled his nose at her, a habit left over from their childhood.

She slapped his arm with the fan. "Look at them," she ordered again. "If we don't do something soon, it will be too late."

"Just what do you want me to do, dear sister? There's no way we can stop her from falling in love with him."

"Maybe not, but we can certainly persuade him to leave."

"Tori might go with him."

"Never," Lila said. "She didn't leave with the last one we ran off, and she won't leave with this one. Tori would never forsake RiverOaks, especially for a Yankee."

Tori suddenly realized where her hands were and jumped back in her seat as if someone had sucker-punched her. "Oh, I'm sorry," she mumbled again. She felt her face flush, and a hot, searing heat burned her cheeks.

"I'm not," Rand said. A wicked gleam lit his blue eyes as he continued to watch her.

Stanton chuckled, but watched Rand shrewdly, assessing him. He liked the boy, but something about him bothered Stanton, some familiarity he couldn't put his finger on.

Rand rose and sauntered to the sideboard. He handed Stanton a cup of coffee, poured two more, and moved back to where Tori remained on the settee.

Tori reached for the cup, her fingers touched his, and a shock of warmth raced up her arms. He didn't release the cup, and she didn't pull her hand away, but rather continued to gaze up at him, mesmerized.

"Do something, Chance," Lila hissed. "Now!"

Suddenly the cup flew from Tori and Rand's hands. It shot straight up in the air between them, and both watched it, too shocked to react. As it arced into its descent, the cup dipped toward Tori and milk-cooled coffee poured forth.

She saw it coming, like a small brown tidal wave, but there was no time to flee its path. The warm liquid splashed against her face. Tori jumped up from the chair, sputtering, as creamy brown rivulets streamed from her hair, ran down over her forehead and cheeks, and dripped from her chin onto her breast. "Of all . . . the . . . the . . . despicable . . . horrid . . ." She wiped coffee from her eyes and pushed wet hair from her face. "If I could kill you, I swear I would."

Rand's mouth hung agape and he stared, shocked, at Tori. Was she nuts? What the hell had happened? Damn, he'd thought his own temper was bad. He grabbed a napkin and began to dab at her face and hair. This was all he needed. A silent stream of curses raced through his head. He had intended to somehow get through that barricade of coolness she'd erected between them so that he could do what he should have been doing since the moment he'd arrived. He had thought to be charming and attentive, but the evening was quickly turning into an episode of Laurel and Hardy, rather than the Rhett and Scarlett scenario he'd planned.

Tori slapped his hand and the napkin away. "Never mind," she said, her tone sharp. She wiped her own napkin across her face and saw by the black mark she left on it that she'd also managed to smear mascara across her cheek. "I have to get upstairs, anyway." *And when I do I have a few choice words for two very stubborn and meddling relatives,* she thought silently. She bent and kissed her grandfather, mumbled something in his ear, and turned back to Rand. "Good night, Mr. Mitchell," she said, and hurried toward the foyer.

"Well, that was wonderful," Lila snipped. She looked at Chance as if he were a total simpleton.

"You said to do something, so I did something."

"I meant do something to *him,* not to Tori, you dolt."

Chance shrugged. "Well, I didn't intend it to go that way, but what difference does it make, really? It accomplished what you wanted, didn't it?"

Tori turned from the window in her room and began to pace. She couldn't sleep. Her mind was like a runaway carnival ride. It wouldn't shut off and it wouldn't slow down, and she couldn't control its direction. Every time she closed her eyes, his image was there. Every time she made an effort to think of the business, of the harassing phone calls from that Mr. Jason Newhall with his never-ending offers to buy Rouchard Travel, her mind rebelled and skipped back to thoughts of Rand. Her concentration was gone, kaput, unless it was directed at him, and that scared her. She had never before been this engrossed in a man, this obsessed. Not even with Tom, and she'd loved him. She didn't love Rand—did she?

She stopped in her pacing, the question stuck in her mind like a stalled train, chugging, huffing, and blowing heat and smoke, and threatening as all get-out. No, it was impossible. She shook her head. She'd known him for barely six days. Anyway, how could she love someone and not know it? And she did not believe in love at first sight. That was ridiculous. She was infatuated, that's all. He was an attractive, very sexy man. She wouldn't be normal if she didn't notice that.

"I like him."

Tori turned at her sister's voice. Krissy sat in the center of the old canopied bed, her legs crossed Indian-style.

She smiled and sat on the edge of the bed. "So, you like him, do you?"

Krissy threw her head back and laughed. Long dark waves of hair slid from her shoulders and down her back. "You'd better believe I like him," she said. "And if circumstances were different, dear sister, I'd snatch him from you."

Tori laughed, too, while she tried desperately to stem the tears that stung her eyes. Krissy would forever be seventeen years old. She would never experience the thrill of her senior ball, never make her debut into society, or know the passion of loving a man, of feeling his arms around her, his lips capturing hers.

"He seems awfully nice, Tori." She absently twisted a lock of her hair around one finger. "He likes you, I can tell. And he's loads better than that old Ashford."

"You never did like Ash, so you'd probably say you liked Dracula better, wouldn't you?"

Krissy giggled, then turned serious. "No. Ashford's a wimp. And he's sneaky. Rand brought you flowers himself, because he thought of it. Ashford got his from Aunt Lila."

Tori frowned, confused. "What? How could Ash get flowers from Lila? He can't see her."

"She had Uncle Chance put them in Ashford's car so he'd give them to you. I heard her talking. She says Ashford isn't romantic enough."

"Not romantic?"

"Yep. And she's right. He's not romantic. Lila wanted to help him and she knows you like flowers." Krissy began to fade.

"Wait. Where are you going?" Tori asked, suddenly frantic for her to stay.

"I can't stay for too long yet, Tori. Mama says the only reason I can get through so soon is cause I was young and had a lot of energy. She and Papa keep trying, but they can't do it yet at all."

"Krissy?" She looked around the room and tears filled her eyes, but there was no sign of her sister. "Krissy, come back to me tomorrow, okay?" she said softly.

There was no answer.

Chapter Fourteen

For long hours after Krissy had gone, Tori lay on her bed, her room bathed in moonlight that streamed in through the open drapes. Everything was against her having a relationship with Rand—any kind of relationship. And it wasn't only that *they* didn't approve, though that was an awfully big part of it. He was too much like Tom, so self-assured, and maybe even a bit arrogant. And Stanton was still grumbling about having seen him somewhere before. Normally that wouldn't bother her, but this time, with Rand, it did, and she didn't know why.

Dawn crept slowly into the room and spread its brilliant glow over Tori, who had fallen asleep only a few hours before. The dazzling light against her eyelids pricked at her unconscious mind and forced her from the restless slumber. The minute she looked at the window and saw the angle of the sun, she knew she'd overslept and was late for work.

"Damn." She scurried around the room, throwing on a pair of chocolate brown slacks, a gold silk blouse, and ran a brush through her hair. She didn't have time to pin it up. At the door to the hall, she grabbed her purse and the blazer that matched her slacks.

"Hey, what's the hurry?" Stanton said, as she practically flew through the foyer. He rolled his wheelchair from the doorway of the parlor toward her. "No breakfast this morning?"

"Don't have time, Gramps. Sorry. I have a meeting this morning, and I'm going to be late as it is if I don't get moving." She bent and kissed his cheek.

"Who you meeting with this time?"

She shrugged. "Some guy who won't take no for an answer about selling the agencies. I keep turning down his offers, and he keeps upping them."

Abram shuffled into the foyer and handed her a small glass of orange juice. "Best drink this, missy. Keep up your strength."

She gulped it down, thanked him, and handed the glass back just as she caught sight of Rand at the top of the staircase, watching her. He had on a white shirt, open at the collar, and tailored to hug the V shape of his upper torso, accentuating the broad width of his shoulders and narrow span of his waist. The pristine whiteness also proved a stark, and complementary, contrast to his bronzed skin, while dark

"Lucky in Love"—a new concept in contemporary romantic fiction.

Now you can start to experience the romantic adventures of modern women whose dreams come true with 4 FREE BOOKS (a $14.00 value).

Did you ever dream of winning the jackpot in the lottery or suddenly inheriting a fortune from someone you hardly knew or finding out that the "junk piece" of jewelry your mother gave you is worth over a million dollars? How would your life change?

Now you can share this fantasy, as Zebra, the leading publisher of romantic fiction, proudly brings you LUCKY IN LOVE. You'll go on exciting romantic adventures with heroines who learn that good fortune is not enough until they find true love.

CHANGE YOUR LUCK WITH 4 FREE BOOKS!

To start your home subscription to "LUCKY IN LOVE", Zebra will send you the first four novels absolutely FREE. There is absolutely no obligation.

GET LUCKY WITH FREE HOME DELIVERY AND BIG SAVINGS!

Each month, we'll send you the latest LUCKY IN LOVE titles for you to preview FREE for 10 days. If you like them, keep them and pay the low Preferred Home Subscribers price of just $3.00 each. That's a savings of $2.00 off the cover price each month. Plus, Free Home Delivery means there are never any shipping, handling or other "hidden charges"— so your savings are even greater.

And remember, you can return any shipment within 10 days for full credit, no questions asked. There is no minimum number of books you must buy, and you may cancel your subscription at any time.

Change Your Luck Today. Fill-out And Mail
The FREE BOOK Certificate. We'll Send You
Your Free Gift As Soon As We Receive It!

FREE BOOK CERTIFICATE

LUCKY IN LOVE

Zebra Home Subscription Services, Inc.

P.O. Box 5214   120 Brighton Road   Clifton, New Jersey 07015-5214

YES, I want my luck to change. Send me my gift of 4 Free LUCKY IN LOVE Romances. Then each month send me the four newest LUCKY IN LOVE novels for my Free 10-day preview. If I decide to keep them, I'll pay the low preferred Home Subscriber's price of just $3.00 each; a total of $12.00. This is a savings of $2.00 off the publisher's cover price. Otherwise, I will return them for full credit. There is no shipping and handling charge. There is no minimum purchase amount and I may cancel this arrangement at any time. Whatever I decide to do, the Free books are mine to keep.

NAME

STREET ADDRESS   APT.

CITY   STATE   ZIP CODE

( )
TELEPHONE NUMBER

SIGNATURE (if under 18, parent or
guardian must sign.)

LILBOB

This is your
best chance
to get
"LUCKY IN
LOVE".
Fill in the
coupon
and mail this
postcard
today.
(See inside for
FREE
OFFER.)

ZEBRA HOME SUBSCRIPTION SERVICES, INC.
LUCKY IN LOVE
120 BRIGHTON ROAD
P.O. BOX 5214
CLIFTON, NEW JERSEY 07015-5214

slacks hugged his long lean legs, defining them perfectly, seductively.

Tori felt a ripple of heat over her skin.

He sauntered down the stairs. "So, you're thinking of selling your business, after all?" He tried to keep his voice even and nonchalant.

"Not really, but this Newhall guy seems to need a face-to-face turn-down."

Rand almost tripped on the last step when she mentioned the name of his vice president. What the hell was Jason doing coming to New Orleans? Hadn't he given him explicit orders to keep digging and prodding? To find those other relatives and to keep bugging her by phone, make new offers? Why was he here? And how the hell was he supposed to get in contact with him now?

Tori opened the entry door. "Have a good day, everyone," she called, and slipped outside. Her heart was pounding a mile a minute. Why did he have such an effect on her? It was maddening.

An hour after she arrived at the office, Rand phoned. She thought about refusing the call, but then he might be tempted to come to the office. She picked up the receiver. "Hello, Mr. Mitchell," she said coolly. "What can I help you with?"

"Well, first of all, you can stop calling me

Mr. Mitchell and go back to using my first name."

She opened her mouth to object, then closed it. It was easier just to go along with him than argue. "All right, Rand."

"Good. Second, you can go to lunch with me."

"I'm sorry, but I have an engagement." With a mountain of paperwork, she added silently.

"With Ash?"

She bristled. "Business, if it's any concern of yours."

"Business," he echoed, as if he didn't believe her.

"I have an appointment with one of my out-of-state managers."

"That's good," Lila said.

Tori's gaze jumped to where the old woman had suddenly appeared at the side of her desk.

"All right, how about dinner?"

"Sorry."

"Breakfast."

"I can't — business."

"Another manager?"

"An appointment with the vice president of a bank who uses our services."

"Lunch tomorrow?"

"No."

Rand's hand tightened on the phone receiver. "You're avoiding me, Tori, and I know that's not what you really want to do. Not if you're truthful with yourself." He couldn't let her turn away from him, and deep down he knew it wasn't really because of business. It was personal. For all his resolve to keep his cool, to keep his mind on business, his emotions were betraying him as they'd never done before.

"I'm sorry, you're wrong. Now, I really must go." She replaced the receiver on its cradle. Her hands were trembling and her heart was fluttering around in her chest like a panicked butterfly trying to escape a net.

"That was good, Tori," Lila said.

She turned to her aunt again and her brow arched upward. "Oh, so you're happy now?"

"Yes."

Tori sighed deeply and laid her head back against her chair. "Well, I'm glad one of us is."

Lila bolted from her seat. "Just remember what happened last time, Tori. I warned you then, and I'm warning you now. Keep your head about you. Yankees are no good. They never have been, and they never will be. Remember that."

Before Tori could respond, which she'd had no intention of doing, anyway, Lila disappeared.

For the next two hours, she buried herself in studying the advertising campaign one of New Orleans better agencies had submitted for her consideration. It was good. Really good. But it needed a few changes. She took a pencil from her desk and began to make notes.

The sound of laughter and raised voices from the outer office broke her concentration and pulled her attention from the papers on her desk. She rose and walked to the door. It opened just as she approached.

"Look," her secretary said needlessly, and walked into the room, though Tori wouldn't have known who it was behind the mountain of colorful balloons if she hadn't heard Sherrille's voice. "They were just delivered for you. Everyone thinks they're great." She tied them to the arm of a chair and handed a card to Tori. "This was tied to one of the ribbons."

Tori didn't need to open the card to know who'd sent them. This wasn't Ashford's style. She opened the envelope, anyway. A smiling cartoon cat was on the card's face. Inside was simply the word "Dinner?" scrawled in a bold script.

"Sherrille, if Mr. Mitchell calls back, please give him my regrets and tell him I cannot have dinner with him," Tori said. She ignored her secretary's frown of disapproval and moved to sit back down behind her desk. "And please close the door when you leave. And hold my calls."

"Even if it's Ashford Thibeaux?"

"Especially if it's Ashford." She hadn't decided what to do about him yet. Tell him again she wasn't going to marry him, obviously, but how?

She stared at the balloons long after Sherrille had left the room. But it wasn't the colorful rubber spheres that she actually saw, but a tall, seductively handsome man, his blond hair touched by the sun, his eyes as blue and glistening as a clear summer sky. Whenever she thought of him, she could remember the feel of his lips pressed to hers, the warm, comforting sensation of his arms wrapped around her, offering strength and support.

She closed her eyes and laid her head back on the chair. She was acting like a romantic ninny. She had tons of work to do and a company to run. She didn't have time to sit and daydream over every handsome man who crossed her path. Anyway, it wasn't as if anything could come of it. She'd given up her dream of a husband, home, and children when Tom had walked out of her life.

A slightly cynical laugh escaped her lips. Walked? No, he had all but run out of her life, and Rand would, too, if she let him in and he found out about *them*. He'd be just like Tom and think she was crazy. That Stanton and Abram were crazy, and the old rumors about her family were all true, that every Rouchard who'd ever lived had been missing a few nuts and bolts.

She straightened in her chair and chuckled. Maybe they were right. Maybe all the Rouchards were a bit off. Why else would they continue to stay on at RiverOaks long after they should be resting peacefully? "Well, I won't," she said vehemently. "When I die, that's it. I'm gone."

Rand waited up for Tori. She hadn't come home for dinner, and the evening had passed slowly. He'd visited with Stanton, even played checkers with the old man, but one eye had always been on the entry door, one ear cocked for any sound of her car in the driveway. After Stanton and Abram had retired, Rand continued to sit in the parlor, waiting. He had to see her. He tried to tell himself it was only to find out what had happened when she'd met with Jason, but he knew it was more than that. He wanted to hold her, to kiss her, to make love to her. He'd gotten almost no sleep the night before, his mind in constant turmoil. He felt guilty as hell because he couldn't keep his attention on business. He lay on his bed, and the image of her lying beside him, her naked body pressed to his length, her breasts crushed to his chest, filled his mind and nearly drove him mad with want. He had never desired a woman so deeply, never become obsessed with the need to possess her, and he hated the feeling. He couldn't control it, and what he couldn't control, he usually avoided. But there was no avoiding Tori. Not unless he wanted to give up the idea of acquiring Rouchard Travel, and he wasn't yet prepared to do that.

He bent down before the fireplace hearth and stoked the small fire that danced there. The tall grandfather clock in the foyer struck eleven. Where the hell was she? With Ash? The thought turned his stomach and caused a surge of anger to well up inside him.

He rose and the glow of a car's headlights flitted across the window. He heard the crunch of tires on the crushed oyster-shell-covered driveway and heard the hum of her sports cars engine as it pulled past the house. Rand turned to the sideboard, filled two glasses with wine, and carried them into the foyer.

Tori ascended the entry steps. Good, the house was dark except for a lamp in the parlor that Stanton probably left on for her. At least she wouldn't have to face Rand. She wasn't up to it. She was exhausted and frustrated with herself, and for all the hours spent in the office she had basically accomplished nothing because all she'd done all afternoon was think about him. Well, she had accomplished one thing: she'd sent Jason Newhall on his way again, but with a sinking feeling that he would be back.

Several years ago she would have probably been dreaming about how Rand would propose to her, where they'd live, and how many children they'd have. That's all she'd wanted then. But that was before she'd realized what it meant to be a Rouchard and contemplate marriage. Especially marriage to someone *they* considered inappropriate. Of course she'd had a taste of their disapproval with Tom. That had also been before her parents had died and she'd found herself thrust from a job in marketing to being president of the company and doing it all.

The entry door swung open. "Good evening, beautiful," Rand said.

Tori tried to ignore the pleasure that rippled over her. She swept past him, set her purse on a skirt table in the foyer, and walked beside him into the parlor. "Where's my grandfather?" she asked, having fully expected to find Stanton there.

"He went to bed about an hour ago."

"Bed?" She looked up at Rand as if he'd just confessed to being Jack the Ripper. "Gramps never goes to bed before midnight. It's a thing with him, and it's only ten."

Rand shrugged. "Maybe he knew I wanted to be alone with you." He took the glass from her hand and set it, along with his own, down on a table, then turned back and slipped his arms around her waist.

Tori tried to step away from his embrace, but it was too late. His arms tightened and he pulled her to him. "I've been thinking about doing this all day, like a starving, stranded man dreaming about the feast he'll enjoy if he's ever rescued."

"Rand, please, we can't . . ." She pushed

168

against his chest.

His hold on her tightened further, a steely grip that held her firmly. "We can, Tori, and we will," he whispered, a bare second before his lips descended to claim hers. His kiss was a brand of fire, burning through her flesh to her soul and igniting the fires within her she had been desperately trying to deny.

The urge to give in to him was strong, but the fear of what would happen if she did was even stronger. She twisted away from him.

"I'm sorry," Rand said.

"No, you're not." She moved to stand by the fireplace, her back to him, her eyes watching his reflection in the mirror that hung over the mantel.

He smiled. "You're right, I'm not. But I thought you might want me to say I was."

How did he always get under her guard? Past the barriers she had so carefully erected around her feelings, her heart, ever since Tom had walked out? Was she so vulnerable that any handsome face could get to her?

"At least stay awhile, finish your wine, and tell me about your day. I'm not sleepy."

She stared at him for a long minute. No, it wasn't just a handsome face. Ash was handsome, too, in a different way. There was something else about Rand Mitchell, something that pulled at her senses, drew her to him, and it gave her the willies because if she let herself become involved with him, World War III was definitely going to erupt in her parlor, and she did not want to go through that. Not again. But he was a guest, and she at least owed him hospitality. "There's not much to tell. I had a couple of meetings, made a lot of phone calls, went over an advertising campaign proposal, and dictated several letters. That's it."

"What about that guy who you said wanted to buy your company. Did you talk with him?" Rand tried to keep his tone light.

"Yes. I think I made him mad."

Rand felt his stomach flip. "How?"

Tori shrugged. "I refused his offer, just the way I told him over the phone that I would. He seemed to turn a very beautiful shade of purple when I said no."

"How much did he offer, if you don't mind my asking?" Rand's right arm hung draped over the chair's arm, and he unconsciously clenched and unclenched his fist as he waited for her answer.

"Ten million."

"Ten million?"

"Plus perks," she added, and smiled. "But I'm not interested. Rouchard Travel is not for sale, no matter what the offer."

"That's a pretty good offer, Tori. Maybe you should consider it. I mean, then you wouldn't have to work. You and your grandfather could travel, see the world, that sort of thing."

"Gramps has no interest in seeing anything outside of Louisiana, and I've traveled to almost everywhere I've ever wanted to go, and more, especially since taking over the company. Checking out the competition, suggested new office sites, tour attractions, branch offices." She sipped her wine. "Traveling is not something I dream of doing, but it is my job. The company was my father's pride and joy. I could never sell it. It would be like . . . oh, I don't know, selling my heritage, I guess."

"Do you own the entire company?" He knew the answer, but she didn't know that he knew.

"No, I own the majority of it, but a few of my relatives have percentages."

"How do you know they won't force you to sell?" He could see the acquisition slipping away from him. Damn, he had to find a way to get her to sell. He'd poured too much money into planning this, setting up accompanying businesses to each location.

"They won't, not if I don't want to."

"How do you know?"

Chapter Fifteen

Tori stared at him, her hand, which held the glass of wine, in midair. His question echoed in her mind. How did she know they wouldn't sell? She thought about it and felt a sudden chill race up her spine. Most of her relatives who held percentages of ownership in Rouchard Travel she was sure would never sell. But there was one she couldn't say that of; her uncle, Morgan Faircreighton. Given a good enough offer, Morgan would sell his shares in Rouchard Travel to Satan and not give a second thought to what she, or anyone else, thought of it. That she was sure of.

She made a mental note to have Sherrille track down Morgan in the morning. Last Tori had heard, he'd gone on some kind of "back to nature" thing in Brazil. She smiled to herself. Maybe if she was lucky he'd gotten himself lost in the Amazon. Fifty years from now the headlines would read "Mr. Faircreighton, I presume?" And fifty years from now she wouldn't care about his shares in Rouchard Travel, *if* they even still existed.

She chuckled.

"Tori?" Rand said. A frown knitted his brow as he watched her.

The smile disappeared and she sat up straight. She recognized that look; she'd seen it on Tom's face several times just before he'd walked out. "Sorry, I was just remembering something." She set her wineglass down and rose. "I really should be getting to bed. I have an early meeting in the morning." She turned away, paused, and looked back at him. "Are you coming?"

"Is that an invitation?" he asked.

The rich honey tone of his voice caressed her overly sensitive nerves, the insolent words a taunt that brought a flush to her cheeks. "Not the kind you think," she said, smiled smugly and proceeded toward the foyer. "Good night."

He waited a good twenty minutes, long enough for her to get upstairs and into bed, then he began to search. There had to be a telephone here someplace. A person couldn't conduct a business as large as Rouchard Travel, as well as open their home to guests and tours without having a telephone. Not to mention having an invalid in the house who had to be eighty if he was a day, and a servant who looked as if he was inching toward a hundred. No, there was a phone, he was sure of it; he just had to find the damned thing.

173

His search was thorough. He scoured the parlor, looked under tables, behind bric-a-brac, even pulled furniture away from the walls to see if he'd missed a phone jack. He searched the dining room next, then the library, the foyer, even the alcove below the wide staircase, and found nothing. He walked into the kitchen, the last room on the ground floor. Well, at least if he got caught now, he could just say he'd wanted to get a snack before going to bed. He looked in the cupboards and moved boxes of food, glasses, and dishes aside. Nothing. He peered behind the refrigerator, the stove, and an old dry sink. Again nothing.

"There has to be a phone here." He sat down on the long bench set beside the table and looked around the room. Evidently he was wrong. He'd looked everywhere and come up empty. Rising to his feet, he moved to a door that led out onto the gallery and opened it. Fresh air wafted in to caress his face, which was now hot and covered with perspiration from his hurried search. Wires. If there was a phone, there had to be wires coming in from the outside. He stepped out onto the gallery, went to its edge and looked up at the roof. Nothing. Discouraged, he turned back toward the door. "How in blazes can a person in this day and age not have a telephone?"

Something tiny and obviously scared skittered across the gallery in front of him and disappeared into the shadows. Rand paused at the movement then reached for the door. If he hadn't been looking down at the threshold he would have missed them: two thin black wires that ran from a small hole in the gallery floor into another hole at the base of the wall. He leaned in past the kitchen door. Underground wires. They didn't go into the kitchen—they went into the adjoining pantry.

"I knew it. I knew they had to have one."

He reentered the kitchen and stepped into the pantry, flicking on a light as he did. A wall phone was beside the door.

"Bingo." He snapped his fingers, picked up the receiver, and quickly dialed his office number. After the second ring, the night operator answered.

"Good evening, Paradise Tours, Miss Lidwell speaking. May I help you?"

"I need to reach Jason Newhall," Rand said in a voice that was barely above a whisper. He assumed he was directly below Tori's bedroom.

"I'm sorry," the operator's voice droned, "but Mr. Newhall is out of town until next week. May I take a message?"

"I need to talk to him now!"

"I'm sorry, but as I said, he is out of town. May I take a message, sir?"

"Yes, you can take a message, Miss Lidwell," he growled into the phone. "You can tell him

175

that you and he are both fired if I don't talk to him within the next five minutes."

"Pardon me, sir?" the shocked operator said.

Rand steeled himself from snapping her head off. It was his own fault she was putting him off. He hadn't informed her who he was, and she was merely doing her job, but that didn't cool his anger any. "This is Rand Mitchell, Miss Lidwell, and I want Jason's phone number—now!" he hissed. He had hung on to his temper all day, but it was about to soar out of control.

The operator rattled off a New Orleans phone number and gushed an apology.

"Thanks," Rand said. He started to hang up but abruptly thought better of it. His hand paused above the receiver. "You did a good job, Miss Lidwell. Remind me to give you a raise when I get back to the office."

He dialed the number she'd given him.

"Vieux Carré House," a deep voice said.

"Jason Newhall's room, please."

The phone rang twice, then Jason answered, his voice heavy with sleep.

"Jason, what in the hell are you doing in New Orleans?" Rand bellowed. His voice bounced off of the pantry walls and shot back at him. He winced. Damn, why didn't he just announce to the world that he'd found the phone? He hoped he hadn't wakened anyone, especially Tori.

"Rand?" Jason asked, suddenly sounding much more alert. "I tried to get hold of you, but that place you're staying at doesn't have a phone, and I didn't want to chance a telegram."

"I'm talking to you from their telephone," Rand said curtly.

"Oh. Well, the operator didn't have a number."

"I thought we had enough connections to get around something as simple as an unlisted number."

"Well, I just assumed there wasn't one, and—"

"Fine," Rand snapped. "So now that we've connected, talk to me. What the hell are you doing here? I thought we had a plan, Jason. I come here and work on the woman, you stay in California and work on the relatives and the legal angle of a forced takeover."

"A forced takeover is out. At least as far as I can tell. The Rouchard woman owns sixty percent, and no one else owns a big percentage. It's split up among about five or six others."

"We already knew that."

"Yeah, but I got a tip that might give us an advantage in this thing and figured I better follow it up."

"What kind of tip?"

"One of my secretaries has an old college boyfriend from New Orleans. She was talking to him the other day, and he happened to mention that his cousin was about to marry Tori Rouchard."

Rand thought of Ash and felt an unreasonable surge of anger. She might as well marry a toad as that simpering prima donna.

"What's the guy's name?"

"The cousin?"

"No, damn it," Rand barked, "the guy Tori Rouchard is supposedly going to marry."

He heard a stirring above him and froze, staring up at the ceiling. Damn, had he wakened her?

"Uh, let me think. It was one of those *Gone with the Wind* names. Rhett."

"Rhett?" Rand echoed.

"No. No, now I remember, it was the other one. Ashley."

"Ashford."

"That's it. Seems this guy Ashford is one of those old-line Southern blue bloods who doesn't believe in having a wife who works. He wants her to sell her company. They've been seeing each other for a while, the way the gossip has it, but now they've actually set a wedding date. Next month, I think. The way my secretary's friend hears it, this guy even has reservations at an old folks' home for the woman's grandfather to move into. Anyway, this could be the break we've needed. I guess this Ashford's been making quiet inquiries around town trying to solicit interest in her company."

Rand felt a distinct surge of disgust for

178

Ashford Thibeaux III. Just the thought of Tori with him made his stomach churn in revulsion. He might be a blue blood, but he reminded Rand of a used car salesman. A slick, con-artist type who would sell his own mother a broken-down heap if he thought he could make a nickel off it.

"What a snake," he mumbled. The spoken words brought him up from his slouched position against the wall. Was what he was doing, or trying to do to her, much better? He shook away the creeping sensation of guilt. What he was doing was different — it was business. He hadn't told her he loved her, as he was sure Ashford had done, nor was he planning to marry her.

A box of oatmeal, on the shelf above where Rand stood, suddenly shot to the edge and toppled over.

It bounced off Rand's head on its way to the floor.

"Son of a . . ." He gaped at the box and lifted a hand to his crown and rubbed the spot where the cardboard corner had jabbed into his skull.

"I figured we'd best take some action before someone else hears of this," Jason was saying. "I know Klondette Travel would be interested. They've been talking expansion for the past few months."

Rand returned his full attention to the conversation with Jason. "I understand she turned you down today."

"Yes, but I've got an appointment tomorrow with her boyfriend. I doubt he'll turn me down."

"He doesn't own the company."

"No, but he has a lot of influence with her."

"Don't count on it."

"You know something I don't?" Jason asked.

"I'll call you back tomorrow night," Rand said quietly, and hung up the receiver.

"This one doesn't scare easily," Chance said, and laughed. He was thoroughly enjoying himself, even if their plan to get Rand Mitchell away from RiverOaks and Tori didn't seem to be working very well.

"Would you be frightened by a box of oatmeal?" Lila asked snidely.

"What do you want me to do? It's not exactly easy to scare someone when he can't see you."

"Humph." Lila pushed against the door of the pantry and slammed it shut just as Rand was about to exit through it. She flipped off the overhead light, grabbed the phone and, faster than lightning, wrapped its coiled cord around Rand's neck. Then she began to pummel him with everything and anything she could push, shove, or throw off of the shelves.

"Hey, what's going on?" Rand yelled, trying

to duck the flying cans and boxes in the dark and having very little success. He veered to one side and nearly strangled himself with the phone cord. Something bounced off of his shoulder, right on the bone, and he nearly bit his lip as pain shot through his arm. He grappled for the phone receiver, which had bounced painfully against his groin, and quickly freed himself from it. A box smashed down on his head, another grazed his temple, and yet another slammed against his chest. He grabbed for the doorknob, found it, and yanked the door open just as a can of creamed corn bounced off his foot. Light from the kitchen flooded the small room, momentarily blinding him, and the hurricane of canned and boxed goods stopped as abruptly as it had started. He stared at the floor, which was now a mountain of dented cans and boxes, some broken, their contents spilled everywhere.

Had they just had an earthquake? He expected them where he lived, in California, especially after the past few years when they'd had so many, but he hadn't thought they really had them in Louisiana. And he didn't remember having felt the floor tremble. Of course, that was the only explanation for what had just happened. Still . . . He remembered that other incident, a day before, when a book had flown off the library shelf and beaned him. There had been no plausible reason for that happening, either, unless it had been an earthquake. And his fall into the pond. He'd been sure he'd felt hands on his chest.

Could RiverOaks be . . . ? He almost laughed at the ludicrous thoughts running through his head. He closed the door to the pantry and walked across the kitchen. Pretty soon he'd start believing in the bogeyman again, too.

Chapter Sixteen

Abram set the last can from the floor back onto the pantry shelf. He looked around the room again, then left it and entered the kitchen. "They ain't never done nothing like that before," he muttered.

"Like what?" Tori asked from her seat at the table.

"Messed up the pantry. Knocked all the cans and boxes of food off the shelves. They must of been spattin' again."

Tori set her glass of orange juice back on the table. "Gramps, you haven't heard anything lately about Morgan have you? Like where he is?"

Stanton bit down on a piece of bacon and chewed it thoroughly before answering. "That good-for-nothing uncle of yours?"

She nodded.

"No, I'm happy to say. Why?"

She shrugged. "I was just thinking of him last

night, that's all. I don't know why." She didn't want to tell Stanton about her fear of what Morgan would do if someone approached him about buying his interest in the company.

"I do, and you've got good reason to worry. That weasel would sell his own mother if he could."

"Gramps," Tori admonished him, and glanced at Rand. She hoped Stanton wouldn't start a tirade against Morgan. She shouldn't have even brought it up.

"You know it's true, missy. Maybe you'd best sic your lawyers on him and buy back his part of the company. Your daddy should have done it a long time ago, anyway. Having relatives for partners is no way to run a business. Especially ones like Morgan."

"They're not full partners, Gramps, and you know it. They just own small percentages of the company in return for the money they gave Dad to help start the business, that's all."

"Anything I can do to help?" Rand said. "In finding this guy, Morgan . . . what's his name?"

"No, thank you," Tori answered a bit too quickly.

"Faircreighton," Stanton said. "But Swindle-creighton would fit him better, if you ask me."

"Oh, Gramps, Morgan's not *that* bad." She laughed. "He's just, well, he's just different."

"Weird."

"I used to do some investigating in one of my

184

jobs, if you need someone tracked down." Rand said.

Tori rose a bit too quickly. Her thigh rammed the edge of the table and nearly sent everyone's orange juice tumbling. "Sorry," she mumbled, and grabbed her purse. She was going to keep a safe distance from Rand Mitchell for the remainder of his stay at RiverOaks. At least she was going to try. "It's not really that important, but thank you," she said to Rand, then turned to her grandfather. "I'll see you at dinner, Gramps."

Rand rose and followed her onto the gallery. When she made no move to acknowledge him behind her, he reached out and touched her arm lightly. His fingers wrapped gently around the curve of her elbow. She paused and looked back at him. "Keep your lunch hour free, Tori. I'll be by around noon." After he made another, very important, call to Jason.

She shook her head. "I really can't, I'm sorry. I have too much work to do, that's why I'm going to the office Saturday, too."

"You have to eat, and so do I. No reason we can't do it together." He'd plan something different. Something special. A picnic. Women liked that, it was romantic, and the ploy had worked dozens of times for him before, and Tori was no different from any other woman, except that she made his blood boil hotter than anyone he'd ever been with before. But he could

185

control that, and use it to his advantage.

An hour after Tori left the house, Rand excused himself from Stanton and also left, using the excuse that he wanted to do a little sightseeing. He stopped at the first pay telephone he found and hurriedly dialed the number of Jason's hotel.

"Jason, what were the names of those relatives you checked out before the old man died?"

"Uh, wait a minute, I've got them written down in my briefcase." He put the phone down but was back within a few seconds. "Harlan Rollsbey, Patricia Sentrum, Thomas Marselle, John Dellos, Morgan Faircreighton, and—"

"Morgan Faircreighton, that's the one."

"One what?"

"The one you need to find. Tori's worried about him selling."

"We couldn't find him last time we tried. The others we found, and they wouldn't sell. Faircreighton was out of the country somewhere and we couldn't locate him."

"So locate him now. Put someone on it. If we can get to him and get him to sell, maybe the others will follow suit. It only takes one loose brick to topple the pyramid, Jason, and this Faircreighton might be just the loose brick we need."

"That still leaves the Rouchard woman with sixty percent, Rand, which I'm sure I don't have

186

to remind you is the controlling interest."

"Let me worry about that, Jason. You just get your hands on that other forty percent." Rand hung up and climbed back into his rental car. He glanced at his watch. Nine o'clock. He had three hours to kill before he was supposed to be at Tori's office. "So why waste them?" he said to himself, and turned the ignition key. He needed to know more about Tori's relatives, and since the Rouchards were an old-line New Orleans family, the most likely place to get that information was the tombs at the local newspaper. He also wanted to know more about Ashford Thibeaux III, and this was as good a time as any. Though, if he was truthful with himself, which at the moment he had no desire to be, that was more personal curiosity than business.

Half an hour later he sat at a table in the tombs of *The Times-Picayune,* surrounded by old newspapers, most open to the society pages.

Harlan Rollsbey, it appeared, was a cousin of Tori's late father. Patricia Sentrum was her mother's older sister, widowed and childless. Both Patricia and Harlan appeared prominently in the papers. Harlan had evidently relocated to Virginia more than twenty years ago, but was still a member and regular face at the balls given by the Mardi Gras krewe he belonged to, Comus. Patricia lived in Metairie and Thomas Marselle, the son of a long-dead cousin of Tori's father, owned a deli in Algiers. John Dellos was the son of another deceased cousin. He lived in a small town downriver from New Orleans and ran a fleet of pirogues that took tourists into the swamps. Morgan Faircreighton was a stepbrother of Tori's father and the family explorer, according to the few articles Rand could find that mentioned him, which were not too favorable. His home base was a bungalow situated in the Florida Keys.

Rand left the newspaper office and found a pay telephone on the street. He dialed Jason's hotel. The desk clerk said Jason was out but offered to take a message. Rand declined and hung up. He couldn't afford to have anyone to connect him with Jason. Not yet. He'd call again later. He glanced at his watch. It was nearly noon. He was due at Tori's office in half an hour, and he hadn't picked up their lunch yet.

Rand drove directly to the small deli he'd spotted near the moonwalk the other night. It had been dark and closed then. Today it hummed with activity, its umbrella-tabled patio crowded with lunching tourists and employees of nearby businesses. The woman behind the counter filled a basket with sandwiches, a small carton of potato salad, plates, plastic utensils, two crystal wineglasses, and a bottle of chilled Chardonnay. With the basket in one hand, he slipped his dark glasses on and walked back out onto the sidewalk. The noonday sun was nearly blinding. He left his car where he'd parked it and crossed the street toward the square, and Tori's office.

"I told you I couldn't join you for lunch." She looked pointedly at Rand over the mound of paperwork piled on her In basket. She felt a warm flush spread over her, as seemed to happen whenever he was near. She tried to disregard it, but the suddenly fluctuating beat of her heart, a kind of flip-flop action, would not be ignored.

"Sorry, Tori," Sherrille said from the doorway, "but he got past me while I was on the phone."

"That's okay."

Sherrille backed out of the room and closed the door.

"What'd you do, post a guard to keep me out?" Rand said, and smiled. He set the picnic basket down on a chair, moved around the side of her desk, before she knew what he was about to do, he leaned down and brushed his lips across hers.

A tremor erupted within her at his touch, a burning heat that emanated from his lips to hers and raced through every square inch of her body. It left her grappling for coherent thought. "No, I just . . . I wasn't . . . I mean, I told Sherrille I wasn't to be interrupted, that's all. It was not directed solely at you, I mean, it was, but . . . no, I mean, it wasn't . . . but . . . ." She was babbling like an idiot again, which she realized was becoming a habit in his company, but she couldn't stop. Her runaway tongue seemed to have a sudden will of its own. "I mean, I have this meeting later this afternoon, and . . . and I keep getting interrupted by phone calls, and . . ."

"And it's time for you to stop, take a deep breath, relax, and have some lunch. With me." He leaned forward and kissed her again. "In the park. Beneath one of those ancient trees you Southerners are so fond of."

"I really don't have time, Rand." Tori clasped her hands together in her lap in an effort to quell the urge to reach out and touch him. She suddenly felt as if all she wanted in the world was to be held by him. Everything she'd tried to do that morning had turned into one big disaster, and she could do with a little comforting, a little borrowed strength.

The advertising campaign she'd been about to approve had fallen through when the vice president of the company called that morning to tell her there were problems within the company that would prohibit them from making a commitment to Rouchard Travel. At this time, he'd added politely, which did her not one bit of good. She needed that campaign now, not in a few months. Then she'd gotten a frantic message from one of the agents in her Baton Rouge office who reported that the manager had walked out in a huff. Another office was having problems with a cruise line it used, another had computer difficulties, and she had two senior citizens from Idaho who were lost in a swamp. They'd wandered away from her cousin John's tour guide and their absence hadn't been noticed until the pirogue returned to dock an hour later.

"You're the president, Tori. Make the time," Rand said. He took both of her hands in his and pulled her from her chair. "Presidents have to eat, too, even hardworking ones."

"Is that a rule you follow?" she asked, and smiled. She suddenly felt better than she had in hours.

"Yes, and if I didn't follow it, my mother would see that I did. She's vehement about her son getting his proper share of food, sleep, and relaxation."

"Sounds like a good mother."

"The best, but a little pushy occasionally." He laughed to lighten his words. "Now come on, no more arguments."

He wrapped one arm around her waist and reached out with his other hand to retrieve the picnic basket. "It's time to eat." She went willingly, no longer feeling the urge to object. The desire to lean on someone, to usurp just a little borrowed strength, if only for a few brief moments, was irresistible. As was the thought that it was Rand who offered the strong shoulder she needed to lean on, the iron force and steel will. But it was more than that, and Tori knew it—

she was just too scared to admit it. Nothing would ever be the same in her life again if she did. Hadn't she tried to go against *them* once in just the same type of situation? And it hadn't worked.

She almost laughed aloud, but instead, only a sad smile curved her lips. Hadn't worked was the understatement of the century. It had turned into a full-blown disaster, with her fiancé's thinking she was the craziest person in the world. She'd been lucky Tom hadn't tried to get her committed. But this was only lunch, not an affair.

She walked beside Rand into the outer office and toward the entry door.

"When will you be back, Tori?" Sherrille called after them.

"What time is her meeting this afternoon?" Rand interjected, before Tori could answer her secretary.

"Three."

"She'll be back by quarter of." He ushered Tori out the door before she had a chance to protest.

"I can't be gone until two-forty-five," she said, as he closed the door behind them and guided her across the walkway toward the square.

"Then maybe I'll let you return by two-thirty. No sooner." He squeezed her waist. "And no arguments, or I'll tell my mom."

Tori laughed. "She doesn't even know me."

"Doesn't matter," Rand replied. "If she hears of anyone not taking proper care of themselves, she swoops on them like an avenging angel and makes sure they change their ways." He laughed. "Believe me, you don't want to be the victim of one of her well-intentioned crusades."

Rand guided Tori to a shaded spot beneath one of the oak trees that dotted Jackson Square. He set the picnic basket down and spread out a thin paper tablecloth.

"Your seat, madame," he said, and bowed mockingly toward Tori.

She curtsied and sat down on the paper cloth. "You thought of everything, didn't you?"

"Not quite," he confessed. "The lady at the deli mentioned using the tablecloth as a blanket, since I told her I hadn't thought to bring one, and I'd hate to see dirt or grass stains on that lovely outfit."

Tori caught the assessing glance he gave her as he referred to her attire; a flowing silk skirt, its green hue nearly the same color as the rich grass that surrounded them, and a white silk blouse, sleeveless, with an open V neckline that plunged just deep enough to flatter but not cross the line between sexy and businesslike. For her meeting she'd brought along a short bolero-style jacket that matched her skirt, but she'd left it in the office. She didn't need it for a picnic in the park.

His gaze traveled over her and finally rose to meet her eyes. She felt suddenly as if she were sitting before him completely naked, as if his eyes could strip her not only of her clothes, but of all her secrets, all the things she had to keep hidden from the world. The sensation made her nervous, and she pulled her eyes from his to stare at the throng of tourists who milled about the walkway that surrounded the square. An outdoor café offered umbrella-shaded tables to lunch at, and next door an ice cream parlor tempted everyone to cool off with a mound of terribly fattening, and deliciously decadent, dessert. On the black wrought-iron fence that surrounded the square, local artists hung their paintings, depicting every scene and landscape imaginable in New Orleans, and hawked them as a little bit of Louisiana to take home to North Dakota, or wherever the tourists had come from.

Rand opened the picnic basket and took out all the food, including the wine and two crystal glasses.

"Hey, remember me?" He said a few minutes later.

Tori turned back to him. "Sorry, I was just enjoying the peacefulness of the scene." She accepted the plate of food he offered her and looked back out at the tourists again. She had been foolish to come with him. No matter how much she'd wanted to, she shouldn't have done it. Any minute now, *they* would show up.

"Tori?"

She turned and Rand handed her a glass of wine. The golden liquid caught the sunlight and sparkled a myriad of glistening colors.

"To lazy lunches in the park." His velvet-soft voice cloaked her with ardor that, without a touch, turned her blood to fire. He clinked his glass against Tori's. "And a beautiful Southern belle."

She lifted the glass to her lips, but her eyes never left his—shimmering pools of blue that drew her into their depths, that held her mesmerized with unspoken promises of all the feelings and things she had always dreamed of having, and had forsaken when Rouchard Travel had become her life, and *the family* her keepers.

Without a word, he reached over and took the glass from her hand, set it and his own on the ground, then leaned forward and pressed his lips to hers. He took his time kissing her, each movement slow, measured, and sensuously gentle. His tongue traced the curve of her lips and tenderly, with only the barest trace of pressure, forced them to part. Her lips brazenly allowed him entry into her mouth, and the first touch of his tongue to hers, as flame to flame, ignited the sleeping passions within her that she had struggled to contain ever since his arrival at RiverOaks. A trembling weakness of need spread through her body, like a prairie fire, con-

195

suming everything in its path, igniting every cell of her body, every muscle and fiber, with a need she was helpless to deny.

Oblivious of the time and place, of the bright sunlight and milling tourists all around them, Tori allowed a faint moan of pleasure to escape her throat, the sound swallowed by his lips as they continued their tender ravishment of hers. She leaned into him, her body telling him what her lips could not.

He had not touched her with his hands, had not pulled her toward him, or crushed her body against his, yet it was the most sensual, seductively passion arousing kiss Tori had ever experienced. Time and their surroundings had ceased to exist, and reality and reason vanished as thoroughly as if her memory were a slate that had been wiped clean. At this moment, this split second in time, nothing mattered to her but Rand Mitchell, the feel of his lips on hers, the gnawing ache that his touch aroused deep within her, and that it continue, that this sweet torment of her senses go on forever.

"Way to go, bro," a young teenager said as he sauntered past.

Chapter Seventeen

At the teenager's brash interruption, Rand felt himself hurled back to reality and reluctantly raised his mouth from the honeyed offering of hers. That kiss had shaken him more than he wanted to admit.

Lost in a world of sensuality, Tori was a little slower to react. She stared at Rand in bewilderment, her gold-flecked brown eyes dark with passion, her breasts rising and falling rapidly with the ragged acceleration of her breathing.

He reached out and traced the line of her cheek with the tip of his finger, a touch as light and gentle as the caress of a wafting midnight breeze. It stoked the hunger that had erupted deep within her at his kiss.

"I guess this spot isn't exactly as private as I had hoped," Rand said, with a laugh that was little more than a whisper of sound. "Maybe tonight I can find a better place."

Tori struggled to her feet. "I really do have to

get back to the office, Rand." She brushed a hand across her skirt to smooth the wrinkles that weren't there, and picked up her purse. "Thank you for the lunch, but I can't make dinner . . . really. I have an appointment then."

"We haven't even been out here an hour, Tori. At least finish your lunch." He rose to his feet and took one of her hands in his. Her slim fingers disappeared within the embrace of his strong hand.

"I can't." She pulled her hand free. "I have some things to do before my meeting this afternoon." She turned and fled in the direction of her office.

"Damn," Rand said, and followed that one curse with a string of silent ones in his head. For every one step forward he seemed to achieve with her, it always resulted in two steps backward. "Well, not this time, Miss Rouchard," he vowed. "Not this time." He gathered up the remnants of their picnic, dumped them in a nearby trash can, and walked from the square to where he'd left his rental car parked earlier. He had at least five hours before she'd leave the office for the day, and he had several things he needed to accomplish before then, like get hold of Jason and find out if he'd made any kind of progress at all.

He stopped at the local historical society first. There was something he needed to check out — Ashford Thibeaux III. He had a niggling curiosity to know exactly who and what Ashford was, whether it helped in his business dealings with Tori or not.

The tiny curator of the historical society, Mrs. Boseau, who looked like everyone's image of a grandmother, was more than happy to accommodate Rand and showed him file after file on the Thibeaux family. Evidently they were not only more prominent in New Orleans society than the Rouchards, they were better regarded.

"Oh, my, wonderful family, just wonderful," she gushed, and handed him a newspaper clipping on Ashford. "Too bad about the parents, though. Passed away a few years back, and now poor Ashford, about to marry that Rouchard girl."

"Poor Ashford?" Rand echoed, puzzled.

The woman clicked her tongue. "Well, maybe not poor Ashford, really. But the children. They'll be the ones affected by it all. I mean, with the mother's genes and all, how can they help but be affected."

"Affected by what?" Rand asked.

"Why—" she looked around as if wanting to make sure no one was close enough to hear and dropped her voice to a whisper"—it's been rumored for years that the Rouchards have all been a little—" she made a circular motion with her finger at the side of her head "—touched."

"Crazy?" His brows arched in surprise.

Mrs. Boseau nodded. "Of course none of

them has ever been committed or anything, but still . . ."

"What's behind the rumor? I mean, why do people think the family's touched?" he asked, using her wording.

"Well, I've never seen anything of the kind myself, you understand, but I've talked to people who have. The Rouchards talk to people who aren't there."

Rand nodded, remembering all the times he'd wondered who Tori had been talking to when he'd seen no one else around, and she wasn't addressing him. She'd always claimed she was talking to herself, but it never seemed that way. "Yes, I see what you mean. But to get back to Ashford. Where does his money come from?"

"The family business, of course. A law firm, one of the best in town. Ashford practices, too, but not criminal law like his father did. Mostly contracts, I think. Big corporation stuff."

"And the firm is solid? No financial problems that you know of?"

The curator appeared shocked and slapped a hand to her nearly flat breast. "Why, mercy sakes, no. Thibeaux and Thibeaux goes back years. I mean, literally, years. They helped to defend many a young man after *the* war and get their properties back, bless their souls."

"The war?" Rand said, totally confused. "Vietnam?"

"The War between the States," the woman

said coolly, as if suddenly affronted by his lack of understanding.

He left the historical society an hour later, located a pay telephone and called Jason's hotel again. He was still out.

"Damn it!" Rand slammed down the receiver. "How in the hell can I run a business if I can't even find out what my own vice president is doing?" He glanced at his watch. It was only three. He still had at least another three hours. He plopped another quarter in the phone, dialed the operator, and told her to put a collect call through to his office in California. A minute later he had the attorney for Paradise Tours on the line.

It was a go-nowhere conversation. Morgan Faircreighton hadn't been located, to the best of their knowledge, and no, even if Rand managed to acquire the forty percent of Rouchard Travel, they couldn't force Tori to sell. They could make her life miserable, but they couldn't force her to sell. Well, he'd already known that, but then he had been in that situation before and he knew human nature. If a person was given enough problems, enough reasons to want out, he'd sell at a much lower price than he'd originally held out for.

Rand wandered around the quarter, killing time, browsing through one souvenir store after another. He purchased presents for his sister, his niece and nephew, and ordered them shipped back to California, and checked out the tours of several historic buildings. Not that he was all that enthused about the buildings, but if Paradise Tours was going to extend into New Orleans he should have an idea of what to include in their packages. After visiting the Beauregard House, he glanced at his watch. It was nearing six-thirty. If he wanted to catch Tori before she left the office, he'd have to get back there.

He got to the door of Rouchard Travel just as Sherrille was locking it. "Where's Tori?" Rand asked.

Sherrille gave him a funny look, shrugged, and started to turn away.

"Come on, Sherrille. We were supposed to have dinner together. I'm a little late because I stopped to buy her something." He held up the bag, hoping to convince her. "Did she go on to the restaurant without me?" Rand practically held his breath. If Tori had made dinner arrangements with someone else, or been picked up by Ashford the wimp, Sherrille would know he was lying.

"Well, she did say something about dining out tonight, but she didn't mention it was with you," Sherrille said a bit defensively.

"Sorry, but believe me, we had a date. She's probably ticked off at me for being late, and to make matters worse, I can't remember what restaurant she wanted to go to." He tried to seem helpless, which was a feat for him.

"The Court of Two Sisters, around the corner on Royal. It's one of her favorites," Sherrille said. "But *I* didn't tell you where she is—understand?" She winked.

"You got it," Rand said, and smiled. "I owe you one, Sherrille." He made a mental note to send her a box of candy, but not until he knew for certain the next time Tori would be out of the office. No sense revealing he had a co-conspirator in Tori's camp.

Five minutes later, Rand walked through the shadowed porte cochere of the elegant old restaurant and tipped the maître d' handsomely in a subtle but effective bribe to get him to show him to Tori's table.

She was seated in the courtyard. The sun had already slipped low enough so that the sky was a pinkish gray and the restaurant had turned on all of its lights. The roof of the patio was a trellis of spreading vines from an ancient wisteria that grew against one bricked wall of the patio. The thin, gnarled vines, all heavily covered with lush green leaves, wove their way overhead, and sprinkled in among them were tiny flickering lights that resembled dancing fireflies.

Tori sat at the far side of the courtyard. The tiny flame of a small, glass-enclosed candle that sat on the table before her cast a golden glow over the thick ebony waves that framed her face and brushed her shoulders.

Rand felt the breath catch in his throat and a

burning knot of desire tighten his groin. Every time he saw her, he thought her more beautiful than the time before, and wanted her more.

He walked to Tori's table and sat in the chair across from her. She glanced up from her menu in surprise. "Rand. What are you doing here?"

"Having dinner with you, I hope. Or are you meeting someone?"

"No, I'm alone," she said, and smiled. She knew she should keep as much distance between them as possible, that a relationship between them, any kind of relationship, would only bring trouble. Yet, Tori found her resolve to reject him dissipate whenever she looked into his eyes. She had just about convinced herself that not only should she not see him again, but that she didn't want to. Now his appearance had instantly brightened her mood, which had been gloomy, and shattered all her good intentions.

"The troublemakers are otherwise engaged this evening, Tori," a voice drawled in her ear. "At least for now."

She spun around and looked over her shoulder. Dominic Rouchard, his gray Confederate uniform a fitting accent to the court's surroundings, stood directly behind her chair. She frowned in confusion. Otherwise engaged?

"Trust me," he whispered. "It is nothing to concern yourself about. Enjoy your evening with him." Dominic nodded toward Rand and smiled that serene smile that Tori had always loved.

"The others may be wrong this time, Tori. Trust your heart. It will know more than they."

Tori opened her mouth to respond, but before she could make a fool of herself by talking to the wall in front of a restaurant full of people, and Rand, Dominic disappeared.

"Something wrong?" Rand asked, and leaned to look past her.

She turned back and reopened the menu she'd set down on the table. "Oh, no, I just, umm, I just heard a buzzing noise behind me, that's all."

"So, beautiful, how did your meeting go this afternoon?"

A tuxedo-clad waiter appeared at their table before Tori could answer. They each ordered, and when he disappeared, Tori spoke.

"Okay, I guess. I met with my attorneys."

"Oh? Something wrong?" The hair on the back of his neck prickled. Had Jason finally made her an offer she couldn't refuse? Or had Ashford actually managed to talk her into selling the company and marrying him? He couldn't believe the latter. It had to be Jason's offer.

"Yes and no," Tori answered. "I have been getting some pretty good offers to sell the firm, as you know."

"So why not take one of them?" Rand asked. He could feel his heart racing, but whether because of what Tori was saying, or merely because of her presence, he wasn't sure, and he was in no mood to analyze it.

She shrugged. "I can't."

"Can't? Why? You own the company, don't you?"

"Again, yes and no. I own the controlling interest, but I have relatives who also own percentages. But it's not that."

"Then what is it?" The question came out a little more anxious and demanding than Rand had intended.

Tori looked at him curiously for a second, then sighed. "I just don't feel it's right. My father practically put his soul into building up the company. I just wouldn't feel right selling it, even if I wanted to."

"Which you do?" he prodded.

She shrugged again. "I'm not sure. I never really wanted to be the company's president, but then I always thought my father would be around for a long time. It just didn't work out that way."

"What happened?" Suddenly Rand was more interested in Tori than in her business.

Her eyes glistened over with unshed tears. "They had gone to a party, my mom, dad, and younger sister, Krissy."

He remembered she'd referred to a Krissy that first night as they'd been sitting in the parlor, when she'd slapped at her skirt and told "Krissy" to stop it. Could what the woman at

206

the historical society said be true? He dismissed the thought away as ridiculous. Tori Rouchard was as sane as he was. He nearly laughed. Of course, sometimes his mother did say he was crazy.

"It was late when they left. They didn't even make it out of town. A drunk in a pickup ran a red light, lost control of his truck and swerved across the road. They were hit head-on."

"I'm sorry," Rand said, and reached across the table to take Tori's hand. "Were they . . . ?"

She nodded. "Instantly, except for Krissy. She lasted a few hours, but she never regained consciousness." A tear fell from the corner of her eye. "Maybe she knew somehow that it would be better this way. The doctors said that if she did live, she'd be paralyzed. Her spine had been broken in the crash."

Rand moved to the chair beside her and, with his free hand, brushed the tear from her cheek. "And you were left alone," he said, but it was more statement of fact than question.

Tori smiled then. "No, not alone. I have my grandfather and Abram. And I have the company. *And a whole lot of relatives that refuse to leave this earth,* she thought wryly.

"Yes, the company," Rand repeated. He felt like the worst snake in the world.

Their dinner arrived and he purposely changed the subject. "I should have ordered what you did." He affected a teasing pout and fixed his gaze on her salmon. He hated fish, but she didn't know that, and all he wanted to do at the moment was make her smile.

It worked, and the transformation tugged at his heart. Tori should never have to cry, he thought to himself. She should never be given reason to, and again Rand felt a sharp stab of guilt.

"That can be easily fixed." She laughed, cut the piece of fish in half and transferred a portion to his plate before he had a chance to refuse it.

"Okay, but you have to have some of my steak," he said, and plopped half of his filet mignon onto her plate.

For the remainder of their meal the mood remained light. Rand purposely steered clear of any discussion of business, or her family. He asked dozens of questions about New Orleans, both about the present-day city and about its history, and found himself mesmerized as she recited tale after fascinating tale.

"I always thought of pirates like Jean Lafitte as murdering thugs who were feared and loathed," Rand said, after she mentioned the pirate's name. "You know, like Bluebeard."

"A lot were, though I think the movies have made them seem worse than true life. In fact, many were well respected and considered nothing more than businessmen. Jean Lafitte and his brothers operated out of New Orleans for years, and were very popular, most of the time."

"Is this a recital of one of the tours your agency gives?" Rand said, and chuckled.

Tori blushed. "Yes. I guess I get carried away when I start to talk about our past."

"It's natural. It's both your history *and* your job. I envy you that." And surprisingly, that wasn't a lie.

"I've bored you enough with it," Tori said. God, but she felt good. Better than she had in a long time, and she didn't want the evening to end. She didn't want to go home, to face *them,* to return to her everyday life.

Rand took her hand in one of his and, with the other, pressed a finger to her lips. "You haven't bored me, Tori. You could never do that." He looked deep into her eyes and felt himself being drawn into a fathomless chasm where nothing existed but those beautiful, fire-specked brown eyes. He lifted a hand to her chin, and with the side of his bent forefinger, he nudged her face upward, just slightly.

His lips brushed gently, lightly, across hers. "Let's take a carriage ride."

She nodded and they left the restaurant, her hand firmly tucked in his.

"Your hair is the same, rich velvety color as the night," Rand said. He had draped an arm around her shoulder and his fingers entwined themselves within the long waves of her hair, letting the glistening ebony strands slip slowly, teasingly, from his grasp. "And like silk." He pressed his lips to the curve of her neck.

The clip-clop of the carriage horse's hooves on the paved street echoed throughout the now nearly deserted quarter. Only a few shops remained opened and most of the tourists were either dining, riding in other carriages or riverboats, or indulging in some other evening activity. Their driver was good. He'd recognized Tori at once, smiled a welcome, and then kept his face staunchly directed forward, toward the horse and road, giving Tori and Rand all the privacy a deep-seated carriage could offer.

Rand's free hand slipped to her waist and his arm encircled her. He pulled her closer, and she was suddenly aware that this was what she had wanted all evening. He was going to kiss her again, and she was going to let him . . . again. The thought both thrilled and scared her. There was no turning back this time. She had already lost her heart to him. The battle was over, it was time for the surrender, and later, after he'd left her, for she had no doubt he would leave her, she would face the aftermath, the pain, alone. But for now she could no longer deny her feelings for him. She wanted him to hold her, to kiss her. She snuggled into his embrace. She wanted him to love her.

Chapter Eighteen

For what seemed an endlessly long moment in time, Rand looked into Tori's eyes, his arms holding her welded within his embrace. She could feel his warm breath on her cheek, his heartbeat against her breast, hard, fast, yet steady, and the aura of masculinity that exuded from him to envelop her. She inhaled and the fragrance of his cologne wafted about her, a subtle blend of spices that reminded her of old sailing ships and open seas. His eyes held her prisoner and drew her into their midnight depths that she knew, in only a few more seconds, she would become lost in forever.

With tormenting slowness, Rand lowered his head toward hers. And just when Tori thought she would go mad with longing, his lips claimed hers and he crushed her against his length. Her entire body shivered with pleasure at the touch of his lips on hers, a kiss that was both a gentle caress and a savage demand, branding her his, body and soul. And she gave no argument, no hesitation to his unspoken command, but rather met his passion, his need, with her own.

As his tongue slipped between her lips, filled her mouth, and flicked hot, searing flames wherever it touched, Tori felt her body harden with intense hunger, her nipples turn to pebbled peaks that ached for his touch, and her flesh yearn for his caress.

"Rand," she murmured feebly, when his lips moved to nuzzle the delicate curve of her ear.

"I want to make love to you, Tori." His voice was a deep, musical whisper in her ear, a mellifluous aria that intoxicated her senses further and heightened the passion that burned within her, and that she no longer attempted to stem.

She shivered with pleasure and offered an answer with her body rather than words. Her lips sought his and she kissed him brazenly, her tongue sparring with his, a fiery duel, each touch stoking the same fires within him that burned deep in her, lending fuel to the gnawing need that was like a sweet, all-consuming ache, and wrapping him in the velvet cloak of her mounting desire.

He tore his lips from hers and held her tight against him, as if fearful she might disappear, and leaned forward toward the carriage driver.

"Take us to the Vieux Carré House, driver," he said, and settled back in his seat to pull Tori nearly onto his lap. He was taking a chance, he knew, going to the same hotel that Jason was staying at, but he had no choice. He didn't know the hotels around here, and he didn't want to waste time trying to find them.

"The Royal Orleans, Henri," Tori said to the driver. She looked at Rand. "It's bigger, and more likely to have an available room."

The man nodded and turned the carriage onto St. Louis Street.

Rand brushed his lips across hers. "A room, a shack, a tent—it doesn't matter, as long as I can love you," he said, and kissed her again.

The old driver pulled the carriage up before a sprawling pale yellow building that bespoke elegance and other, older, times.

Rand climbed down and paid the driver, giving him a generous tip, then reached up and, placing a hand to each side of Tori's waist, lifted her easily from the carriage to the ground. He slipped a proprietary arm around her shoulders, and they turned to walk into the hotel.

The entry was ablaze with light from a crystal chandelier, while the pale yellow arches on the opposite wall from the doors remained in shadow.

To their left was a bank of marble steps leading into the main lobby. They ascended them together, but Tori took a seat by one of the arched windows as Rand registered. Nervousness suddenly overwhelmed her. She entwined her fingers in her lap. She looked at Rand, then at the door. What was she doing? Had she lost her mind? She started to rise from the chair. Maybe she could make the door before he turned around.

Rand walked away from the desk and approached Tori. "Come on, beautiful."

Her apprehension disappeared as quickly as it had come. She placed her hand in his and rose. He wrapped an arm around her waist and held her close as they walked to the elevator.

At the door to their third-floor room, Rand had the ridiculous urge to sweep her up into his arms and carry her across the threshold. He caught himself just in time and instead rammed the key into the door's lock and nearly broke it off.

He was playing with fire. He knew it as well as he knew he was nearly helpless, at least at this moment, to do anything else. He could no sooner walk away from her now than he could throw himself off the roof of this building. He had come to New Orleans to learn more about the woman who headed the company he wanted to merge with his own, to discover out why she kept refusing every offer proposed to her, and to find out just what it would take to change her mind. But he hadn't intended to get emotionally involved with her. It was a hazard he had not foreseen, and one he had never before encountered.

A crystal-shaded lamp set on a mahogany table to one side of a white marble-faced fireplace glowed softly and cast an amber hue over the ivory-toned room. Rand pulled Tori inside and immediately drew her into his arms. "I have wanted to make love to you since the moment I laid eyes on you, Tori Rouchard," he said, his voice a husky drawl.

He moved one hand to the plunging neckline of her blouse, and trailed a finger along the open V to pause just above the place where a small pearl button clasped the fabric together between her breasts. He felt her sharp intake of breath at his touch, and the slight tightening of her hands on his arms, and smiled. "Do you know how many times I dreamed of doing this?" he asked. His fingers undid the button. "And this?" He undid another button. "And this?"

His head lowered to the subtle rise of flesh above the lacy edge of her brassiere and his lips gently, deliberately nuzzled the smooth skin there. He breathed in the scent of her, of magnolia blossoms and sultry Southern nights, and knew he would never forget it; the fragrance that seemed to him so uniquely Tori would haunt him forever.

She felt her breath catch in her throat at the intimate touch. His head lifted and their eyes met. Her heart, already accelerated to a thudding, out-of-control pace, hammered ever faster at the reflection of raw desire she saw glisten in his eyes—the same, she knew, as was in her own.

He moved to kiss her, and as his head slowly lowered, her gaze roved over his rugged features. The glimmering light of the crystal lamp touched the silken strands of his blond hair and transformed them to threads of precious gold, and shadowed the deeply curved hollows beneath his chiseled cheekbones. Thick lashes lowered over deepset blue eyes a split second before his lips met hers.

With a groan deep within his throat, Rand dragged her against him, her breasts crushed to his chest, her waist encircled by the viselike grip of his arms. His mouth crushed down upon hers, a savage demand that stole her breath and left her trembling.

Her arms closed around his shoulders and she returned his kiss. Her own tongue hungrily probed the depths of his mouth, exploring its inner warmth, and at the brazen liberties she took, she felt a shudder course through his body.

Desire turned her languid in his arms, a delicious warmth, like flowing, hot honey, spread through her limbs as he continued to ravage her lips and his hands slid over her back in a sensuous caress. Her breasts tingled against the rock-hard wall of his chest, and as she shifted deeper into his embrace, her hips grazed and met his and she felt the hard evidence of his arousal against the lower part of her stomach.

His kiss infused her body with energy, electrified every cell and fiber, and at the same time rendered her helpless, stole her will and drained away any hesitation that might still lurk within her.

With all the willpower he had in him, Rand slowly pulled his mouth from hers. "I want to love you," he whispered, and brushed the thin veil of silk blouse from her shoulders. "I need to love you." He pressed his lips to the curve of her ear and released the lone button that held her skirt to her waist. Both skirt and blouse fluttered to the floor with a soft rustle and fell in a circle of color at her feet. His fingers deftly released the hook of her brassiere, and with a quick flick of his finger at the thin satin straps that looped her shoulders, the frail garment fell away.

His eyes never leaving hers, Rand bent forward and touched his lips to first one, then the other breast, while his hands gently pushed her half slip and panties over her hips and let them, too, flutter to the floor.

Tori's body instinctively arched toward him and her fingers kneaded his shoulders while his tongue slowly, teasingly, laved her pebbled nipples, hot point meeting hot point, tasting, savoring the feel, the pleasure it brought.

His mouth traveled sensuously over the

mound of her breast, her throat, and finally, as
Rand rose back to his full height, recaptured
her lips. He cupped her buttocks with his
hands, pulled her roughly against him, crushed
her hips to his and then moved one hand to en-
circle her breast. His strong fingers stroked and
caressed, his thumb circled rhythmically over the
pulsating, taut nipple, and the touch pushed
Tori's passion ever higher, her need for him
deeper, nearly all-consuming.

For the very first time in his life, Rand found
himself totally ruled by his emotions, uncaring
of what this act might bring, the results that
could affect him forever. The feel of Tori, naked
in his arms, giving herself to him, was like none
he had ever experienced before. She affected
him in a way no woman ever had, and maybe
ever would. He could no sooner deny himself
the pleasure of her passion than he could deny
himself breath. Nor did he want to.

The searing ache of desire that had erupted
within Tori, the gnawing need that had roiled
deep within her, tightened ever further at his
teasing caresses and the assault of his lips. Suddenly she wanted him as naked as she was so
that her hands could roam his body, could in-
duce the same blinding, bewitching stirrings in
him that he had caused to flame in her.

Not pulling her lips from his, she slid her
hands beneath the lapels of his sports coat and
pushed it from his shoulders. He straightened

his arms so that the garment fell easily to the floor, while Tori's hands unbuttoned his shirt. Her fingers roamed over the contours of his chest, and she thrilled at the feel of the powerful muscles beneath her touch, the mountainous range of might and strength, and the silky hair that curled across the taut flesh.

Moving his lips briefly from hers, letting them trail the curve of her jaw, Rand shrugged out of the shirt, but he refused to cease his own assault on her body, his hands on her breasts a steady foray into her passion. He felt her fingers slip downward and hesitate at the belt that still held his slacks secure around his waist. His lips moved to hers, but before they claimed them again, he whispered against her mouth, "Unbuckle it, Tori." His tongue flicked against the corner of her lips. "Release it so that there is nothing left between us."

Tori did as he asked, as he demanded, her own mind a whirl of desire, her body a conflagration of need that burned recklessly and threatened to engulf her. Only his touch, his caress could satiate that inferno, could tamp it and allow her some semblance of calm and control over her body.

Brashly she released the small gold buckle, then the button of his slacks, then the zipper. Her fingers delved beneath the fabric of his shorts, and she pushed them from his hips. They fell to the floor, and with a slight movement of his legs, she felt him step from his shoes.

Her hands began their own exploration, traveling across the ropy landscape of his shoulders, down the curve of his back and the tight, rounded shape of his buttocks. But that wasn't enough. She slid one hand around his waist, her fingers tripping over his skin with a light touch that caused him to tremble in her arms. Emboldened now with the knowledge that she could, and did, create the same wondrous passions within him that he stirred in her, Tori let her hand slip between them and closed her fingers around the hard arousal that was proof of his need of her.

His body jumped convulsively and his arms tightened around her, roughly holding her to him, pinning her within his powerful embrace. "Tori," he gasped in a shaken voice against her mouth, "do you know what you're doing to me? Do you know how crazy with want I've been for you for the past few days? How I've thought of nothing else?"

With a swell of excitement at his words, Tori let her fingers caress the throbbing, hard length of him as his lips ravaged hers and his hands moved over her body on an exploration of their own.

Before she realized what he intended, and never taking his lips from hers, he bent to sweep her into his arms and carry her to the large bed that dominated the room.

For one long, eternity-filled second, Rand looked down at her beneath him. Her ebony hair spread like a halo of darkness around her head on the white pillow, and her eyes, a dusky cinnamon, glistened with desire. And as his gaze delved into the depths of her soul, hers devoured the expressions that flitted across his face and tried to impress them on her memory to call up later, and savor, after he was gone.

Finally, when she thought she might cry out with want, his mouth closed over hers with an almost punishing demand, his kiss filled with an urgency and hunger that swept the breath from Tori's lungs, and any lingering thoughts of anything or anyone other than him from her mind. Her hands traveled his body, roamed freely over his shoulders, slid sensuously down and across the smooth, curved valley of his back, caressed the sinewy length of his arms, and again encircled the pillar of his need.

"Oh, God, Tori," Rand murmured against her mouth. "You're driving me crazy." He had made love to many women, but none had ever inflamed his desire as Tori did, nor had any come close to touching that place within him that he had kept barricaded from the world for so long—feeling nothing, giving nothing, only taking.

He tried to keep his thoughts rational, tried not to lose himself within the passion he felt for her that was slowly, steadily, engulfing and overwhelming him. But it was a useless struggle. Every other woman he had ever known, ever been with, vanished from his mind as Tori, lost in an intoxicating world of her own, a hot tide of ecstasy sweeping her along to heretofore uncharted regions, returned his kiss with all the fervor she felt, giving all.

Much like a dying man giving up the struggle for life, Rand gave up the struggle against losing himself within her desire. He would worry and face the consequences tomorrow. His hand slid up her thigh and across the flat plane of her stomach to find the small triangle of curls at the joining of her thighs. With a gentleness that was tormentingly sweet, his finger probed intimately and then thrust deeply within her. Small sparks began to explode within Tori's body, and her blood turned to hot rivers of fire that raced through her veins and coursed through a heart beating madly. She moaned her pleasure at this invasion into the secret depths of her being and twisted beside him, her body on fire, aching for him to touch her everywhere. Each movement of his finger as it caressed the small nub of her need was exquisite torture, and each time it penetrated her she felt a stunning passion race through her body that left her quivering and aching for more.

"Oh, Rand, love me," Tori pleaded against his lips. "Love me."

Her words were nearly his undoing. He pushed her legs apart and lifted himself above her. In one swift but gentle movement she felt him fill her and settle his weight atop her. A moan of rapture slipped from her lips.

As his tongue wreaked havoc within her mouth, exploring all the hidden delights there, the hard shaft of his need, moving slowly in and out of her, wreaked havoc with her entire body.

He slipped one hand under her hips and, as he thrust deeply within her, drew her up to meet him. His mouth deserted hers and slid seductively down her throat, his lips leaving small spots of searing flesh behind wherever they touched. His mouth closed over one breast, and his tongue laved and curled around the taut peak, as his teeth gently grazed it and brought a cry of bliss from her lips as she thrust upward against him.

Tori writhed beneath him, matching her moves to the rhythm of his thrusts, every nerve of her body a live wire of sparking, sizzling pleasure, all of her senses centered on his movements within her, his tongue on her breasts, his hands on her flesh.

"Oh, yes, Rand, yes," she said, the words a velvety purr. She lifted her hands to his head, her fingers entwined in his hair, and she pulled him up to her, needing his mouth on hers again.

He groaned and pinioned her lips beneath his, filling her mouth with his tongue, a savage assault that might have been punishment for the bewitching effect she had on him, or begrudging surrender to the enchantment of her.

With his next surge into her, Tori felt an incredible pleasure sweep over her. Wave after wave of the most exquisite feelings she had ever experienced invaded her, filled her, burst within her. They hurled her through a timeless, spaceless, chasm, an infinite void that swirled with blinding stars and rainbows.

With a shudder, Rand groaned and released himself in her, his body quivering from the force of pleasure that coursed through him as he spilled his seed within her.

She felt his body tremble violently with the power of his release, and then he lay quiet, his weight like a comforting blanket atop her. Moments later he moved to lie beside her, his limbs still entwined with hers, his head resting half on the pillow, half on her shoulder. She could hear the raggedness of his breath, and feel its warmth on her breast as he lay still and waited for calm to return to his body.

They lay quietly for long moments, unmoving, and then deep inside her a tight, hungry knot of desire rekindled, and the gnawing ache, faint now, but definitely there, erupted within her as her body yearned for him again.

As if sensing the change in her, Rand pressed

his lips to the curve of her throat. His hand covered her breast, and his fingers gently kneaded the tip of her nipple back to its rigid, pebbled peak of hunger.

Chapter Nineteen

Rand leaned on the iron balustrade and stared out into the night, his gaze roaming over the sleeping city. The quarter lay quiet now, a stark contrast to its daytime hours. Only the bawdy dens on Bourbon Street, which never closed, would still have tourist activity at this hour, but that was several blocks away, out of both sight and sound of the hotel. The sloping, slate roofs of the old buildings shone beneath the glow of a lowhanging crescent moon, while the structures themselves, with their lacy wrought-iron balconies and ancient cypress shutters, dwelt within the shadows, their pale, faded stucco facades hidden by the night, shrouded until morning's light.

Occasionally a street sweeper would drive past, or a lumbering garbage truck. He had been standing in that same spot for over an hour, and he'd seen both. Other than that, the streets were deserted. The quarter and the newer city beyond it, the skyscrapers that loomed above the horizon, were as empty and quiet as if New Orleans had been evacuated and Rand were the only person left behind.

Except for the woman who lay peacefully asleep in the room behind him. Rand turned and looked-through the open French doors at Tori. What the hell was he supposed to do now? He knew what his conscience was telling him, but he rarely listened to that little voice. If he did, he'd never be as successful in business as he was today. He had to think about this logically, which was proving difficult to do as his emotions were suddenly a tangled web, his mind and heart in total conflict—something that had never happened to him before, something he had never allowed to happen.

So why this time? That was the other question that haunted him. How had Tori Rouchard broken through his barriers? And what was he going to do about it?

He had come here to get her to sell Rouchard Travel. His people had tried buying it from Tori's father several times, and he'd rejected every offer, as she had since. They had been in the process of going after what few relatives there were who held percentage of ownerships in the firm, but had stopped when her father died, Rand figuring Tori would most likely sell instantly. He'd been wrong. Jason had even proposed the idea of starting from scratch in the Southern states, setting up their own stores and relying on the reputation of Paradise Travel that was established throughout the West, as well as the accompanying PR and advertising firms they owned to bring in the business. But Rouchard Travel had a virtual vise grip on the Southern travel agency market, especially the corporate market. Obviously the old rumors that the Rouchards were "touched" hadn't hurt their ability to create or run a successful business.

Rand shook his head. In the end he had decided to take matters into his own hands, as he'd done several times before in similar business dealings. Jason didn't like Rand's way of doing business, but that didn't concern him. Jason didn't own the company, Rand did. But in the past few days, he had to admit, business had not been the most important or constant thing on his mind.

A car pulled up in front of the hotel entrance below the balcony. Rand watched its occupants walk into the hotel and then he looked back at Tori, smiling to himself. He had never met a woman quite like her. She brought out a side of him he hadn't thought existed anymore. He wanted to protect her from the world, keep her beside him, and love her forever. That last thought stopped him cold. Forever? What the hell was he thinking?

Forever was the same as happily ever after, and he knew there was no happily ever after. Not really. He'd learned that lesson early, just before his tenth birthday, when his father had walked out on his mother because she wouldn't quit her job as an interior decorator. She'd made more money than her husband, and the man's pride hadn't been able to handle that, or being a part-time father. So he'd just quietly walked out of their lives and never looked back, not even at his children. A few years later Rand had watched his sister's husband leave her and their two kids. His acting career was going nowhere, but her steady role on a soap opera was garnering her top honors. George had left her for another woman: a groupie. Rand shook his head. No, there was no happily ever after, and he'd do best to remember that. Especially with women who needed a career. He took a deep breath, filled his lungs with the dank, humid air that had settled over the quarter, and walked back into the room.

She awoke slowly, her lids fluttering open as he brushed a finger across her lips and looked down at her.

"Good morning," Tori said, and smiled.

Rand's fingers tangled in the long waves of her hair. He slid down on the bed beside her. "Good morning, beautiful." Overcome with a surge of need that shot through him like a bolt of lightning, he pulled her into his embrace, drawing her naked form to his, allowing his muscled contours to fill the valleys of her subtle curves, his finely honed, taut planes to press against, and meld, with hers, every shadow between them erased and filled.

Again, as the night before, all of his intentions, his vows of self-control, were swept from his mind the moment she snuggled into his embrace. He breathed in the scent of her, luxuriated in the satiny feel of her, and captured her mouth with his to taste the exotic mystery of her. He felt himself immediately drowning in his need for her, the satiation of their lovemaking the night before vanished from his body, and the gnawing ache as deep, as intense, as if he had never yet touched her. She was like an intoxicating drug that he could not get enough of, that he craved with his entire being. He covered her with his body, his hands moved to explore anew the promises of her passion, the subtle curves that had given him so much pleasure only a few hours before, and now enticed him anew. For a short time he once again allowed himself to forget the cares of his world, the plans, schemes and driving, blinding ambition that had brought him to New Orleans, to Tori, and just let himself enjoy the rapture of the moment, of his melding with her.

Not once since last night, since Dominic had come and told her Lila and Chance were "otherwise detained" had she thought of *them*. Now, as she lay on the bed, draped only in the thin sheet, the soft roar of Rand's shower in the background, her mind seemed incapable of thinking of anything else. Where were they? Had they been here all along? Had they watched?

She smiled at the ridiculous thought. No, she could rest easy that they hadn't watched her and Rand make love. Lila would have never stood by quietly and witnessed Tori making love to a "filthy Yankee." She sat up. But they could come any moment, and if they did it would mean nothing but trouble. She threw the sheet from her and scrambled from the bed just as Rand stepped from the bathroom.

A knot of desire tugged at her, a yearning deep within her that began to grow as she looked at him. He stood in the doorway, a white towel around his hips and secured by a tuck at his waist. His deeply tanned and muscular body glistened with tiny beads of water.

"It's still hot." He caught her gaze with his, and a smile tugged at the corners of his mouth. He knew exactly what she was thinking, what she was feeling, for beneath the towel, his body was hardening from those same stirrings.

Tori looked from his eyes, to the towel, and back up at his eyes.

"The shower," he said, and laughed. "Something else is definitely still hot for you, but I

231

was referring to the shower. I left it on for you, and the water's hot."

"Oh." She felt a flush of embarrassment and hurried past him to step into the glass-enclosed shower. The cascading hot water engulfed her instantly, streamed over her face and turned her thick mane of hair to a flat cap of black. Suddenly the soap fell from its wall tray to the floor and hit her foot. She jumped back and gaped at it. *They* were here! She looked around frantically, expecting at any moment, any second, to come face to face with Lila's scathing glare, or Chance's mocking eyes.

"Where are you?" she demanded through clenched teeth.

"I'm right here," Rand said. He opened the shower door and leaned forward. "At your beck and call. Why? Need someone to scrub your back?"

Tori jumped at his appearance, nearly flattening herself against the tiled wall. She had expected *them* to appear, not him. She pulled herself off the wall and tried to laugh. The sound escaped her lips as more of a squeaky mew. "Sorry, I didn't realize you were so close."

He feigned a hurt look. "Well, if you're not going to let me scrub that lovely back, the least you can do is hurry up and get out of there so we can get some breakfast. I'm starving."

It was Sunday morning, and the Court was crowded, but Rand noticed that somehow the maître d' always seemed to find a table for Tori. And not just *any* table, but one of the best. "What do you do, keep the maître d's around here on retainer?" he joked, as they settled into their chairs in the courtyard.

Filtered rays of sunlight streamed through the trellised roof of green wisteria.

"It's called Southern hospitality," Tori said, and laughed. "And good business. Most of the better restaurants in the city are included on one or another of our tours, and they want to stay that way. One of the perks of owning the company, I guess."

They ordered, and minutes later, as a mountain of food was slipped before Rand, he began to ask the questions that had nagged at the back of his mind ever since they'd made love. "Being president of a firm as large as Rouchard Travel must be pretty stressful. Did you always want to take over for your father?" He slipped a forkful of scrambled egg and diced ham into his mouth and watched her carefully.

"I never wanted to do it," Tori said.

Her answer surprised him so much that he nearly choked on the egg he'd been about to swallow. A quick sip of coffee gave him back his composure.

Tori's smile disappeared with her words and a sad look came over her face as memories of her family filled her mind.

"I'm sorry, I didn't mean to remind you of unpleasant memories."

She shook her head. "It's okay, they're not unpleasant really, just . . ." She shrugged and took a sip of her coffee. "Truthfully, I didn't even want to go to college, but I had nothing better to do, and my dad wanted me to go. So I did. Then, when I graduated, he wanted me to work in the firm. I had majored in marketing in college, so—" her eyes clouded for just a moment as she remembered that time "—my dad appointed me the director of marketing. A position that hadn't existed before."

Rand smiled. "Sounds like nepotism to me."

"Definitely," Tori said, and they both laughed. "But I enjoyed the job, and I think I did it reasonably well."

"What did you really want to do? Deep down?" he prodded.

"Have kids."

His eyebrows raised. "By yourself?"

"I think that's a little impossible, don't you?" She laughed again, and realized how good it felt. It had been a long time. "No, I wanted the standard old dream all little girls want. You know the one—a husband, a nice house, a few animals, and a lot of kids. Some little girls grow out of that dream. I never did."

He felt a shock of surprise. He'd pegged her for a real career woman, someone who put business before everything else. He had figured that was her real reason for not selling, that she loved the power of her position, the recognition and acknowledgment it gave her from other businessmen, maybe even the same ones who still thought her family was "touched." And he'd been wrong. It was like a weight suddenly lifted from him, and the cold, hard barrier he'd erected around his heart, the wall that had kept everyone out for so long, started to crumble. "You could still have all that," he said softly, and reached across the table to take her hand, "if you sell Rouchard Travel."

Her expression grew suddenly serious and she shook her head. "I can't."

"Because your dad built it into what it is?" He echoed the words she'd said earlier on the subject, and unconsciously drew his hand back.

"Yes."

He looked long and deep into her eyes. This was not what he'd wanted to hear. He had wanted to believe she was high on power, and that all he had to do was find the right incentive and she'd sell. And he didn't want to think of business right now, either. All he really wanted was to be with her. "Let's go on that swamp ride your agency gives," he said in an attempt to lighten the mood and change the subject.

It worked. Tori laughed. "I'm not exactly dressed for a swamp tour," she said, and looked down at the silk skirt and blouse she had worn since the day before.

"So? Neither am I. We'll stop at a shop and buy something for both of us. Come on," he said quickly when he saw her hesitation. "It's on me." He took her hand in his again. "It'll be fun. And I want to spend the day with you."

Tori hesitated for only a moment. She hadn't been to John's in a long time, and as she recalled the quiet beauty of the swamp, and the fact that she would be with Rand, the idea was too much to resist. Anyway, it was Sunday, her day off. "All right, but let me visit the powder room before we leave the restaurant." She rose and made her way into the restaurant's interior, but rather than enter the ladies' room, she approached the maître d'. "George, can I use the phone in the office?"

The man nodded, and Tori hastened toward a small door that was out of sight of the courtyard. She slipped behind the manager's desk and dialed the private number for RiverOaks.

Abram answered on the first ring. She smiled. How was that man always where he was needed? If she didn't know better, she'd think he was a ghost, too, materializing wherever he wanted, whenever he wanted.

"Abram, this is Tori."

"Yes, missy."

"I—I'm sorry I didn't call last night. Is everything all right there?"

"Yes, everything's just fine."

"I'm going to stay in town today, Abram. Well, no, actually that's not right. I'm going out to John's place today, to take a ride into the swamp. Mr. Mitchell is with me."

"Yes, missy, we figured that. Your grandfather said to tell you, if you called, to have a good time and not worry about nothing here. We're fine." He didn't bother to tell her Ashford had been by the house twice the night before looking for her, or that Stanton's parting words to the already upset man had caused him to nearly run his car into one of the trees that lined the drive.

The modern pirogue slid noiselessly through the water after Etienne cut the small outboard motor attached to its stern.

"Everybody off!" he shouted, and cackled merrily.

Rand gawked at the frail-looking old man as if he'd lost his mind. "Off?" he echoed in disbelief.

Tori rose and held out a hand to him. "Come on, it's okay. We're going to take a walk in the swamp."

Normally he would have been unable to take his eyes off the long, lean length of her legs, exposed to him in all their golden glory by the high-cut shorts she wore. As it was, all he could do was stare into the swamp. "In there? We're going in there?"

The other four passengers on the pirogue also hesitated to rise. Tori smiled. That was the natural reaction of almost everyone on the first tour of the swamp. It was breathtaking to look at from a distance, but nobody actually wanted to go into it, especially on foot.

"Only a short way," Tori said reassuringly.

"But what about those?" Rand pointed to the huge hulk of a dead oak tree. It lay on its side, half of its massive trunk settled into the black water, and draped, curled and hanging, all over its gnarled and leafless branches, were hundreds of glistening black snakes.

"They're asleep," Tori said simply.

"Yeah, but what if they wake up?"

Her laughter was like tinkling chimes in the quiet swamp. "They'll take one look at the group of bumbling, chatty humans stomping through their home and slip into the river, most likely as deep and far away from us as they can get."

"Yeah, right," Rand mumbled beneath his breath. He didn't like snakes. Or spiders, or anything else that crept, crawled, or slithered its way through life.

Kind of like you, a little voice said in the back of his mind.

"And that alligator sunning itself on the opposite shore over there?" he asked, but at the same time he rose to his feet, unwilling to head a mutiny or appear a coward in front of the

238

woman he loved. Love? He immediately denied the emotion; he was not in love. But the rational denial was too late as the initial thought sent him almost tumbling onto his face when he tried to follow Tori from the boat. His foot caught on the curve of the pirogue's bow and he flew forward, saved from landing face first in the muck by Etienne's swift reaction. The old man shot past Tori and, grabbing one of Rand's arms, whirled him around and flopped him on the opposite side of him, feet first.

A frown tugged at Tori's brow, and she looked around suspiciously. "Are you here?" she whispered, and waited for Chance or Lila to respond.

Nothing happened.

She walked a few feet from the group as Rand helped the others from the pirogue and continued to watch Etienne, obviously surprised at the old man's strength. "If you two are here, please behave. Just let me enjoy myself, okay?"

Again there was no answer.

Tori clenched her teeth and took a long breath. "All right," she said finally. "Don't answer me, but if you are here, don't do anything, please." She turned and began to walk back to the group, then paused and glanced over her shoulder. "If you do, I'll make you sorry. I promise."

"Ah, *chérie,* you ready now?" Etienne said as she approached.

"You want me to bring up the rear?" Tori asked.

"*Oui*. I take the lead, you and your friend the rear."

The old man waved his hand for everyone to follow and the group proceeded into the swamp, the two women tourists tightly holding on to their husbands, who both looked as if they were about to turn green.

The group inched its way along a narrow path of land that ran through the stagnant black waters of the swamp. No one except Etienne and Tori looked at the scenery; they were too busy watching where they put their feet, as the path was barely a foot and a half wide and only about six inches above water level.

Rand suddenly felt as if he were six years old again. His mind was alive with horrifying visions of giant alligators and long-fanged snakes, all mad with hunger, all watching the small group trek innocently into the creatures' lair, all lying in wait until just the right moment to strike.

"Heads," Etienne called out. He bent down suddenly but continued to walk forward.

Nobody seemed to know what he was trying to tell them until a second later. The first person behind Etienne, one of the husbands, jerked to a stop, grunted, and began to wave his arms in front of him, as if trying to ward off some invisible creature. His wife screamed, began tearing at her hair and slipped from the path. Her feet disappeared in the murky water, which caused her to begin dancing in fear and thrashing her way back up to the path. The second couple, in front of Rand and Tori, whirled around and bolted for the boat. The woman pushed Tori against the bulbous trunk of a cypress tree that grew from the dark water. Rand managed to jump to a small piece of land just before being run down by the husband. But his move had been a bigger mistake than being pushed into the water by the panicked tourist.

His face and head were suddenly engulfed by a wispy veil that felt like a thousand sticky hairs. It clung to him and seemed to crawl over his flesh, an invisible cloak that sent a shudder of revulsion through him. He slapped at his arms, and wiped his hands hastily over his face and head in an effort to free himself.

"Hold on!" Tori yelled, and ran toward him. "Stand still before you hurt it."

Hurt it? What the hell was on him? He tried to stifle a very strong urge to jump into the water to rid himself of whatever it was that had attached itself to his body and barely succeeded. He didn't want to find out what might be waiting for him in the water.

Tori grabbed a dried piece of brush from the ground and swiped it at the side of Rand's head. A plunk sounded behind him as something fell into the water. He whirled around and stared at the rippling circle. "What the hell was that?"

"A spider."

"Prehistoric, I'd say, judging from the sound of the splash."

"My hero," she said laughing.

Rand pulled her into his arms, oblivious of the others around. He held her tightly against him, suddenly needing the feel of her close to him. "I may not be good in the swamp, Tori, but I am good at other things."

"Oh, really?" she teased. "Like what?"

He smiled slyly and a wicked gleam sparked in his eyes. "I think you know the answer to that."

His lips descended on hers, and his tongue filled her mouth, its sweet caresses and dueling flicks sending her senses reeling even faster. His arms crushed her to him, breasts to chest, hip to hip, until there was no shadow of light between them.

"Thunder and blazes!" Etienne suddenly yelled.

Tori spun in Rand's embrace just in time to see the old guide topple from the narrow path and splash, back first, into the water. He came up sputtering and cursing a string of Cajun expletives that would have shocked the other tourists if they'd been able to understand them.

Then she felt Rand's arms leave her, the security of their embrace ripped away from her.

"Lila, no!" she screamed, but it was too late. With a look of total confusion and horror etched on his handsome features, Rand toppled backward, arms and legs outstretched, and landed flat on his back in the water. He sank immediately. "Rand!" She jumped into the water and grabbed for him, her fingers tightly gripping his shirtfront and pulling him toward her. He clasped his hands around her upper arms and, using her as leverage and balance, managed to get to his feet.

"Why the hell did you push me?" he roared suddenly. His eyes blazed with fury as he shook his limbs to rid them of as much water as possible.

"I didn't push you," she shot back, angry that he would even think such a thing.

"Well, someone did, and you were the only person near me." He climbed back onto the path and trudged toward the pirogue without a backward glance or another word.

Tori looked around again. So *they* were here, after all. She sighed deeply. She couldn't ignore their demands any longer. If she did, things would only get worse.

Chapter Twenty

"I found him," Jason said. "And he's willing to sell. I'm having our attorney draw up the papers now. He's going to express mail them to me so that I'll have them in the morning, for my meeting with Faircreighton."

Rand inched farther into the pantry but didn't close the door. If everything on the shelf began to fall on him again he wanted to be able to get out of there quickly. "How much does he own?" Rand whispered into the phone.

"Twenty percent."

"Why so much more than the others?"

"He put up more money than the others."

Rand knew he should be elated by Jason's news. This was the break they'd been looking for. If Faircreighton sold, there was a more than good chance the others would, too. So why wasn't he jumping for joy? Why did he feel so rotten? He knew the answer—he'd just been trying his damnedest to ignore it. "What about the others?" he asked. "Have you talked with any of them since Faircreighton said he'd sell?"

"Yes. Harlan Rollsbey, the cousin in Virginia. He's on the verge. Needs a fresh infusion of cash for his own business. It's been hit hard by the recession. And Marselle's deli isn't doing too good, either. In fact, it's only hanging on because of the monthly checks he gets from Rouchard Travel."

"What about Patricia Sentrum and Dellos?"

"The lady will be harder. She doesn't need the money. John Dellos is doing okay with his swamp tours, but he might do better with a little more cash. I haven't approached either of them again, but I will in the morning. Oh, and I met with that guy, Ashley . . ."

"Ashford."

"Yeah. Anyway, you were right; he talks a good game, but when it comes right down to it I doubt he has much influence over the Rouchard woman."

"I'll check in with you around noon. If you need me for anything and you're out, leave a message at the desk of your hotel."

"Right."

Rand hung up the phone and slipped from the pantry. Suddenly everything was going exactly the way he'd wanted it to, and instead of feeling great, he felt like hell.

"Missy, you'd best hurry this morning," Abram said, knocking on Tori's door only seconds after her alarm had gone off. She'd purposely given herself an extra half an hour to sleep.

"Now what?" She yawned. "Have *they* gone on the warpath because we couldn't have our *soirée* last night?"

"No, it's not *them,* it's your office. Miss Sherrille called a bit ago, said you'd best get in there as quickly as possible. Some kind of trouble with Mr. Faircreighton."

"Morgan?" Tori felt a sense of dread.

The old servant nodded. "I'll have your coffee and juice ready for you when you come downstairs. Mr. Stanton is waiting in the kitchen."

She nodded and closed her door. Damn. Jason Newhall had gotten to Morgan, she just knew it. She could feel it. While she was lazing around on swamp rides and letting her foolish heart flutter over Rand Mitchell, Newhall had tracked down Morgan and made him an offer her uncle obviously couldn't refuse. She whipped around the room, jumping in and out of the shower, running a brush through her hair, and throwing on a pair of white slacks and a chocolate brown tailored blouse. She grabbed a white blazer, slipped into her pumps, and hurried from the room. If Morgan hadn't actually signed any papers yet, maybe there was still

246

time to head this off.

"Good morning, Gramps." She gulped down her orange juice.

"What's good about it?" he grumbled. "I told you that fool cousin, or uncle or whatever he is to you, would pull something low-down if you didn't get to him first."

She bent down and kissed his cheek. "I'll take care of it, Gramps, don't worry." Her tone was cheerful, her words confident, but that was the exact opposite of what she felt. If Morgan sold, and he owned the largest percentage after her, what would the others do?

Luckily it was early and the roads were clear, commuter traffic not yet having turned to gridlock. She made it to the office in record time. "All right, Sherrille, what's going on?"

"Faircreighton left a message on the machine. I got it when I came in this morning. He said to tell you he'd had a very generous offer to buy his share of Rouchard Travel, and if you couldn't top it, he was selling out."

"The little weasel," Tori mumbled.

"My sentiments exactly. I thought he was family."

"He is, but we don't like to admit it. Did he leave a number where I can contact him?"

Sherrille nodded. "The Vieux Carré House."

Tori's brows soared. "That's pretty fancy for Morgan."

She hurried into her office and dialed the number of Morgan's hotel. She was put through to his room and he answered on the first ring. *Hmm, anxious,* Tori thought.

"Tori? Good, I see you got my message. I wouldn't have called so early, but the other party in the matter seems in quite a hurry to wrap this up."

Morgan's nasal-sounding voice grated on her nerves, as it always had. "Can you come to my office, Morgan?"

"Well, if I have to, but we can handle it on the phone, Tori. He offered me a million dollars. Now, normally I wouldn't sell, you know that, but, well, Anita wants to buy a new house and settle down on the Keys."

"Anita? Who's Anita?"

"My wife. We married in Peru when I was there a few months ago. She was my cook."

"Congratulations," Tori said halfheartedly.

"Thank you. Now, can you better Mr. Newhall's offer?"

"Newhall," Tori muttered, as if it were a dirty word.

"Yes, do you know him?"

"We've met."

"Well, Tori, I hate to press you, but if you can't . . ."

"Morgan, it will take me some time to raise that kind of cash. I'll call you back tomorrow morning, but don't sign any papers before you hear from me. Promise?"

"Well, okay, but no later than tomorrow morning, Tori. I have to get back home to Anita."

Tori quickly called her accountant and, over his objections, ordered the man to get the money together. One million two hundred thousand and drawn up as a cashier's check.

The phone on her desk rang just as she was breathing a sigh of relief at having talked to Morgan before it was too late.

"Tori, it's your cousin Harlan," Sherrille said.

"Harlan?" Tori repeated. Her heart began to sink in her breast. Harlan never called her. That meant this had to be bad news. She waited for Sherrille to connect them. "Harlan, what can I do for you?" she said, forgoing any pleasantries and getting straight to the point.

"Tori, sweetheart, it's so good to hear your voice. We really should see each other more often."

"Yes, Harlan, now what is it you called about?" She wasn't in the mood for Harlan's gushing.

"Well, I received a rather interesting call this morning, and, well, I thought I'd better contact you about it. Professional courtesy, you know?"

"Professional? Has this something to do with your interest in the firm?"

"Well, yes. I've had an offer to buy it. A very generous offer, I might add."

"And you're considering accepting it if I can't come up with a better one, is that it?" Her tone was hard and curt, and she couldn't help it. She felt like the captain of a ship whose crew was suddenly beginning to mutiny.

"Well, I wouldn't have put it quite that way, dear, but since you did, yes, those were my thoughts exactly."

A few minutes later she nearly slammed the phone down. Her day was swiftly and steadily going straight into the gutter. She spent the remainder of it arranging for more monies to be drawn from her accounts, and stocks to be sold, and trying frantically to contact the others who owned interests in the company. John, unfortunately, was out on an all-day swamp tour, Patricia had flown to Nashville to attend some kind of music award ceremony with her latest beau, a country singer, and Thomas seemed out on never-ending deliveries. At least that's what his assistant said every time she called.

By six o'clock she was almost a basket case. And then Ashford walked into her office. She nearly groaned in defeat. *This* she didn't need, not tonight.

"*Chérie,* whatever is the matter with you." He took hold of her hands and pulled her from her chair. "I have been calling you for two days, and I stopped by RiverOaks last night, twice. I was even out there a little bit ago. When Sherrille wouldn't put me through to you, I thought maybe you were home ill. And your grandfather—" he made a face of dislike "—he wouldn't tell me a thing, either."

"I was . . ."

"Never mind, it's not important now. You can tell me later. Right now we have reservations at the Court. We have a lot to discuss and plan. Our wedding is in less than four weeks, *chérie*, and I've been very busy.

"Ash, I'm not—"

He grabbed her purse and her jacket and ushered her out the door. "Come on, *chérie,* we're going to be late.

They weren't, but it wouldn't have mattered, anyway. The Court always found her a table, no matter how crowded they were.

"Ash, listen, I—"

He poured her wine. "I took the liberty of ordering the flowers today, Victoria. My secretary uses that little shop on Royal, La Fleur, so I just had her call them and tell them what I had in mind. Oh, and Mademoiselle's is putting aside several gowns for you to look at. I told them you were traditional and would probably like one of those old-looking things, like those they wore before the war. You know, a hoopskirt and the whole bit. They're expecting you to come by tomorrow, around ten-ish."

"Ash . . ."

"I know, I'm doing it all, but, well, it was really only a few phone calls. Oh, and the best news—" he fairly beamed with smugness "—I talked to a man yesterday who is very interested in buying the company."

Tori's temper soared, but before she could open her mouth and retort, their dinner arrived. She glanced at it and almost gagged. Not that the food wouldn't be delicious—it always was—but at the moment food was the farthest thing from her mind. "Ash, will you listen to me?" *Because if you don't,* she thought to herself, *I'm going to lunge across this table and strangle you with your tie.*

"Well, of course, *chérie.* Did I make the appointment time too early for you?"

"No, the time's fine, I mean, no, it's not. What I mean is . . ."

He stretched an arm across the table and patted her cheek with his long fingers, then returned his attention to the almondine trout on his plate. "I know, *chérie,* this is all happening so fast, but now that we're doing it, I wonder why we've waited."

"Because it isn't right," Tori snapped. Her temper flashed and she frantically grappled with herself to get it back under control. Several other patrons seated nearby turned and stared at her outburst. She lowered her voice and tried to smile. "It's not right between us, Ash."

"Of course it is. I love you and you love me." He filled his mouth with a piece of trout.

"No, I don't love you, and if you're truthful, Ash, I don't think you love me, either. You like being with me because it's comfortable, you don't have to constantly worry about putting up a front, we know each other. But you're not in love with me."

"Yes, I am," he said calmly, and speared another piece of fish.

Tori sighed. "Ash, I'm not going to marry you. And I'm not going to sell the company." She lifted her wineglass, and as she did she glanced at the other occupants of the courtyard. She halted abruptly at a pair of dark blue eyes.

"We'll postpone it then, just a few months, until this little anxiety attack you're having is over. I understand. It's probably better, anyway, what with this big case I'm about to undertake. I really shouldn't take any time off for a honeymoon, and it wouldn't be right not to go on a honeymoon. As for the company, we can always find another buyer when you're ready"

Rand glowered at her, a look of controlled rage on his face, eyes dark, piercing, unreadable.

She tried to smile and nodded.

He didn't acknowledge the friendly gesture.

Instead, he tossed two twenty-dollar bills on the table, stood, and walked from the restaurant.

Boy, this was really her day. Tori set the wineglass back on the table before her fingers could crush it. What was this? Murphy's Law in effect, and all directed at her? Everything had gone wrong from the moment she'd opened her eyes that morning. Maybe she should have just stayed in bed.

"You're just feeling a bit nervous, *chérie,* but we'll still have to pay on the suite at the home for Stanton, or they'll give it to someone else."

She stared at Ash, not really hearing anything he was saying. Who was she trying to fool? She had tried to walk away from Rand Mitchell, told herself it was best, that *they'd* only ruin everything, anyway. And she was miserable. Maybe it was time she stopped worrying about what *they* would do, and what Rand would think once he found out about *them,* and listened to her heart. Isn't that what Dominic had suggested?

She glanced at the table where Rand, only moments before, had sat. Maybe *they'd* been right before, about Tom. Maybe he had been wrong for her. But maybe *they* were wrong this time, and she'd never know if she didn't follow her heart.

"Victoria, did you hear me?" Ash asked. He sounded slightly miffed.

"Uh . . . ?"

"We will postpone it. I'll get hold of everyone: the cathedral, flowers, and such. But I must advise you to reconsider this business about keeping the company. Now is a very good time to sell it."

"Ash—" her tone brooked no argument "—listen to me very closely." She felt as if she were talking to a five-year-old, but since Ashford seemed too preoccupied with his own thoughts, she had no choice. "We are not, I repeat, *not* getting married. Not now. Not in a few months. Not ever. I love you like a brother, Ash, but that's all. I am not *in* love with you. I am not marrying you and I am not selling the agency. Period."

Ash patted his napkin to his lips. "You're upset, Victoria, that's all. A little rest would do you good." He stood and held his arm out to her.

She pulled her car into the carriage house and felt an instant wave of disappointment wash over her. Rand's rental car was not there. She walked slowly to the house. How had her life turned into such a mess?

"Hi, honey, come on in here," Stanton called from the parlor.

She kissed his cheek and slumped onto the

settee, kicking off her shoes and releasing a long sigh.

"You take care of Morgan?"

"Not yet. But Harlan's in on this, too." No sense hiding the truth from him. Somehow he always found things out, and she had a sneaking suspicion it was Abram whose pipeline to every other servant in the parish was the source.

"Humph, two snakes in the grass, those two. Always told your daddy that. Where's Rand?" His immediate change of the subject jolted her.

"I don't know. I dined with Ash at the Court and I saw him at another table there, but he left before we did. I thought he'd be here already."

"You give Ashford the old heave-ho like I been telling you to?"

She smiled. "I told him I wouldn't marry him, if that's what you mean."

"Good, now maybe he won't come around anymore. Dandified wimp."

At that moment Tori heard the front door open and close. She turned and peered into the foyer. Rand walked past the doorway on his way to the stairs.

"Hey, there, young fella," Stanton called out. "Come on in here and sit a spell."

Rand reappeared at the doorway, hesitated, then entered. "Good evening, Stanton, Tori," he said, his tone rather formal. "I was going to retire early tonight, I have, umm, some business to see about tomorrow."

Stanton nodded. "Have some coffee with us first, why don't you?"

With those words, Abram magically appeared with a tray of steaming coffee.

Rand brushed past Tori and, rather than sit next to her on the settee, which she'd expected, positioned himself on the tall wing chair opposite her.

"So, how's your vacation going?" Stanton questioned.

Rand nodded. "Nicely. Your granddaughter is a very good guide. I'll recommend her highly to my friends."

Tori felt as if he'd just thrown a bucket of cold water over her. That's what she was to him? A tour guide? And maybe a little pleasure on the side? She felt fury heat her breast, and her eyes stung with indignation.

"I told you Yankees were no good," Lila said. She suddenly appeared beside Rand and glared down at him, her arms crossed over her flat chest. "He's just like all the others, Tori: crude, greedy, and thoughtless."

"Leave her alone, Lila," the general said from across the room. "You lived your life, let Tori live hers."

"Don't talk to me that way, you traitor," Lila retorted, and turned her back on Ambrose. "She

257

wouldn't be smarting right now if she'd listened to me in the first place."

"If she listened to you all the time, she'd never do anything," Dominic said, "or love anyone."

Chapter Twenty-one

So, once again she'd been wrong and *they'd* been right. It hurt, but this time it also made her angry. Very angry. How could he be so . . . so . . . cold. Tori paced the length of her room, spun, and retraced her steps, like an angry tigress, unsure of what to do. Suddenly she stopped. But wasn't that exactly how she'd been treating him since he'd accused her of pushing him in the swamp yesterday? Coldly and distantly?

She knew she hadn't pushed him into the swamp, but how was he supposed to know that? She'd been the only person close to him. At least the only person he could see. And, she reasoned, it was better this way, if they were cool to each other, then the sparks that simmered between them would have little to no chance of igniting again. He'd leave RiverOaks in a few days and that would be that.

The thought of his leaving hurt, and Tori knew it would hurt even worse once he was gone, but it was best this way. Now all she had to do was convince herself that was true.

With a deep sigh, she slipped into bed and closed her eyes. She had a big day tomorrow and needed rest, especially if she was going to have to deal with Morgan and Harlan. Elmer Fudd and Buggs Bunny. She chuckled softly into the dark, but as images of Rand invaded her mind, the chuckle faded and the smile on her lips died.

"Where the hell have you been, Jason?" Rand hissed into the phone. "I tried to call you yesterday." He was getting better at this; at least he hadn't yelled and woken everyone up.

"I was wining and dining our little friend, Faircreighton. The man really is an aborigine, Rand. He may have been born and raised in New Orleans and come from a good family, but he's straight out of the backwoods now."

"So, did he sign?"

"Yes. We have his percentages, and he has our one million dollars."

Instead of a surge of triumph, Rand felt a distinct plummet of his spirits, straight down to his toes. He tried to shake away the disheartening feeling, but it refused to be banished. What the hell was the matter with him? Isn't this exactly what he wanted? "What about the others?" He peered around the pantry door into the kitchen to make sure no one had entered while he'd been talking.

"I heard back from Harlan Rollsbey. He's flying in later this morning. And Marselle is ready to listen. I have an appointment with him this afternoon. Dellos still says no, and I found out from Sentrum's maid that she's due back in town tonight."

"Good. Where are you meeting Harlan?"

"Brennan's, for lunch. Why?"

"I may join you."

"Is that a good idea? I mean, the woman might see you."

"It doesn't matter anymore. What time?"

"One."

"I'll see you then." He hung up the receiver and stepped out into the kitchen.

"I see you've discovered we're not quite as authentic as we advertise," Tori said. Her voice was like a cold breeze, biting and hard.

Rand stopped. How much had she heard? He watched her, trying to decide, and then realized, as he'd told Jason, it really didn't matter anymore. After he'd yelled at her in the swamp, accused her of pushing him into the water, everything had changed between them and she'd made it quite clear on the ride back to New Orleans that she preferred it that way. And that was fine with him. He never should have let

261

himself get emotionally involved with her, anyway. Business was business and pleasure was pleasure, and they were a deadly combination when mixed together. "I saw Abram answer it the other day." He shrugged, trying to ease the tautness that suddenly gripped his shoulders. "I needed to call my office and didn't think anyone would mind. I'll pay for the call."

"That's not necessary." She poured herself a glass of iced water from the refrigerator and turned to leave the room. "But please don't tell anyone we have a phone here. We like our guests to feel they've left the labors of the real world behind when they stay at RiverOaks. Most don't want to call their offices and tend to business."

He stared at the empty doorway long after she'd left. Had she heard his conversation? Or were her remarks innocent comments rather than barbed words that seemed to zero in on exactly what he'd been doing? He didn't know, and though he knew he shouldn't care, he did. Damn it, he did.

The room turned suddenly chilly, as if all the warm air had been abruptly sucked out of it. He felt a frosty breeze cut across his cheek and turned to look at the back door. It was closed, but even if it hadn't been, that wouldn't explain the draft or sudden drop in temperature. It was summer, and hot. Even now, at midnight, the air outside was humid and warm. He looked around the room in confusion. The refrigerator door was closed, as was the pantry's. There was no reason for a cold draft in the kitchen . . . yet there definitely was one.

Rand shivered, but not entirely from the cold, and left the room. He needed to go over some of the papers he'd brought with him, refresh his mind on Harlan Rollsbey and the others. He sighed deeply as he climbed the staircase and thought back on his conversation with Jason. They were on the verge of accomplishing what they'd set out to do. So why did he feel so down? As if he'd just lost everything, which was ridiculous.

The coldness followed him. He felt it on the stairs, in the hallway, and swirling around him like a winter breeze while he paced his room.

He shivered. "Damn it, I can't get sick now," he mumbled to himself, and climbed beneath the covers of the ornate poster bed. If he was coming down with something, it must be a doozy because he was freezing, yet he didn't feel all that bad. He'd left the heavy blue damask drapes that adorned the windows open and moonlight filled the room, touched each piece of antique furniture, and shone a reflection from their polished surfaces. He ignored it all and looked up at the sunburst pattern of the drawn silk canopy overhead. The covers cut some of the chill, but not all, and he could still feel it, all the way to his bones.

By morning, he'd slept little. He felt drawn and irritable. The coldness had left him only a few minutes before dawn, right about the same time he'd faintly heard Tori's alarm clock go off. He remained in his room until he heard the crunch of tires on the shelled driveway. With a glance out the window he assured himself she'd left for work, and went downstairs.

"You just missed Tori," Stanton said, when Rand entered the old kitchen.

He nodded, voiced a few pleasantries, and excused himself. He'd get a leisurely breakfast in town, over which he could enjoy browsing *The Wall Street Journal,* something he usually did religiously and since coming to New Orleans hadn't done at all. Then he'd call the office, and at one, meet Jason and Rollsbey. If Jason seemed to have this thing well on its way to a successful end, maybe he'd book himself a flight back to San Francisco for this afternoon.

But somehow that latest thought didn't sit too well with him.

Tori sat at her desk and stared out the window that gave a view of a small courtyard. A fountain in the center sprinkled steadily, its spray glistening silver in the morning sun, and the scent of the several dozen azaleas wafted in through her open window.

She tore her eyes away from the scene and picked up a pen, but her hand remained idle, poised above a pad of paper, still. "Can we raise more money today if that's not enough?" she said into the telephone receiver that rested on her shoulder.

Half a minute later she slammed the phone down on its cradle, only to hear it ring again almost immediately. She glared at the flashing light on the phone, then, with a sigh of resignation, picked up the receiver. "Yes, Sherrille?"

"It's your grandfather on the line. He wants to talk with you."

"Gramps? He never calls unless it's an emergency." She felt her heart thud in fear. Had something happened to Abram?

Sherrille left the line and Tori heard Stanton's voice. "Tori, you there?"

"Yes, Gramps, what's wrong?"

"Nothing. Me and Abram just been talking. About Rand and where we've seen him before. Remember, I told you we both had this feeling we'd seen him somewhere?"

"And you remembered where?" Not that it mattered anymore, she thought, except to satisfy their curiosity.

"No, but we got an idea. Can you stop at the library sometime today and pick up a few things

265

I ordered?"

"Like what?"

"I asked the clerk to put aside one of them who's who books."

She smiled. Rand Mitchell would have to be an awfully important person to be in *Who's Who*, but there was no harm in humoring Stanton and Abram in their little investigation. She'd send Sherrille to get the book. "Okay, Gramps, I'll bring it home to you." She hung up, slumped back in her chair, and closed her eyes against the world. Right now she didn't like it much. And the reason wasn't all because of this business with Morgan and Harlan trying to sell her out. She couldn't fool herself into believing that. Rand Mitchell was constantly at the back of her mind, invading her thoughts, keeping her from putting her whole concentration on anything. Letting her guard down, even just a little, allowed thoughts of him to totally take over. It was especially bad at night, when she lay in bed staring up into the darkness. Her body yearned for his touch, to be held by him, cradled in his embrace. She ached to feel the press of his lips on hers, his hands on her breasts, his body melded with hers, loving her.

She sighed again, so deeply that a shudder shook her body and a tear fell from her eye. "Sometimes I think it would have been better if I'd been in that car, too," she murmured.

"Don't say things like that, Tori."

She opened her eyes and, seeing who her visitor was, smiled. "Hi, Uncle Dom."

The fact that her tone held no cheer did not escape his attention, nor did the defeated slump of her shoulders. "You're giving up, Tori," he said, "and that's not like you. You've always been a fighter. What's wrong?"

She shrugged. "Everything. My whole life seems like it's taken a nosedive into the sewer."

"And there's nothing you can do to try and fix it?"

"Well, I've got my accountant trying to cash in enough stocks and bonds to raise the cash to buy out Morgan and Harlan. Normally that wouldn't be a problem, but I've put so much into negotiations for a new location in Florida, and the remodeling of the offices in Mississippi in the last two months that the company's a little cash poor at the moment."

"And is that all that's bothering you?" he persisted. His tone was soft and drawing.

"Well, no."

"The young man?"

She nodded. "Everything was going so well. Maybe not everything. Lila and Chance did cause some trouble, but it was going well in spite of their pranks."

"And you fell in love with him?"

She nodded again. "Yes." She took a deep

267

breath. "But I know it won't work. *They* won't let it."

"You can go against them, Tori. They're not always right, you know. Lila didn't want me to marry Laura."

She looked at him, shocked by his words. "She didn't? You never told me that? Why not?"

"She didn't like her. But I didn't care, and neither did the rest of the family. When I proposed to Laura, they appeared, and that's all the blessing I needed. And Lila came around—" he smiled "—eventually."

Dominic had always had a way of subtly admonishing her so that rather than make her feel angry or resentful, she felt guilty and determined to right whatever wrong she'd been pouting about. But this time it was different. She wanted to believe him, but she couldn't. Lila and Chance would never accept Rand, and she knew, no matter what she told herself, that she could never give up RiverOaks. It was her home. Her heritage. And *they* came with it.

The bell on her phone jingled again and Dominic abruptly disappeared. She picked up the receiver. "Yes?"

"Morgan Faircreighton's here to see you," Sherrille said.

A start of surprise brought Tori out of her chair and to the door of her office. She opened it and tried to smile at Morgan. It didn't work, and she gave up. He hadn't changed since the last time she'd seen him, ten years before. He was still skeleton thin and hawkish in appearance, and his clothes hung on him like rumpled rejects. "I thought you were going to wait for my call."

He smiled sheepishly and rushed past her into her office, all the while keeping his gaze averted. She returned to the seat behind her desk, but he declined a seat and instead paced nervously about the room.

"Morgan, what is it?" Tori demanded finally.

He stopped his fidgeting and turned his bulging brown eyes on her. "I've sold my share of the company."

She came out of her chair like a ball exploding from a cannon. "You what?"

"I sold." He smiled weakly. "They offered me a million dollars, Tori, and, well, I talked to Anita on the phone last night and she wants me to come home, and she's found this cute little cottage she wants to buy, and . . ."

"I thought we had an understanding, Morgan. You were not going to do anything until we talked again."

"Yes, but, well, they offered . . ."

She slumped back into her seat. "Never mind. Have a happy life, Morgan. Goodbye."

He hurriedly from her office.

Morgan had owned twenty percent. That meant Jason Newhall now owned one-fifth of Rouchard Travel. The thought turned her blood cold. It wasn't a controlling interest by a long shot, but it was enough so that it made her nervous. Maybe, for enough money, he would sell it back to her.

Several hours later she had done enough talking to, pleading with, promising, and nearly bribing both her accountant and the bank that handled her accounts so that she felt comfortable again. She could offer Jason a fifty-percent return on his money, enough profit for anyone. By tomorrow she'd most likely be able to up the offer, if she had to. She buzzed Sherrille. "See if you can get Jason Newhall on the line. He did leave his number with you, didn't he?"

A minute later, Sherrille buzzed back. "He's not in. The desk clerk said he made Mr. Newhall reservations to lunch at The Court of Two Sisters today, for one o'clock."

"Good." She glanced at her watch. Twelve-thirty. "I think I'm starting to get hungry."

"I won't need a table today," she said to the Court's maître d', "but I would appreciate it if you would direct me to Mr. Newhall's table."

A moment later, Tori walked across the courtyard. She had nearly tripped on the flagstone

270

when she'd seen Harlan sitting at the table with Jason Newhall, but quickly composed herself.

"Good afternoon, gentlemen," she said sweetly. "Mind if I join you?"

The two men looked up at her, obviously stunned by her appearance at their table. Harlan seemed to turn white and looked as if he wished he could crawl under the table. Jason rose to his feet and motioned at an empty chair across from him. "Please," he said.

Tori slipped into the chair. "Well, Mr. Newhall, I understand you've been quite busy." She turned to Harlan. "And so have you, obviously."

"I—I did phone you, Tori."

"Yes, gracious of you." She turned back to Jason, "Mr. Newhall, let's get down to business, shall we? You bought Morgan Faircreighton's share of my company this morning. I'd like to make you an offer to buy it back." She glanced at Harlan. "And if dear cousin Harlan here wants to sell, I'll buy his share, too, at a nice profit to you, of course."

Jason cleared his throat. "I'm sorry, Miss Rouchard, but Faircreighton's shares are not for sale. And neither are Mr. Rollsbey's."

She turned to Harlan. "Harlan, how much do you want?"

He shook his head and smiled smugly. "You'll have to ask Mr. Newhall that, Tori."

271

"You've already sold out, then?" she said, though by the look on his face she knew there was no need for an answer.

Rand stood in the shadows of the porte cochere, watching the trio at the table in the courtyard. He had spotted Tori just before stepping into the courtyard himself, the black brilliance of her long hair glistening in the sunlight like cascading ebony waves. But they hadn't seen him, and though he'd told himself it didn't matter anymore, he hesitated to show himself, to reveal to her that it was he who wanted her company, not Jason. And standing there, watching her, witnessing the sudden sag of her shoulders as Jason obviously refused to deal with her, or worse, lay his cards on the table as to exactly what he was doing and wanted, Rand felt his insides begin to twist and churn, felt a rending in his heart that threatened to leave a void which would torment him forever.

Suddenly the acquisition of Rouchard Travel didn't seem as all-important as it had. Even the very reason that he so desperately wanted the company escaped his mind. All he could think of was how it was affecting Tori. Though all he could see was the back of her head and shoulders, Rand's imagination was a vivid one. In his mind he saw her eyes as she stared in dismay at

Jason, golden brown pools that glistened with tears. He saw her lips quiver, those full, sensuous lips that had kissed him and taken his breath away. He felt her hands tremble, and sensed how shattered her heart must have been.

He took a deep breath and silently cursed himself. She had told him how much the company meant to her, and he had ignored her, as he had the feelings burning deep within him that stirred every time she came near. Suddenly everything was clear to him. Now, when Tori would turn from him, hate him, if she learned the truth, he came to realize and admit how much she meant to him. How could he have been so blind? So stupid?

"Well, not anymore," he growled, and took a step onto the patio. But he stopped before he could take another as Tori shot up from her chair.

"You will not get controlling interest of Rouchard Travel, Mr. Newhall, now or ever." Her angry voice cut through the quiet afternoon like the steel edge of a well-honed knife, sharp and cutting. "I own that, and I have no intention of selling, or being forced out. You can tell whoever you work for that he has a definite fight on his hands, and if it's an agreeable partner he's looking for, he can forget it! Rouchard Travel is mine, and I neither want nor need a partner." She whirled abruptly and stormed from the restaurant, her shoulders held back stiffly, her face a drawn mask of determination and rage.

Rand stepped back into the shadows as she passed and she brushed past him without noticing his presence.

"What the hell was that all about?" he muttered to himself. He glanced at Jason and Rollsbey, thought about approaching them, and thought better of it. Rollsbey just might say something to Tori about meeting him, and he wasn't prepared for that yet. He had too many things to do in order to change this disaster he had created.

Chapter Twenty-two

But fixing things with Tori proved a lot more difficult than he'd anticipated. For one thing, she wouldn't talk to him. She was polite and gracious. She would respond to his comments when directed to her and answer his questions, but she would not prolong a conversation, nor would she accept any of his invitations to breakfast, lunch, or dinner.

He thought about just grabbing her, forcing her to remain still and listen to him, and announcing that no one, not Jason Newhall, not Rand Mitchell, not anyone, was going to take Rouchard Travel from her. But he couldn't do it that way. He needed to make her understand that the things he'd done had been planned long before he'd realized he was in love with her. And he did love her, but she would have to be convinced of that, too.

So his campaign began.

On Wednesday he sent flowers to her office — dozens of them, of every color, shape, and scent the florist could find. She accepted his calls that afternoon, but politely declined his invitation to dinner, and did not return to RiverOaks until well after midnight. He'd fallen asleep in a chair and hadn't heard her come in.

On Thursday he sent her candy — enough to feed an army, but when he phoned, Sherrille insisted Tori was in a meeting and couldn't be disturbed. Yes, she knew about the candy, Sherrille said, and had instructed her to thank him, but no, she could not go to dinner with him.

On Friday, a few minutes before noon, a tuxedoed waiter from Antoine's arrived in the Rouchard offices pushing a tray laden with salads, gumbos, breads, and desserts. Rand knew she was there because he'd been sitting on a bench in Jackson Square for over an hour. He'd seen her come out once, talk to someone, and then reenter her office. He waited until after the waiter left, then walked to a pay phone and called.

"Sherrille? How do you ladies like the lunch?" he asked when she answered.

"It's delicious, Mr. Mitchell, thank you."

"Good. I thought since Miss Rouchard is too busy to lunch with me, I'd make sure you all enjoyed a good meal. May I speak with her?"

"Oh, I'm sorry, but she's closed herself up in her office and instructed me not to interrupt her."

"Not even for me?" Rand said, his tone light

276

and teasing. She'd helped him once; maybe she could be cajoled into doing it again. It was worth a try.

She laughed. "Sorry. She's in a real mood today, and I don't feel like losing my job."

Rand hung up and looked across the street at the glass front of Tori's office. What was she upset about now? He'd ordered Jason to back off. Was someone else approaching her about selling? Or was there something else wrong?

He felt icy fingers suddenly close around his heart and a sinking feeling in his stomach. Was she seeing Ashford again? Had he, in her vulnerability, convinced her to marry him, after all?

"Over my dead body," Rand vowed.

Fifteen minutes later he was standing in the shop of one of New Orleans' most exclusive jewelers. He looked at rings, watches, pins, jeweled barrettes, and bracelets, but after an hour of browsing he decided on a small gold heart encrusted with diamonds and hanging from a delicate gold chain.

But that evening Tori didn't come home. Stanton said something about her visiting a relative, but Rand had the depressing feeling that it was Ashford she was visiting, not a relative.

The next morning she was up and gone before he got downstairs, which had been the norm ever since that day in the swamp, the one Rand thought of as their last "real" day together. He slipped the small velvet box into the pocket of his black slacks and, after having coffee with Stanton, left for town. He wouldn't go to her office until noon, but he wanted to make sure she was there, and that she didn't leave.

He stopped at the Café Dumonde across the street from the square and purchased a cup of café au lait and several of the huge, square powdered doughnuts that were the staple of the café, and what it was famous for. According to Stanton, who seemed to have guessed what Rand was up to and recommended the place, the doughnuts were called beignets and the café had been serving them for more than a hundred and forty years.

Rand found an empty bench in the park that gave him a clear view of Tori's office, sat down, and pulled one of the doughnuts from the bag. He bit down on it and white powdered sugar puffed up in a cloud around his face.

"Oh, great," he mumbled, and waved a hand at the settling powder. He wiped it from his face, feeling a bit foolish, and wrapped a napkin around the remainder of the doughnut before biting down on it again.

At ten to twelve he stood, deposited the bag and cardboard cup in a garbage can, and sauntered easily toward Tori's office. His fingers played with the velvet box in his pocket, but he couldn't quiet get a smile on his lips. He was too nervous and though he hated to admit it, scared. What if she didn't return his feelings? Maybe that was why she'd backed away from him so abruptly. Rand swallowed, hard. Was this what it had been like when his mother lost his father? Had she felt as if the world had just been pulled from beneath her? As if there was no reason to go on living?

He opened the entry door. Sherrille and Tori stood in the doorway to Tori's office. Both women turned at his approach.

Suddenly this seemed like the hardest thing he'd ever done. He fingered the velvet box. "Tori, can I talk to you for a few minutes?" He moved up beside her, and the nearness of her was instant intoxication to his senses. The urge to reach out and pull her into his arms was almost irresistible.

Sherrille quickly retreated to her desk, but Tori remained standing in the doorway. She shook her head. "I really have a lot of work to do, Rand. If you need a guide I'm sure Sherrille can assign one to—"

"I *need* to talk to you," he said, his tone leaving no room for argument or refusal. To make sure she did neither, he clasped a hand about her arm and half-pushed, half-urged her into her office. He kicked the door closed behind him.

Tori turned, which she found out was a mistake. He swept her into his arms, crushed her against his chest, and his lips descended on hers. His mouth moved over hers with ravaging intensity, commanding an acquiescence from her she was powerless to withhold, demanding a response she was unable to suppress. His tongue sought hers and caressed its length while his hands traveled over her back. Each touch, each flick of his tongue, stroke of his hands and crush of his arms drained her of the resistance that had dwelled within her for the past week and filled her with a hunger stronger than any she had ever known.

When he finally did pull his lips from hers, Tori found herself breathless and weak, and her resolve against him banished as thoroughly as clouds in a windstorm.

"Now will you listen to me?" His own breathing was rapid and shallow, and each movement of his chest pushed against her breasts, teasing her senses, taunting her desires, and leaving her little choice but to surrender to whatever it was he had in mind.

"Yes," she whispered.

"I've been going half out of my mind this past week." He placed a finger beneath her chin and nudged her head upward, forcing her to look at him. "And all because of you."

She knew she should resist him, should twist her way out of his arms and demand he leave her office, her life. But she couldn't. She couldn't send him away, and she couldn't give him her love. Tears stung her eyes and she tried to blink them away.

Rand reached into his pocket and, continuing to hold him to her with one arm, pulled out the tiny velvet box and flipped it open. "I know this doesn't make up for what I've done, Tori, but, if you'll let me, I'll keep trying."

She frowned. For what he'd done? She was the one who should be apologizing, for *them*. "But you haven't done anything."

He smiled sadly. "Yes, I have."

"It's beautiful, Rand, but I can't accept it. Really."

"It was made for you, Tori." Releasing her, he plucked the heart from the box, looped the chain around her neck, and fastened it. He stepped back and looked at the sparkling diamond heart as Tori ran an appreciative finger over it. "It was definitely made for you." He pulled her back into his arms. "And so was I."

She tried to push him away at that. This was wrong. *They* would show up any minute. She had to get him out of here. "Rand, please, we can't . . . it's impossible . . . you and I just aren't . . ."

He tightened his embrace around her. "I have a confession to make Tori, then if you want me to go, I will."

She stopped pushing against his chest and stared up at him, puzzled. A confession?

"I love you."

"What?" She laughed. Obviously she was hallucinating. She hadn't had breakfast or lunch, and her body was rebelling. Rand wasn't really here, he hadn't kissed her, held her, or given her a diamond necklace, and he certainly hadn't just told her that he loved her.

This was not the reaction he had expected. "Tori, did you understand what I said?"

She looked up at him. This wasn't a hallucination. "I'm sorry." She blushed. "I think I just misunderstood what you said."

"I said I've fallen in love with you."

Before he knew what was happening, her lips were on his, her arms wrapped around his shoulders, her fingers entwined in his hair. She kissed him hungrily, all the pent-up emotions she had denied for so long, had been afraid to reveal, pouring from her to wash over him like a warm wave. When she finally pulled away, her eyes were gleaming with happiness. "I love you, too."

He smiled, but instead of feeling better, he suddenly felt worse. The fear that had been eating at him, gnawing at his insides for the past week, threatened to consume him. He felt guilty as hell, and he hadn't told her the truth about himself, but if he did, what then? Would she hate him? Order him out of her life as the snake that he was? He pressed her closer and buried his face in her hair. He couldn't tell her . . . not yet. He'd find a way to fix things, he just needed a little time.

A knock sounded on her door. Tori pulled away from Rand, much as she didn't want to, and turned expectantly. "Yes?"

Sherrille entered. "I'm sorry, Tori, but your cousin John Dellos is here and he says it's quite urgent he talk to you."

Tori turned to Rand. "I have to see him, but if that dinner invitation is still open I'd like to accept."

"I'll be back at six," Rand said. He brushed his lips across her cheek and then walked from her office. He waited until he was outside before he allowed a frown, which had tugged at his brow the moment he heard Dellos's name, to settle. What did Dellos have to discuss with Tori that was *urgent?* He had a sinking feeling in the pit of his stomach and headed for the phone booth on the wharf across the street.

Halfway there he changed his direction. He would go to Jason's hotel. This was something they obviously needed to discuss face to face.

He found the Vieux Carré House with little problem, getting turned around only once. The desk clerk rang Jason's room.

"I'm sorry, sir," the young man said, "but there is no answer. Would you care to leave a message?"

Rand shook his head and turned to go, but as he passed the hotel's lounge on his way out, he saw Jason sitting at a table with a rather rotund elderly man. He approached and slid into the vacant chair between the two men. "Jason, we need to talk."

"Rand, I'm glad you're here. This is Mr. Thomas Marselle."

"Hello," Rand said briskly, but his gaze remained riveted to Jason's. "Can this wait until later, Jason?" he asked, indicating whatever business his vice president had with this Marselle person.

"Actually, we've just concluded our business." Jason stood and offered his hand to the pudgy man, who also struggled to his feet, his massive weight making it a difficult and slow procedure. "Thank you, Mr. Marselle. It was a pleasure doing business with you."

"Jason, what's going on with . . ." The identity of the man half-waddling, half-walking out of the lounge suddenly struck Rand like a lightning bolt between the eyes. He stared after him, and then jerked around to glare at Jason. "Marselle? Tori's cousin Marselle?"

Jason's face creased in a wide, satisfied grin. "That's the one. We just bought his shares." He raised a glass of mineral water in a toast. "Three down, two to go."

"Are you crazy? I told you to back off." The thundering growl of Rand's words caused a surprised Jason to nearly drop his glass.

"Back off? What are you talking about? I thought you wanted this company, at whatever the cost."

"I do, I mean I did. But that's not important anymore. Why did you proceed with this after I ordered you to stop?"

"You didn't."

"I what?" Rand's fingers gripped the chair so tightly his knuckles turned white, but it was better than the alternative, which was smashing them into Jason's face.

"Look, you left me a message that said something about you wanting to handle things, which is fine, but I was already in negotiations with this Marselle guy and I couldn't reach you. I waited for you to call, but you didn't. I even left a message with Lidwell, but you didn't call the office, either, so I did what I thought was best, which was go after this guy's interest in Rouchard Travel. And I got it."

Chapter Twenty-three

He spent the remainder of the afternoon wandering the quarter, sitting in the square and staring at her office front, and meandering along the moonwalk. And all the while he'd been trying to decide what to do, how to tell her the truth, and he had come up with no way to do it. At least not one he was comfortable with. No matter how he put it to her, she'd end up hating him, and he couldn't bear that.

Rand leaned on the railing of the moonwalk and let his gaze roam over the wide river, its murky waters gently lapping past New Orleans on the way to the Gulf of Mexico. She'd probably like to see him drown in the river once she learned who he was. He sniffed disdainfully. She had turned every conception he'd had about life and love completely around and upside down. Except for one thing: her company. She'd claimed she wanted nothing more than a mate, a home, and kids. He'd never realized it before, but that's exactly what he'd been looking for in a woman, though he also hadn't realized he'd been looking. But what about Rouchard Travel? She said she would never sell it, so where did that leave them even if she did accept and forgive what he'd done? Or tried to do. Could he accept a wife who was as successful in her career as he was?

A sardonic chuckle bubbled from his lips. Tori didn't have *just* a career—her company was one of his company's main competitors, and their roadblock to expanding into the Southern states. Even if they were married, without her giving up Rouchard Travel, that wouldn't change.

Unless they combined the agencies, he thought, and smiled. He turned and walked across the street to Tori's office. By the time he entered her front door, he felt as if his heart were lodged somewhere in his throat, strangling him.

"Sherrille, have you located that little weasel yet?" Tori snarled from her office, her voice snapping through the otherwise quiet room like a whip.

"His wife said she doesn't expect him back until late, and the deli says he's gone until tomorrow. I've called his club, but they haven't seen him. I don't know where else to call."

Tori appeared at her open office door, a gleam of fiery rage burning in her eyes. "So

287

help me, if I get my hands on that little . . ." Her eyes met Rand's and her features were abruptly transformed from anger to joy. "Rand," she said, and moved toward him.

He took both of her hands in his. "What's the matter?" he asked, not sure he really wanted to know, but then he had a sneaking suspicion he already did. She was looking for Thomas Marselle.

"One of my other cousins is thinking about selling."

"How do you know that?"

"John, my cousin who runs the swamp tours, told me. He came by right after you left this afternoon. Said Marselle stopped by and tried to talk him into going, too."

"Going where?" Rand asked, though he knew very well where.

"To a meeting with Jason Newhall."

She mistook his silence for a question.

"He's that man I told you about who keeps hounding me with offers to sell. He managed to talk my uncle and one of my cousins who own percentages in the company into selling, and now he's after another cousin."

Rand felt his stomach plummet to the ground. He couldn't tell her. Not yet. Not when she was in this kind of mood. He'd tell her tomorrow, when she'd calmed down. Or maybe the day after, when things didn't look so bad to her, when she'd had a chance to reassure herself that none of her other relatives were going to sell out. Because they weren't, unless someone else was trying to buy their percentages.

They walked from her office to Brennan's and were seated at a table on the screened porch overlooking the courtyard.

"Feel a little better?" Rand asked. He held her hand across the table, his thumb slowly and gently caressing the small mounds of her knuckles.

"Only when I don't think about that horrid man."

"Then don't think about him," Rand said, wishing the problem was really that simple.

The rays of the setting sun gilded the courtyard below and settled a rosy glow over the area, bathing everything and everyone in its warmth and hue. They ate their dinner in near silence, Rand giving Tori time to recompose herself, time to relax and try to put the day's trials aside for a while. And it worked. When they finally left the restaurant, the sky had turned dark and her mood light. He slipped an arm around her shoulders and they made their way back to the square, and then across the street to the moonwalk.

"I've come here several times since my arrival," Rand said. "I like it."

"Are you a romantic, Mr. Mitchell?" Tori

teased. She slipped an arm around his waist.

"Only with you, Miss Rouchard." He turned and wrapped her in the circle of his arms and drew her tenderly to him. His kiss was a gentle melding of his lips to hers, his tongue in her mouth a tormentingly sweet stroke that touched her deeper than even his lovemaking had, and left her shaking in his arms. It was a kiss of promise and love, asking nothing in return, merely giving, and it brought tears to her eyes.

He felt the moisture of her tears on his cheeks and pulled away to look at her. "What's the matter, Tori?" She shook her head and smiled up at him. "Nothing, except that I want you to make love to me. Now. Tonight."

He crushed her to him for several long minutes, praying silently that this would not be the last time she would ask him that.

He entered her slowly, savoring the feel of her flesh enveloping his, the warmth and moisture of her wrapping around him, drawing him deeper into her. At this moment, nothing mattered to him but Tori, that she love him as he loved her. He felt her hands on his back, holding him to her, as her legs twined about his and she pushed her hips up to meet his. Rand let his hands travel over her body, his fingers caressed each curve of flesh, but his touch was light, almost teasing, as a feather run across her skin.

His lips traveled over her face, kissing her eyelids, her cheeks, the curve of her jaw, but teasingly avoiding her mouth. He nuzzled the long column of her neck, let his tongue taste the hollow of her throat, and breathed in the magnolia scent of her perfume that clung to the tiny basin of flesh just behind her earlobe.

He held himself back, wanting to savor this time with her as long as he could. Several times, when he'd sensed Tori's release building, he had slowed his caresses and forced himself to pause within her until he felt her settle again, and then he had started the climb to the pinnacle they both yearned for all over again.

Afterward, they lay quiet for long minutes, savoring the feeling of being together. Her head rested on his shoulder, and she lay with one arm draped over his bare chest. Both stared up into the night, their ceiling a blanket of unpenetratable blankness, broken only by a brilliant splattering of stars, and a huge, low-hanging golden moon. All around them the soft sounds of the animals who made the swamp their home, and the night their day, pierced the otherwise eerie stillness of the stagnant black waters and moss-draped thickly grown trees.

He shifted position on the floor of the shallow pirogue her cousin John used to take tourists into the swamp, and unconsciously tightened his embrace on her, drawing her even nearer, pressing her naked form to his and branding the image of her length on his flesh. Calm had returned to the exterior of his body, and even his breathing, but his insides were still churning, nervous, but not from passion, not this time. It was fear that ate at him now, gnawed at every cell and fiber to remind him that there was still a lie between them, a lie that could destroy this newfound love he had discovered and tear it away from him, but a lie that had to be revealed. He inhaled deeply of the humid tangy odor of the swamp air and released it slowly. But not now, he decided. He couldn't tell her now, and destroy this moment between them. Tomorrow, in the light of day, when they were both calm, he would take her someplace quiet and tell her, explain everything to her. He would find a way to make her understand, for if he knew nothing else, he knew one thing; he couldn't lose Tori. No matter what she chose to do, maintain a career, be a housewife and mother, or combine all three, nothing in his life would really matter again if he didn't have her there to share it with him. He knew that as surely as he knew that if she walked away from him now, he would be nothing more than an empty shell of a man for the rest of his life.

He turned to her, and she snuggled deeper

into his embrace. "Tori, will you marry me?" The words slipped out of his mouth with no warning, a message from his heart, reaching out to her and ignoring the turmoil of his conscience.

"Yes," she whispered against his neck. Her lips pressed to his flesh. "Oh, yes."

They made love again then, joined in the ritual that bound all living things, blending their bodies for life, their souls for eternity. They soared to new heights together, the promise of forever between them, no matter how fragile, an intoxicant to the senses, drugging them against reality, and the trials yet to face.

In the shadows, standing beneath one of the giant oak trees that grew so abundantly in the swamp, Dominic Rouchard appeared. The pale gray of his Confederate uniform blended with the ghostly moonlight that filtered down through the thick, gnarled branches of the ancient tree, making him nearly invisible, though there was only one person who could see him, anyway, and she was not looking. A sad smile curved the corners of his mouth. He had come to warn her, but this was not the time.

Dawn crept over the swamp in a slow, steady stream of amber light. It touched first the far-off horizon, then spread its fingers of gold to the tops of the tall trees that had stood in the quiet swamps long before any human had dared ventured there. It moved between the branches, caressed each leaf and limb, and banished the last bits of night as it melted each drop of dew and finally settled onto the ground to kiss the earth and shroud it in warmth.

Tori awoke first, the light of day a brilliant glow against her closed eyelids. She sat up and looked around, then glanced hurriedly at her watch. "Lord, the tourists will be here any minute." She twisted around in Rand's arms, still holding tight around her waist and nudged his shoulder. "Rand, wake up." She bent down and pressed her lips to his. He stirred. "Wake up, sleepy, or we're liable to be the main attraction here in a few minutes."

His eyes fluttered open, long flaxen lashes opening to the daylight, and deep blue eyes looked up at her, but he didn't stir. "Come back here," he murmured, pulling her to him.

She laughed and struggled to resist. "Rand, John's going to be down here any time now to prepare the pirogues for the first onslaught of tourists, and if we don't get dressed they're going to get a real show."

He couldn't have sat up any quicker if she'd stuck him with a pin. "Tourists?" He looked around, getting his bearings, and then, as she had done, looked at his watch. "We've been here all night," he said, as if she didn't know that.

Tori quickly slipped back into her black slacks, deciding to forgo the nylons. She stuffed them into her purse.

Rand grabbed his clothes, but getting into his pants while sitting in a pirogue proved harder than getting out of them had been. The shallow boat began to sway violently as he twisted and turned. Finally, leaving a laughing Tori behind, he rose and stepped from the boat. It dipped with his movement and instead of meeting dry land, his foot splashed down into a foot of water, black, murky water. He scrambled to shore and stared down at his wet foot as if to make sure it was still there, his mind telling him he couldn't be too sure.

Within minutes they were both dressed and in the car. Tori sat close to him on the seat, her hand resting on his thigh. "Do you want to go into the Quarter and have breakfast before we go back to RiverOaks?" Rand asked.

She shook her head. "No, we'd better get back." Her mood had turned suddenly quiet and serious, and he'd noticed the faint shadow of a frown had appeared on her brow.

"What's wrong?" His heart nearly contracted in panic. Had she changed her mind? Could he have talked in his sleep? Mumbled out the truth?

She shivered. "I don't know, I just have this

feeling I need to check on my grandfather and Abram."

He looked at her, puzzled. "Can you sense when something's wrong?"

She smiled, but it was obvious her mind was preoccupied. "Not usually." She suddenly thought of *them*. She didn't normally need physic warnings or hunches—*they* were usually around to tell her what was going on. Alarm coursed through her. It wasn't like them to leave her in peace for so long. She hadn't seen Lila and Chance now for a couple of days, and if she knew anything, she knew that meant trouble.

Chapter Twenty-four

"I think next week would be great," Rand said. He squeezed the hand that Tori had laid on his thigh, while his other hand remained on the steering wheel. That gave him a little over seven whole days to come up with a way to tell her the truth.

"Next week?" She laughed. "You are kidding? What about your family?"

"I only have my mother, sister, and nephews, and they'll be here, I can guarantee that."

Tori laid her head on his shoulder. Everything in her life suddenly seemed perfect. Well, not everything. She still had to contend with *them,* but this time they were going to listen to her, not the other way around. And somehow she'd get Jason Newhall to sell her back the interest he'd bought from her greedy relatives. She peeked up at Rand as he put his attention on driving the car. But everything that really mattered was perfect.

He felt her watching him. "What are you

thinking about, beautiful?" He was almost afraid to ask.

"Just how much I love you," she whispered, and leaned to press her lips to his cheek. "But . . ." She looked suddenly apprehensive and pulled slightly away from him. "There's something about me I haven't told you."

He almost choked. Something about her? He shook his head. No, this wasn't the time for confessions. If she made one, then he'd have to make his, and he wasn't ready. He hadn't figured out how to do it yet without it ending with her hating him. He pulled her close again. "Whatever it is, Tori, it can wait. All I know right now is that you're here, and I love you. Nothing else matters." He looked down at her anxiously. "Does it?"

"No." She smiled and snuggled up against him. "At least I hope not."

He pulled the car to a stop in front of the wide entry steps of RiverOaks.

The fact that something was definitely wrong assailed Tori the moment they stepped onto the wide front gallery. A bloodcurdling shriek pierced the still morning air, and was immediately followed by a cackling laugh.

"Oh, no." She rushed for the front door and slammed it open in her haste. It crashed against the doorstop and its impact caused the narrow windows set on either side of it to shake precariously. She ran into the foyer and stopped, horror-struck, in the center of the wide room.

Rand entered practically on her heels, his imagination conjuring up everything from a gun-toting maniac trying to kill Stanton and Abram, to monsters from another planet trying to abduct them, to Satan risen from the depths of hell to claim their souls. In his haste to get to the rescue of the old men, who were obviously in trouble, and to keep Tori out of harm's way in her zeal to also get to them, Rand nearly ran her down when she stopped. He clutched her shoulders and found them trembling, then followed her gaze to the second-floor landing of the staircase. His heart nearly stopped its racing beat altogether at what he saw.

"Lila, stop!" Tori screamed. "Stop!" But the calamity continued.

Rand wasn't sure what confused him more, the ordeal that was happening on the landing with the two elderly men, or Tori's scream at someone named Lila who, as far as he could see, wasn't even there. His puzzlement and shock rendered him momentarily immobile.

Tori charged up the stairs. This was absolutely the worst thing Lila had ever done, and if Tori could get her hands on the woman, she'd strangle her.

Abram thrashed wildly from the loop of drape he had been hung in, his bony old legs kicking back and forth, his hands gripping the fabric as he jerked and twisted his body in an effort to free himself. But his feet were a good two feet from the floor, and the drape was wrapped tightly and securely around him, holding him in place, a prisoner suspended in midair. "This is it, missy!" he yelled. His old voice cracked beneath the strain and anger of the moment. "I'm gonna call a preacher out here for sure now. Afraid to meet their Maker, that's what."

"No! Don't do that!" Tori screamed. She was only halfway up the wide staircase when one of *them,* still without showing themself, grabbed hold of the handles of Stanton's wheelchair and pushed him forward.

"Whoa!" Stanton bellowed uselessly. His gnarled old hands gripped the wheelchair. "Who the hell's behind me?" He jerked around and swatted at the air.

The chair zoomed from one end of the landing to the other, swerved toward the window, and cut abruptly away just before crashing into it.

A high-pitched laugh cut through the air again to blend with Abram's screaming threats and Stanton's bellowing curses, but Rand heard only the latter two.

"Tori, what the hell's going on?" he yelled, and charged up the stairs after her, finally finding his momentum. Whatever was happening, it was unearthly, and he wasn't sure he wanted an explanation, even though he'd asked for one.

Tori lunged for Stanton as he and his chair went speeding past the landing. She missed, narrowly, and nearly landed on her face instead. The chair came to a jerking stop, spun, and headed straight for the stairs.

"No!" she screamed.

Rand looked up just in time to see Stanton, his face a blend of fear and outrage, roll toward him.

"Oh, Lord," Rand moaned. He bounded up the last few stairs, making his already wide stride stretch even farther and straddle four stairs in one leap. With an almost superhuman effort, he reached out to catch Stanton, who was nearly at the edge of the stairs.

"If you don't like me now, old woman," Stanton bellowed loudly, "wait until I get to where you're at! I'll make you sorry you were ever born, let alone died."

Rand's fingers touched the old man's hands, which were still gripped tightly about the chairs armrests, but just as they did, the chair was yanked to the side, and out of his grasp.

"Here I come, Josephine," Stanton yelled to his deceased wife. His mass of gray hair whipped about his head as the chair sped in first one direction, then the other, then roared back toward the stairs.

Behind it, Tori made a grab for the handles. The chair turned, shot forward, and collided with Rand, who was just lunging toward it. The

301

crash knocked him backward and off his feet. His back was slammed into the wall and, a split second later, the breath knocked from his lungs as the wheelchair and Stanton, as well as his blanket and the old .45 that always rested in his lap, tumbled into his lap in a tangle of metal, wool, and thrashing limbs.

Seeing that Stanton was safe from harm, at least for the moment, Tori whirled around and ran for Abram, who was still beating at the drape that held him prisoner and cussing a blue streak that surprised even her. Pushing a chair under him, which still left a good three or four inches between its seat and his feet, she climbed up on another and yanked at the knot of fabric tied at the old man's back. The drapery suddenly unraveled and Abram fell to the chair. Tori grabbed at him.

"That's it, missy," he sputtered, and climbed to the floor on still-shaking legs, but the trembling that controlled his limbs was caused by anger rather than fear. "They've gone too far this time. I'm getting the priest out here, I swear. Then we'll be rid of them once and for all."

"You'll never be rid of us, old man," Lila sneered. Her face suddenly loomed up over Abram's shoulder, but only Tori heard the snide words and saw the spite flashing in her aunt's eyes.

"*I* will be, if you don't stop this," Tori threatened.

Realizing she was talking to someone behind him, Abram jerked around. "It was that old witch, wasn't it?" he asked.

The end of the drape curled up in the air and swirled around Abram's head.

"Stop it," Tori demanded. "Or I'll do exactly as he said."

The drape suddenly dropped back down and fell against the wall.

From his seat on the floor beside Stanton, who'd managed to right himself into a sitting position, Rand watched in mesmerized fascination. Whatever was going on, he'd never seen anything like it before, and he wasn't quite sure he wanted to see it again, though Tori appeared on the way to getting things under control somehow.

"Which of you are here?" she demanded.

"I am," Lila snipped tartly, and reappeared before Tori.

"Who else?"

"No one. I didn't need any help to handle two crotchety old men."

"Chance didn't help you do this?"

Lila sniffed. "No, the coward."

"I am no coward, Lila, and you know it," Chance thundered, appearing beside her. His eyes flashed fury at the insult. "But I did tell you enough was enough. If Tori is so attached to this young man that she'd defy us, then so be it. I will not purposely do anyone physical harm to get my way, which is obviously more than I can say for you."

"Oh, pssh," Lila said, and turned her back to him.

"Pssh, yourself," Tori said childishly, but she was so infuriated that she didn't know what else to say. "Go away now, and stay away, at least for a while."

They both disappeared.

She turned toward her grandfather and Rand, and it suddenly struck her: he'd seen what happened. She nearly moaned, but swallowed the sound before it could escape her lips. This is exactly what she'd been afraid of, that *they* would do something horrendous like this in front of him before she'd had an opportunity to explain about them, if that was even possible.

"Let's help them get downstairs," she said to Rand, hoping to postpone talk of what had just happened.

Abram was already making his way down the entry stairs. Tori righted Stanton's wheelchair and Rand, getting to his feet, lifted the old man into it.

"Give me my gun," Stanton said.

Rand laid it in the old man's lap. "How do we get him down?"

"Very carefully," Tori said, and laughed nervously. Stanton's room was on the first floor. He hadn't been upstairs in years, ever since the riding accident that had put him in the chair, so she had no practice in getting him down the staircase.

"I'll hold him from the front, to prevent the chair from rolling out of control, and you maneuver from behind while holding the handles," Rand said.

Ten minutes and a lot of teeth-clenching later, they had him downstairs.

"You'd best heed Abram's words this time, girl," Stanton said, still smarting from the attack.

Tori pushed him into the parlor and sat down on a chair opposite him. Rand settled into the one next to her. They could hear Abram's busying himself in the kitchen. Rand gave the old servant credit for being alone in the other room after what had just transpired.

"What happened, Gramps?"

"That damned old woman got a bug up her—"

"Gramps.".

He scowled. "Ashford was here. He wanted to talk to you."

"And?" Tori prodded.

"And I told him to drop dead."

"Oh, Lord. And?" she urged again.

"I told him you were with Rand, and he needn't bother coming around anymore."

"And Abram?"

Stanton shook his head. "Abram didn't do anything, except agree with me and show that

305

milksop to the door."

"Oh, Gramps. And that's what started this?"

"The old bat obviously figured if she got rid of me and Abram, you'd listen to her threats and start seeing Mr. Wonderful again."

Tori smiled, though she was still angry, both with *them* and with her grandfather. "She wouldn't have hurt you, Gramps. None of them would. Lila only wanted to scare you into being quiet, not get rid of you."

"Well," he huffed, "you could of fooled me. Thought I was on my way to meet your Grandma Josephine for sure."

"I'll have a talk with Lila . . . with all of them."

"Excuse me," Rand said, leaning forward in his chair and propping his elbows on his knees, "but just who are you going to talk to? And, as long as I'm asking, who were you yelling at up there? Who's Lila?"

Tori wrung her hands. "I tried to tell you earlier, in the car, remember? When I said there was something about me that you didn't know."

He nodded. "I remember, but what's that got to do with this . . . this whatever it was that happened?"

Her insides began to churn and quiver. She averted her eyes and looked everywhere but at him. "Rand, my family isn't like others, we're . . . different. We don't . . . I mean, my dad's side, and anyone who marries into it doesn't

". . ." She turned her eyes back to him and swallowed hard. "When the Rouchards die, Rand, they . . . we don't leave RiverOaks." There, she'd said it.

He stared at her as if she'd just told him she was from another planet. "You . . . don't leave? You mean you have your own family cemetery here?"

"No, I mean we don't leave. Well, maybe for a while, to adjust, but then we come back. Our spirits stay forever."

A frown drew his brows together and his eyes narrowed. "Your spirits stay?"

Here it comes, she thought, *the conviction that I'm crazy.* "That's right. Every Rouchard who has ever lived at RiverOaks over the years is still here."

"And that's who you've been talking to? Ghosts?"

"Right."

"And that's who caused this . . . this scene upstairs?"

"My great-great-great-aunt Lila was angry with Gramps and Abram. And me. She and one of her brothers, my uncle Chance, want me to marry Ash and they were afraid I would become involved with you." She continued on before he could comment, the words pouring from her lips like a torrent. "My uncles, Chance and Dominic, both died in the war, and Lila had to struggle with managing the plantation alone af-

307

terward. She had some very hard times. To them, Rand, you're a Yankee, and they still hate Yankees."

He smiled. "You *are* kidding?"

She shook her head and did not return his smile. "No, I'm not."

He took a deep breath, rose to his feet, and moved to stand beside her. He took her hands in his and drew her to her feet. "So, where does that leave us?"

She stared up at him, surprised by his words. She had fully expected him to walk out the door without a backward glance, exactly as Tom had done. "I—I don't know."

"Yes, you do, Tori," Dominic said at her shoulder.

She smiled at him. He was right. This time was different from the last. "Wish me luck, Uncle Dom?" she asked, her eyes filling with tears.

He leaned forward and Tori felt a cool caress on her cheek as he kissed her. "You do not need luck, Tori," he whispered, "you have love."

She turned back to Rand, who was watching her intently. "It's a long story, but one that, if you really love me, you need to hear."

"Go on," he said. "Tell me."

She closed her eyes and took a long, slow breath, and when she reopened them, he saw the fear that sparkled there, and his heart ached to hold her, and reassure her. But he remained still, waiting. "Long ago the Rouchard who built this house, Hippolyte, died before his only son married. But Hippy didn't leave. He stuck around and rejected every girl his son brought home, until finally, when his son was about to despair of ever marrying, Hippy gave his approval to the one girl who could see him when his son proposed. That is our family tradition, Rand. If you propose to me again, here at RiverOaks, and they appear to you, then we can marry, and love, and be happy. But if you still can't see and hear them, then our relationship is doomed."

"Then I guess—"

A pounding crash against the entry door interrupted Rand and drew their attention.

Ashford ran into the room, waving a handful of papers over his head, a triumphant gleam in his eyes. He pushed himself between Rand and Tori, forcefully breaking Rand's hold on her hands.

"Ash," she protested.

He stuck his face in hers. "I knew there was something about—" he paused and glared over his shoulder, then whipped his face back around "—*him* that I didn't like. Do you know who he really is, Tori?"

"Rand Mitchell."

"Right. Randall Kane Mitchell, owner and president of Paradise Tours."

Her mouth dropped open and hung agape at

his words. Paradise Tours was the name of the company that had tried to buy Rouchard Travel when her father had been alive. It was as big in the West as Rouchard was in the South.

Stanton slapped his thigh. "I knew I'd seen you before," he said to Rand, "on the news. There was something on about how you been opening advertising agencies to promote your own tour services. Entrepreneurial, they called it."

Tori glanced quickly from Rand to her grandfather and back to Rand.

"And he's the one behind that man who's been hassling you about selling, too," Ashford offered.

She looked past Ash to Rand. "Is this true?"

He nodded. "I wanted to tell you, Tori, but I didn't know how."

"And all of this other—you and me—was that just part of the plan to get my company? Acquisition through seduction?" She felt a deep rending in her heart, as if it was breaking.

"No. I mean, at first, yes, but I didn't plan on falling in love with you. It just happened."

"I told you," Lila whispered in Tori's ear.

"Oh, shush, I don't need to hear from you right now," Tori snapped.

Ash, thinking she meant him, took a step back. "Well, if that's the thanks I get for trying to warn you . . ."

She moved past him without answering. "Why

didn't you tell me last night? Or was that part of the plan, too?"

He wanted to reach out to her, to draw her into his arms, but he knew she wasn't ready to accept that yet. "I was afraid to, Tori. Ever since I was ten years old, and I watched my dad walk out on my mom because she made more money than he did, I swore I would never fall in love with a woman who had a career she wouldn't give up."

"And you thought I wouldn't give up mine?"

He shrugged. "You turned down every offer Jason brought to you, so I figured you were one of those hardnosed businesswomen, the kind who live for deals and power."

"So you decided you'd come yourself and out-deal me by using a little charm?"

"Yes. But I didn't realize it would backfire, and I'd fall in love with you." He pulled her into his embrace then, no longer able to resist. "I was wrong, Tori. I know that now, and I'll do whatever I have to do to make it up to you. You have to give us a chance."

"I do?"

"Tori," Ashford whined. "He's only trying to charm you again."

"Someone shut that fop up," Chance snarled.

"Put a lid on it, Thibeaux," Stanton ordered.

"Well, I never," Ash said, and puffed indignantly.

"You love me Tori, and I love you. I don't

care if you want to keep working, I don't care if you want to open twenty more offices, or fifty, or a hundred, and oversee all of them." He brushed his lips across hers lightly. "I love you, Tori Rouchard, more than anything in the world, and I need you in my life. Will you marry me?"

She turned her face away from him and looked around the room. They were all there, all thirty-five of them, and Krissy, too, and she thought, when she looked toward the archway that led to the ballroom, she could faintly detect images of her mother and father. She looked back at Rand. He was smiling and looking at them, too.

"So, these are the famous Rouchards," he said.

She stared at him in surprise, not daring to believe, afraid to hope. "You can see them?"

Epilogue

Tori stepped from the rear entry door of
RiverOaks and paused on the gallery to catch
her breath. She still couldn't believe this was
happening.

Overhead the morning sun shone brightly. Its
pale rays filtered through the thick, gnarled
branches of the many oak trees that dotted the
landscape of RiverOaks, and settled on the wide
expanse of lawn, turning the lush blades to a
blanket of glistening emerald. Ribbons of white
satin had been strung between the massive
trunks of three of the trees to create an altar,
while yet more were attached to the branches
themselves, entwining within the prickly curtains
of gray Spanish moss that draped gracefully all
around. Several dozen white wrought-iron chairs
had been rented, and more ribbons, both white
and pale apricot, had been attached to the
chairs at the end of each row, creating an aisle.

Birds chirped in the trees, a soft hum of conversation emanated from the guests who had

seated themselves in the chairs, and organ music played in the background.

Tori straightened the off-shoulder capped sleeves of her gown, the same gown that Laura had worn so long ago when she'd married Dominic, and looked at her sister. "Are you ready, Krissy?"

She nodded. "I have the ring right here, sis," she said, and held up the twisted gold band Tori had chosen as Rand's wedding ring.

"Then let's not keep Rand waiting," Tori said. The organist noticed her approach to the stairs and immediately began to play a lilting version of the traditional wedding march. Krissy moved down the steps proudly, her head held high. She paused as Tori stopped to kiss Abram's cheek and take Stanton's hand.

The four of them moved down the aisle together, Krissy in the lead, Tori walking beside Stanton, and Abram bringing up the rear, pushing Stanton's chair.

Rand turned to watch her approach, his face alight with the love that filled him, his eyes gleaming with unshed tears of happiness. Never before had he seen her look more beautiful. The voluminous folds of her gown swayed gently as she walked, the huge hoopcage beneath her skirt moved slightly with each step she took, and the silk of her petticoats rustled softly. The antique ivory silk, the hue a result of the gown's age, shimmered beneath the sun's glow, and the tiny seed pearls embroidered within the Valenciennes lace that trimmed the plunging neckline reflected a myriad of minute spots of color.

She had pulled the sides of her hair back, away from her face, and pinned it behind her ears. The long waves flowed freely across her shoulders, a black veil of satin that contrasted richly with the magnolia flesh of her bare shoulders and the silk of her gown. A thin veil of lace, embroidered at its scalloped edges with flowers and vines, covered her face and hung down her back.

Rand felt the pride and love he felt for Tori swell within his chest. This was the woman he had waited all his life to possess, the woman he would give up a kingdom for, the woman who now held the key to his heart, and always would.

They said vows that each had written especially for the other. Rand took the ring from his best man, who was also his six-year-old nephew, and slipped it on Tori's finger.

Tori felt a tap on her shoulder and turned.

"It's your turn now, Tori," Krissy said, and held out the gold band.

A murmur of shock and exclamation broke out behind them. Rand looked past Tori's shoulder and saw Krissy holding up the ring, but to everyone else present he knew the ring would seem to be suspended in midair. He smiled. His family was in for a lot of surprises when they visited RiverOaks, so they might as well start to get used to it.

Tori took the ring and slipped it onto Rand's finger. He lifted the veil from her face and, drawing her into his arms, claimed her lips with his own. "I love you, Tori Mitchell," he said huskily.

With their arms held tightly around each other, Tori and Rand turned back to their guests. He looked to his left, caught his mother's eye, and winked.

Tori nudged him gently. "Look at Lila," she whispered.

He moved his gaze to the right bank of chairs, where Stanton and Abram sat. Beside them a handsome couple suddenly appeared to him and Rand realized he was looking, for the first time, at Tori's parents. He heard her little mew of surprise as she, too, saw them, and pulled her close. Thirty-five other Rouchard family members sat on what everyone else thought of as empty chairs. Rand found Lila easily, her black dress a stark contrast to the white chairs and colorful gowns of the other Rouchards present. He watched her lift a lace-edged handkerchief to her face, sniff, and dab quickly at the corners of her eyes. He smiled. The world was full of surprises, and at River-

316

Oaks, he was assured of at least two things: a beautiful, loving wife, and a life that would never be dull.

FEEL THE FIRE IN CAROL FINCH'S ROMANCES!

BELOVED BETRAYAL (2346, $3.95)

Sabrina Spencer donned a gray wig and veiled hat before blackmailing rugged Ridge Tanner into guiding her to Fort Canby. But the costume soon became her prison—the beauty had fallen head over heels in love!

LOVE'S HIDDEN TREASURE (2980, $4.50)

Shandra d'Evereux felt her heart throb beneath the stolen map she'd hidden in her bodice when Nolan Elliot swept her out onto the veranda. It was hard to concentrate on her mission with that wily rogue around!

MONTANA MOONFIRE (3263, $4.95)

Just as debutante Victoria Flemming-Cassidy was about to marry an oh-so-suitable mate, the towering preacher, Dru Sullivan flung her over his shoulder and headed West! Suddenly, Tori realized she had been given the best present for a bride: a night of passion with a real man!

THUNDER'S TENDER TOUCH (2809, $4.50)

Refined Piper Malone needed bounty-hunter, Vince Logan to recover her swindled inheritance. She thought she could coolly dismiss him after he did the job, but she never counted on the hot flood of desire she felt whenever he was near!

DISCOVER DEANA JAMES!

CAPTIVE ANGEL   (2524, $4.50/$5.50)
Abandoned, penniless, and suddenly responsible for the biggest tobacco plantation in Colleton County, distraught Caroline Gillard had no time to dissolve into tears. By day the willowy redhead labored to exhaustion beside her slaves . . . but each night left her restless with longing for her wayward husband. She'd make the sea captain regret his betrayal until he begged her to take him back!

MASQUE OF SAPPHIRE   (2885, $4.50/$5.50)
Judith Talbot-Harrow left England with a heavy heart. She was going to America to join a father she despised and a sister she distrusted. She was certainly in no mood to put up with the insulting actions of the arrogant Yankee privateer who boarded her ship, ransacked her things, then "apologized" with an indecent, brazen kiss! She vowed that someday he'd pay dearly for the liberties he had taken and the desires he had awakened.

SPEAK ONLY LOVE   (3439, $4.95/$5.95)
Long ago, the shock of her mother's death had robbed Vivian Marleigh of the power of speech. Now she was being forced to marry a bitter man with brandy on his breath. But she could not say what was in her heart. It was up to the viscount to spark the fires that would melt her icy reserve.

WILD TEXAS HEART   (3205, $4.95/$5.95)
Fan Breckenridge was terrified when the stranger found her near-naked and shivering beneath the Texas stars. Unable to remember who she was or what had happened, all she had in the world was the deed to a patch of land that might yield oil . . . and the fierce loving of this wildcatter who called himself Irons.

Available wherever paperbacks are sold, or order direct from the Publisher. Send cover price plus 50¢ per copy for mailing and handling to Zebra Books, Dept. 4054, 475 Park Avenue South, New York, N.Y. 10016. Residents of New York and Tennessee must include sales tax. DO NOT SEND CASH. For a free Zebra/ Pinnacle catalog please write to the above address.